TO DAVID + PASHA,

GREAT WARM + LOVING FRIENDS
WHOSE GIFTS DON'T ALWAYS FALL
ON FOREIGN, HIDDEN LANDS
BUT ONTO THOSE BLESSED NEARBY.

WITH LOVE, AARON

the day the
televisions
stopped

S. B. Sutton

the day the televisions stopped

Harcourt Brace Jovanovich, Publishers

New York   San Diego   London

HBJ

Requests for permission to make copies of any part of the work should be mailed to:
Copyrights and Permissions Department, Harcourt Brace Jovanovich, Publishers,
8th Floor, Orlando, Florida 32887.

- Library of Congress Cataloging-in-Publication Data
Sutton, S. B. (Silvia Barry)
The day the televisions stopped/S. B. Sutton. — 1st ed.
p.   cm.
ISBN 0-15-123994-0
I. Title.
PS3569.U8977D38   1992
813'.54 — dc20   92-6732

Printed in the United States of America

First edition
A B C D E

For June and Melvin Sutton,
with love and respect

Acknowledgments

I am thankful to Clark Abt for a fine critical eye, to Phyllis Andersen for friendship and encouragement, to Tom Guinzburg for making magic, to Imre Halasz for love and inspiration, and to Harriet Wasserman for good humor and advice.

the day the televisions stopped

M a r i a ' s S t o r y

 "One day a long time ago, in the middle of an important soccer match," Maria said in a tone her children and grandchildren recognized as the beginning of one of her stories, "the television screens suddenly went blank."

"Was I still a baby, Nana?" asked Paolo.

"Oh my, no. You weren't born yet, your mother was a baby, and your uncle Gilberto was a very little boy. It happened when I was a young woman, much younger than your mother is now."

"Then it must have been a *real* long time ago," teased Teresa, who admired the persistence of her grandmother's vanity into advanced age.

"I'm not an antique, child," Maria observed crossly. "I only said it was a long time ago because that's the way stories are supposed to begin. Not only was I young, but some men believed I was pretty."

"Your grandmother was the most beautiful woman in all Amazonas," said Serita.

Maria suddenly and for no good reason remembered the very short dress, made of a shiny emerald green fabric matching her eyes, that she had worn with black pantyhose and high-heeled patent leather shoes the time she had been in Manaus at Carnival and danced the lambada with an exciting man. What *was* his name? And what had become of pantyhose? She must ask Teresa.

"Nana?——"

"Where was I? You ask too many questions and make me lose my place."

"Right at the beginning, when the television screens went blank," said her daughter-in-law.

"Well, let me back up a little . . ."

This is the tale Maria told.

On Friday June 21, 2002, in the nameless shanty town in the province of Amazonas where we lived, more than a hundred people—nearly all of them men, many of them, like your grandfather, casual laborers trucked into the region by the Brazilian government to help build a new highway—had assembled in the dusty street outside the whorehouse where the toothless whore Gloria had been persuaded by appeals to her sense of patriotism and a cash donation to bring her television (the only one in town with which, during her leisure hours, she followed the Mexican soap operas, and which she often used for professional purposes in conjunction with her videocassette recorder to play one of her four pornographic films) outdoors, connect it by three extension cords to her generator, and place it on the hood of a pickup truck so that everyone could watch the World Cup match between Brazil and Hungary.

Gloria, who thought soccer was boring even as played by the champion Brazilian team, did not watch the game. Instead she and her girls patrolled the edges of the crowd to make sure no one ran off with the television set. Meanwhile the men cheered their heroes racing up and down the field in the great Barcelona stadium where one hundred and thirteen thousand or more people had paid scalpers' prices to witness the event.

The Hungarians countered the Brazilians' grace and speed with cunning, tenacity, and a suicidal goalie whose daring leaps and dives stopped all but one Brazilian attempt. Midway through the game the Hungarians put the ball into the net to tie the score at one all, precipitating despair in front of the whorehouse; a few minutes later a Hungarian player deep within his own territory committed a foul so dastardly with respect to private anatomy as to prompt the referee to award Brazil a penalty kick. The officials stopped the game while the injured athlete was carried off the field; partisan fans rose out of their seats; the television replayed the misdemeanor in slow motion while the commentators discussed potential incapacities; the Hungarian goalie paced the terrain in front of his net, talking to himself . . .

. . . And at that very moment Gloria's television went blank with a small sound like the sighing of wind through river grasses.

The men stared numbly at the box perched on the hood of the 1983 Ford pickup, and the screen stared back at them with a blind eye the color of cataracts. The sportscasters' chatter yielded to the barking of a stray dog.

Even before the men recovered their senses, Gloria, convinced her television had broken, went berserk and attacked the nearest spectator who happened to be my husband Paco—your grandfather—who was then hardly more than a boy. And believe me, Paco was afraid because even though he had never been with her (he had no reason, my dears, to ever want to pay for the attentions of Gloria or her girls) he knew her terrible temper by reputation. She ripped his shirt (he had only three; luckily he hadn't worn his good plaid one that day but the one he had on was his favorite, a blue T-shirt that said, I Survived the Second Millennium in gold letters) and clawed at his back like a jungle animal, drawing blood the color of her painted fingernails and leaving wounds which I tended later that evening with a poultice of herbs.

"My name is Paco," he protested when he found his voice. "I never touched the television. My wife is Maria. I am the father of four children."

Gloria interrupted her assault.

"Maria?" she asked. "Which Maria?"

"My Maria," Paco explained. "The Maria who does the washing. The one with the green eyes who sings songs."

"Ah," Gloria said. "*That* Maria! The one with the smile who doesn't take care to cover her breasts."

Gloria was jealous of me, especially because of my teeth which have always been perfect. Paco understood this and defended my virtue.

"She is beautiful, my Maria," he said, "a modest woman, a mother. I am sorry about your television."

"I curse your Maria and your four children," Gloria screamed, yanking a handful of his black hair. "You're a murderer like the rest of them. You killed my television set. Do you know how many ugly men I had to screw to pay for it?"

Three strong men pulled Gloria off Paco. The rest of them, eager to find out what had happened with the penalty kick, began fiddling with the buttons on the television and checking the connections on the extension cords and inspecting the generator. Through these experiments they determined that the electrical current was still flowing from the generator through the wires into the television and that, although none of the channels came in, the set could be turned on and off.

"Gloria!" one of the men announced cheerfully, "your television isn't dead. You see? It can go on and off." He demonstrated by pushing the appropriate buttons, and indeed the screen changed from dark to milky white when he turned the set on.

"What good is it to me if I can't see anything on it, you

fool?" retorted Gloria. "And get your filthy hands away from it. Go away, all of you. You can forget about Gloria and her girls until you either fix my TV or get me a new one. As of this moment, our services are suspended."

The men groaned. After a while somebody remembered that the bar and the barbershop had radios, and the crowd split into two radiocentric clusters to hear what had transpired in Barcelona and whether the kicker had scored, leaving Gloria alone as she wished, to mourn the remains of her television.

Later that evening, after celebrating the soccer game which was won by Brazil, a few of the men tried to repair Gloria's television but since none of them knew more than a hummingbird about electronics, all they accomplished was the discovery that the VCR did not work either—or, rather, that the power came on and the tape advanced, but nothing showed up on the television screen, not even the static at the beginning of the film—which, as you can imagine, poured *molho* on Gloria's anger, and she threw them out of the house and locked all the doors.

Now your grandfather Paco, as I have always told you, was a kind man, and even though the whore Gloria had destroyed his favorite T-shirt and carved ugly marks on his back, he felt sorry for her (and perhaps a little guilty because, after all, the television had stopped while he was watching it) and sorrier yet for the men in the road gangs who had no wives or girlfriends and would have nowhere to go while the whorehouse was closed down. Being smarter than the others, Paco knew better than to try to fix the television himself, but he thought he knew someone who could, so on Monday morning he went to the *chefe* of his gang, Rodrigo, who was one of Gloria's regular clients, and suggested that they tell the assistant engineer (a bald, lonely government man from Brasilia, with a university degree, whom I sometimes caught eyeing me while I was hanging the laundry) what had happened and ask for his help. Rodrigo approved Paco's plan, and they went together to the assistant engineer who listened to their story without speaking a word, although they could see he was agitated. When they finished, he exploded with laughter.

"You mean you haven't heard?" he asked, wiping his eyes.

"Heard what?" Paco replied, because they had heard nothing except that Gloria's VCR was also broken, which was not funny.

"It's the same all over Brazil," the engineer explained. "Nobody has television. They all went off at the same time. In São Paolo there were riots in the streets because of the game."

"That's impossible." Rodrigo frowned.

"But I swear it's true. Listen"—the engineer reached across his drawing board and switched on a radio—"the president made a speech about it an hour ago, and everyone is talking about how there is no television."

Paco and Rodrigo stood in the engineer's trailer and heard the deep voices of the newscasters and from time to time the whiny voice of the president who said the government considered television failure a matter of urgency, that the cabinet had been meeting since Sunday, that scientific experts were studying the situation, and that he was certain reception would be restored in time for the World Cup final, three weeks hence.

"I don't understand any of this," Rodrigo complained. "How could such a thing happen?"

"How should I know?" The engineer shrugged. "I guess we'll just have to wait for the experts to tell us."

"I don't think this is funny at all," Paco declared gravely. "In fact, it is serious."

"No doubt you're right, Paco," replied the engineer, "but I couldn't help laughing when you started to tell me about Gloria."

Paco and Rodrigo looked at each other. Gloria! Oh my goodness! In their consternation over the national failure of television, they had forgotten about Gloria.

"When she hears about this, I'm sure Gloria will pardon you and open up again," said the engineer. "At least I *hope* so. You have my permission to go back to town now and try to work things out with her."

But Gloria would not believe Rodrigo when he shouted into her window what he had heard from the engineer and on the radio, namely that all the televisions in Brazil had gone on the blink and therefore hers would work just as well as before as soon as they solved the problem, whatever it was, and so she should unlock her doors and resume business at once because the men would get horny and fights would break out in the highway gangs if she didn't.

Gloria stuck her head out the window and took out her plastic teeth. She opened her mouth wide and rolled the tip of her pink tongue provocatively around her gums. "You want Gloria, honey, you bring her a new TV. Gloria wants a Sony. No gringo shit! And throw in some new videos. I'm tired of the old ones."

"Gloria, I beg you," Rodrigo pleaded. "We could bring you a hundred Sonys, a new generator, and Mr. Sony himself and you still wouldn't have any TV because there isn't any TV to have."

"What kind of crap is that, 'there isn't any TV to have'? What's that supposed to mean?"

"Exactly that. The radio said there's no TV in Brazil. It doesn't work: no picture, no sound, no VCR."

"You insult me, you pig!" Gloria sneered. "I may be a whore, but that doesn't make me an idiot. What you say is impossible!"

"Go on. Listen to the radio. You'll hear. The president himself has made a speech about it."

"Ah! You mean the same president who said last month there is no more inflation in Brazil? The same president who promised dental clinics in all the provinces? The same president who announced two years ago that this highway was finished? The same president whose goons stole the last election? I'd sooner believe Tanya Mamou who gets her information from chicken gizzards.

Get your fat belly away from my window, Rodrigo, before I die laughing. And you too, Paco. Go home to your Maria and her boobs, but beware—they'll soon be hanging down to her knees!"

Gloria popped her teeth back into her mouth and retreated into the shadows of the house, slamming the shutters behind her.

"This is serious," Rodrigo muttered. "As long as the television isn't working, she isn't going to open up."

"Don't worry," Paco consoled. "They'll fix it. The president promised it would be fixed in time for the championship."

"That's three weeks away. Already the goats are beginning to look good to me. You see the small one over there, with the big eyes. Her name is Belita. She looks like a virgin, no?"

• • •

"Mama," Gilberto laughed. "Stop it! You're exaggerating!"

"The secret of storytelling is to know when to exaggerate," Maria observed dryly. "Excess in the proper place and in exact measurement is essential to any story."

• • •

When Paco came home that night he told me about the televisions. Naturally I blamed it on the United States because, in those times, the gringos were behind many of the incomprehensible events that occurred on our continent. Perhaps, I suggested, they wanted us to have a new president and they had captured the television reception to embarrass the old one; whatever the gringos wanted (and it was not always obvious what they wanted, or why they wanted it), it wouldn't matter to us because nobody paid attention to the poor people in Amazonas. But Paco shook his head and said no, that even though he did not understand exactly how television worked, he was certain that not even the gringos could capture the reception. Then I saw the trouble written on his face, so I told him not to worry, that they would fix it. He replied with riddles I could not answer.

"Who are *they?*" he asked. "And what is it that must be fixed?"

In the night when he thought we were all sleeping, my husband left our hammock, picked up his wreck of a guitar, and tiptoed out the door, and I knew he had gone behind our shack to sit under the flamboyan tree beside the stream where I did the washing. I parted the curtains on the moonless sky, and for a while I listened to him strumming ruined songs on that old guitar, warped and cracked in the climate of the Amazon which does not treat humans or their artifacts with tenderness. He must have stayed there for many hours because he had not come back when I fell asleep.

Paco's theory that the gringos had nothing to do with the television was proven correct later in the week when the news reached us over the radio that nobody anywhere in the world had television, including the gringos, and that presidents and kings of all countries were making speeches, and scientists were trying to discover what had gone wrong. The men in our settlement talked of little else because the World Cup final was now only about two weeks away and they still hoped to be able to see it on television and, more importantly, because the whore Gloria (even though Rodrigo and Paco had borrowed a big black transistor radio from one of the bars, turned it up to full volume, and blasted the news reports in front of her window) continued to disbelieve her ears, claiming that all the reporters worked for the government and only said what that bastard the president ordered them to say and, accordingly, it was a Big Lie or possibly a practical joke by some of the men, but in either case she was sticking with her original conditions and would unlock her doors when the men delivered her new Sony and not one minute earlier.

"Women are not logical," Rodrigo sighed miserably, "but Gloria is more illogical than most." He cast a wistful glance at Belita who was up the street nibbling on a corncob.

"Maybe you're right, but this is a most illogical situation," Paco observed. "Nobody seems to understand what has happened. Gloria's theory isn't any loonier than some of the others we've heard."

"I didn't mean the televisions. I am speaking about the whorehouse. She's being unreasonable. It isn't fair to the men, stuck up here in this lousy climate, working their asses off all day, when the only whorehouse for a hundred miles closes down. You have your beautiful Maria, so why should you care? But I tell you, even the assistant engineer is beginning to get short-tempered."

Belita, having devoured her corncob, pranced down the street and nuzzled Rodrigo's back pocket. He reached inside and extracted the end of a pack of Life Savers which she took from his hand delicately with a kiss of her soft lips; she crunched the candy and looked up at Rodrigo with mischievous eyes.

Paco laughed.

"Be patient, Rodrigo," he said. "Everyone promises that the televisions will be fixed in time for the soccer game, which is only two weeks away. And in the life of a man, my friend, two weeks weigh less than the wings of the green dragonfly."

Paco had spoken empty words of sympathy. In fact, he was beginning to doubt that anyone had the power to restore television in time for the soccer game. So he was not at all surprised on July 12 to find himself standing beside Rodrigo in the crowded little bar drinking beer and listening to the World Cup final between Brazil and Finland which, according to the radio announcers, was a classic confrontation between Brazilian agility and Finnish strength and which, as you might expect, was won during the second fifteen-minute overtime by the Finns because in those days grace and skill counted for little in the world, power for everything. I am told that some men wept when the Finns scored the victorious goal, others began to quarrel, and the street filled with fights. As your grandfather observed his companions, he felt a withering of his heart.

At the end of the day, when the rain had washed away the heat, Gloria unlocked her doors. Paco, who chose to believe in the goodness of human souls, insisted she had committed an act of mercy, but I had heard gossip that her girls were threatening to set up independently, so I am still convinced Gloria made a financial decision. Whatever her motives, the reopening of the whorehouse restored the rhythm of the town. And since Gloria owned the only television in town, nobody missed it.

Nobody, that is, except Gloria who worried what had become of the characters in her soap operas, and Paco.

As long as there was television in the world, Paco hadn't concerned himself with it. Like all poor people he sometimes dreamed about owning one, but only after he had acquired a patch of land to farm, a new guitar, a car, a house with electricity and running water, a refrigerator, and a pair of red shoes for me—so you see, a television was pretty far down on his list. As for me, I don't remember television among my dreams: what I wanted most was to learn how to read and for our family to escape this stinking little town that had no past and no future, only a mildewed present. Yet even there I enjoyed happiness with my family and in my imagination, and it was in Amazonas that I started to sing my songs (do you remember, Gilberto, the lullabies I sang to you?), sometimes on Saturdays or at fiestas in front of many people, occasions for which I borrowed Rodrigo's guitar which still held a tune. In that wounded landscape I discovered that every note of a song has a history, a biography—a beginning, a middle, an end—and that some of necessity live longer than others, and some are louder, but all support the song and, therefore, must be sung respectfully, from birth to death. I suppose with such thoughts I would have forgotten the whole television problem if it hadn't been for Paco's obsession.

As I told you earlier, after Gloria reopened her doors the people resumed their former habits, good, bad, and without moral value. However Paco, who had always come home directly from his work on the highway, started going instead to the bar to listen to talk about the television situation on the radio, a preoccupation that eventually began to annoy the other customers who preferred sports or music to long-winded speeches and earnest discussions among scientific experts, politicians, and professors who seemed to have no idea what had caused the failure of television, even less how to fix it. The men in the bar, who were not famous for their patience (most of them carried machetes, and many had used them to hack humans as well as snakes and jungle vegetation) indulged Paco whom they liked for his gentleness (and, if you will forgive my immodesty, for his beautiful wife) until they could tolerate television talk no longer and threatened the owner of the bar with loss of an ear if he did not change the radio to a more lively station. When the bar owner accommodated his patrons Paco, who ordinarily drank one or two beers, became upset and started to drink a strong spirit (I think it was cheap *pisco*) in large quantities until he fell flat on the floor where he lay like a statue, with the men stepping over him, and where he would have spent the night if Rodrigo hadn't carried him back to me when the bar shut down.

Paco awoke the next morning without a hangover (a miracle that perhaps ought to have alerted me to his strange mission) but with the symptoms of an addict who has been deprived of his drug: he could not tolerate the possibility of a day without news of the latest developments about television. He went out to work with the highway crew in the morning as usual, came home in the evening, found fault with the children, quarreled with me, refused his supper, kicked his guitar, and walked out into the night I know not where. He continued this obnoxious behavior (which I did not comprehend and did not bear with sympathy or agreeable temper) for several days until Rodrigo, who pitied him, arranged with Gloria for Paco to listen to the new radio she had acquired for what she grandly called her "parlor," provided he did not interfere with business—which may be one reason why Paco attributed more generosity to the whore than I believe she merited, although as I tell the story it occurs to me for the first time that Gloria, who had lost her friends in the soap operas, may indeed have felt genuine compassion for Paco's condition.

A woman of less self-confidence than myself—whose husband was spending his nights in a whorehouse—would have stolen his children and run away to her mother in Borba, or used a razor blade to render him unfit for other women, but I had reason to trust my Paco, and rather than plot my revenge I lay alone in our hammock at night or sat under his flamboyan tree by the stream trying to invent some way to release him from the curse of television—because, although I prided myself on being a rational woman, Paco was acting so strangely that I was beginning to believe what people were saying, that he had fallen under an evil spell. My seductions, my herbal potions, and the slaughter of a perfectly sound chicken failed to alter the cast of your grandfather's mind. That was when I decided that Tanya Mamou, the *macumba* priestess, had put a curse on him. One night I persuaded Paco to visit her and demanded that she remove the curse. She insisted it wasn't her curse at all, but that she could break it: she lit many candles and chanted and placed her wrinkled hands on Paco's forehead and gave him a foul-smelling liquid to drink, but even she lacked the powers to remove the television curse, and my poor Paco suffered a terrible stomach ache from the drink.

Some days passed until one evening Paco came back to our hut earlier than usual. He caressed the heads of the children, asked your aunt Elena to recite the names of the flowers that grew beside the stream, and placed the palm of his rough hand on my cheek.

"Maria," he announced, "I must speak with Gregorio Fisher."

"Who is Gregorio Fisher?" I inquired.

"It is not important who he is. Only that I must speak with him."

"Whatever you say, Paco, but where do you find this Gregorio Fisher?"

"He lives somewhere in the United States," said Paco, "I think. Maybe in the state of Pennsylvania."

I started to yell at him.

"You're proposing to leave us here and travel to the state of Pennsylvania to talk to some stupid gringo about—I don't know what, but it must be television?"

Paco fixed my hysterical eyes with his own calm brown gaze.

"Don't be loco, Maria. Do you think I would leave my family? We are going together—all of us. We are all getting out of this miserable place and looking for Gregorio Fisher together."

That was my dream, of course, to leave this rotten jungle, but even so the idea of Pennsylvania and the notorious United States immigration police scared me.

"I don't want to go," I cried. "I'm frightened."

"New places are frightening, Maria. But we must go. Only Gregorio Fisher can fix the television."

"Paco," I argued, "I don't give a damn about television. And I cannot understand why you care so much. What does it mean to you?"

"I don't understand it myself, Maria. I know only that I must find Gregorio Fisher and speak with him. Of course you may take the children to your mother in Borba, but it is my greatest wish that you will come with me."

I agreed, as you must guess (otherwise we wouldn't be here today), because even though I was still afraid, I could never resist Paco. He worked through the next Friday, collected his pay for the week, and drank a farewell beer with Rodrigo. Early the next morning we put our belongings on our backs; I hung the baby from my neck while Paco carried your uncle Gilberto, and then your aunt Elena, your uncle Fernando, your grandfather, and I all started to walk to Belém.

· · ·

"And now it is time for bed."

"No it isn't, Nana," Paolo objected, looking at his watch.

"Not for you, maybe," Maria countered, "but I need my beauty rest. Old age plays tricks on me: I rise very early now, sometimes at three in the morning, and I think about—"

"But you haven't finished the story," complained Teresa. "Did grandfather ever find Gregorio Fisher?"

"I'll tell you another story tomorrow, dear."

"Wasn't he the man who glowed in the dark?"

"Gregorio Fisher was a man of exceptional qualities," said Maria, "so naturally there were many rumors about him."

"And what about the televisions?"

"Oh my. That's a very long story indeed. Perhaps it is many stories."

Bertie's Story

"Uncle Bertie, tell us a television story," said one of the cousins, "Please, sir."

Bertie could not recollect whether the lad was a blood relative or one of those stepchildren imported into the family by marriage, but in either case his school seemed to be having a good influence on him, judging by the *please, sir.*

"Yes, Uncle Bertie," said a girl. "A television story."

"Well, I don't know," said Bertie. "How about something else? You've probably heard all my television stories before."

"Even so, it won't be the same. You never tell a story the same way twice."

The family laughed.

The commentary on his narrative habits, though lovingly intended, pierced Bertie's holiday mood by reminding him what he had momentarily forgotten: the little landslides of memory—the misplaced house keys, the scorched soup, and only yesterday the loss of the humblest of nouns (a spoon: the image had been fully formed in his head but he hadn't been able to retrieve the proper word)—that suggested to him an avalanche of the mind. God knows, he'd seen enough during half a century of medical practice to dread the wreckage of memory though did not fear death itself. Well, maybe he was mistaking natural lapses for symptoms (he'd seen that, too); after all, at ninety-seven a man was bound to forget something—though never, it seemed to him, what one would choose to forget.

"Bert darling, don't be an old goose." Helen's reassuring fingers found the back of his hand. "You've always been our best storyteller. Tell them about Paco and Maria."

"Yes, Bertie, c'mon, please, do," the family egged him on.

"I suppose I might be persuaded by a little lubrication," conceded Bertie. "How about some of that pear brandy from the kitchen cabinet. . . . Ah, that's splendid. . . . Funny you should ask about Paco, Helen. I came across that copy of his file just the other day—it's over there, on the shelf next to my desk, son, if you'll hand it to me."

Whisper, the cat, jumped onto Bertie's knees. As he stroked her striped fur, she purred and curled herself into his lap.

This is the tale Bertie told.

As you ought to remember since I've repeated my stories so often, on the Friday of the television failure I had dropped into the hospital to check on one of my patients who wasn't recovering properly from a heart attack. I entered his room and saw he had the TV tuned to the baseball game between Baltimore and the Yankees, so I asked him who was pitching for Baltimore. Poor fellow apologized for not knowing. (Hospitalized patients often retreat to the darkest corners of childhood and desperately try to please their doctors, as if disease were punishment for a crime of which the doctor can absolve them.) Anyway, my patient said he'd been feeling nauseous and hadn't been concentrating on the game. I reviewed his records, listened to his heart and lungs, explained some changes I planned for his medications, and he dozed off while I was writing new orders for the nurses. Neither of us noticed when the television quit, although I did observe that the screen was blank when I got up to leave the room. I didn't think much about it—just turned the damn thing off and drove home. Where, as you also know, I found Helen on the phone trying to call the cable company.

And then, of course, we soon learned that television failure was a global phenomenon. I remember listening to the radio when the reports started coming in from all over the world, hearing one confirmation after another, and feeling in the pit of my stomach a gathering of alarm, akin to an accumulation of gas, way out of proportion to my affection for television. Helen had served a fine dinner on the patio, but I couldn't summon any appetite.

"This is a very serious matter," I declared gravely.

"Don't worry, Dad," one of the boys consoled. "They'll fix it."

"Oh? What is it that must be fixed?" I asked. "And who exactly are *they?*"

"I don't know. Electrical engineers or whatever. Or the space agency. Probably the satellites have gone haywire."

"Just like *they* saved the African rhinoceros?" I retorted. The only African rhinoceros my boys would ever see would be in ancient copies of the *National Geographic* magazine, a melancholic fact of twenty-first-century life that bothered me a good deal more than it did them.

"Bert," exclaimed Helen, "you're letting your dinner get cold. It's not like you to be so negative. Whatever has come over you?"

Well, she had me there because indeed I had no idea at all what had come over me apart from the disagreeable sensation in my gut.

"I can't expect people who have to purchase a greeting card

to say something as elementary as 'you're nice' to be able to cope with a worldwide failure of television," I replied. "Can you?"

To which the boys responded, with admirable logic, "Huh?"

All I could tell them was that I felt absolutely convinced that no committee of Nobel laureates, professors, engineers, or politicians could raise television from the dead. Why? I couldn't say. But, of course, I turned out to be right.

Where I proved wrong, however, was in my prognosis that people would adapt to life without television. Why shouldn't they, I thought: generations before us had gotten along without it; also, my training in the biological sciences had taught me that *Homo sapiens* was a resilient species.

As long as TV failure still had the veneer of novelty and made for good conversation, my prediction held solid. But it began to disintegrate sometime in September when the professional football team owners announced they were calling off the 2002–2003 season because they weren't getting paid by the networks which couldn't collect from the advertising agencies which couldn't persuade their clients to take the financial risk that television would shortly return to normal. An elaborate web of people held together by television football collapsed all because of an inscrutable electronic glitch: just imagine million-dollar quarterbacks, giant tackles, coaches, trainers, masseurs, secretaries, grounds keepers, ushers, hot dog concessionaires, cameramen, sportscasters, grips and gaffers (whatever they are), receptionists, network executives, makeup artists, janitors, statistical researchers, and on into the advertising industry—not to speak of manufacturers of football helmets or sweatsocks, and who knows who else. The cancelation of one program broadcast twice a week dumped all of them out onto the sidewalks and precipitated pathological irregularities in the heartbeat of American life.

For what was a Sunday afternoon in November without the National Football League? How would people know it was

Monday without football? What would the family do after Thanksgiving turkey?

When football was multiplied by soap operas, by the evening news, by kiddie cartoons, by MTV, and by home video you wound up with a result that resembled universal congestive heart failure.

. . .

"Is that the same thing as a heart attack?" asked a grandchild.

"Not quite," Bertie explained professorially. "Congestive heart failure is what we call a clinical syndrome, caused by any number of physiological mishaps, in which the heart fails to propel blood normally. The result is circulatory congestion and diminished blood flow to the tissues."

"Uncle Bertie, do you mean that television was the heart of the whole world?"

"There's a concept called literary license, dear. I'll explain it to you when I've finished my story. But for now, yes, let's say that's what I mean."

Whisper woke up, cocked a skeptical eye at her master, then resumed her nap.

. . .

And indeed—although I couldn't figure out why at the time—people got sick. Halfway through October my waiting room had become so crowded that I practically had to fight my way into my office. The patients, many of whom were new to me, were presenting aches and pains that refused to yield their sources to laboratory tests or imaging technology. These people weren't hypochondriacs; they had genuine complaints, in most instances nothing life-threatening, but nevertheless discomforts that interfered with their lives and refused to remit spontaneously—headaches, fevers, rashes, stomachaches, neuritis, insomnia, chest pains, coughs, hemorrhoids.

I did what a physician is supposed to do: I took thorough histories, made careful physical examinations, and dispatched them to X ray and the labs with orders for whatever diagnostic tests seemed appropriate. Then, two or three days later, the results would come back negative. I'd call the patient with, say, diarrhea and congratulate him, and he'd say, "But Doc, I still have diarrhea," so I'd advise Kaopectate, and he'd say, "I tried that, and it doesn't work," so I'd ask him what he was eating, and he'd tell me he'd been living off whole grain cereals and clear soup for three weeks; so I'd tell him I'd phone in a prescription for paregoric to his pharmacist and that he should come in and see me if his problem didn't clear up.

Meanwhile a number of my chronic patients—people with serious conditions like heart disease, AIDS, diabetes, and lymphoma—who had been getting along nicely, suffered relapses. I had to admit several to the hospital, and there was one period when I had seven deaths in about four days. I became anxious and afraid I was losing my touch, that the diagnostic intuition that had gotten me where I was in academic medicine had gone on strike. Along with that I was extremely tired from putting in eighty or ninety hours a week in the hospital because of my huge caseload.

In fact, all departments of the hospital were overburdened: outpatients were jamming the offices, the inpatient census was running over a hundred percent, the emergency ward filled up every day with gunshot wounds, drug overdoses, industrial accidents, suicide attempts, heart attacks, and the other dreadful urgencies that brought patients in through the E.W. The only department reporting normal traffic was obstetrics which, in principle, presided over the healthy process of childbirth, although we did have a frightful number of crack babies in the nursery. We couldn't send people to other hospitals in Miami because they were congested, too. So we had to discharge patients sooner than we believed was good for them, and we had to set up beds in the solarium and in the corridors.

Finally the director called an extraordinary staff meeting and announced that we had an "epidemic." My colleagues who, like me, had welcomed the meeting as a chance to *rest,* slouched in their seats. I heard a few snores.

"An epidemic of *what?*" inquired the chief of nursing.

Incredibly, the director didn't respond nor did anyone else, even though the answer couldn't have been more obvious if it had jumped out of a giant cake in a G-string. I guess it was a case of a collective collapse of imagination. After weeks of double shifts our brains had transferred to autopilot and couldn't execute any unprogrammed thoughts, certainly not one that involved un-conventional connections between cause and effect.

The problem of cause and effect, by the way—

• • •

"You're going to tell us about Paco and Maria, aren't you, Grandpa?"

"I said I was going to, didn't I?" Bertie responded sharply. Damn! He'd forgotten, even with Paco's old file sitting right there on his lap under the cat. He'd gotten derailed by the hospital. "If I said I would tell you about Paco, then I will! I was just getting there."

He tugged at the file. Whisper, apparently annoyed at what she interpreted as an eviction, jumped down and stalked off in a huff.

• • •

One morning some weeks later, as I was getting ready to leave for the hospital, Helen told me that one of the boys had a fever.

"How much?" I asked, putting on my professional face.

"Thirty-nine point seven."

"Hmmm. That's pretty high for early morning. Maybe I should take a look at him."

"I wouldn't bother," my wife—his mother—said airily. "It's one of those withdrawal symptoms. Nothing you can do."

"Good Lord, Helen," I exploded, "are you telling me my son has been messing around with drugs? How could—"

"Not drugs, Bert. *Television!* All kinds of things are going around. I assumed you knew. That *is* why you've been staying so late at the hospital, isn't it?"

"*Television?* Is that what he thinks he's doing? Withdrawing from television?"

"Of course not! Nobody admits it, but everybody's so spooked. It's obvious, isn't it? The demonstrations in the streets, all the crime and broken windows. And so much sickness."

"THAT'S PREPOSTEROUS!" I slammed the newspaper on the kitchen table.

Helen smiled because she knew I knew she was right.

This is where Paco and Maria get into the story. Let me read you something from Paco's medical file. These are the notes I made when I admitted him to the hospital, on January 10, 2003, according to the record.

Name: Coehlo, Paco

Address: (Here I lied and put in our old address.)

Telephone: 434-9890 (which you may recognize as our old number)

Sex: Male

Race: Mixed; African, S. American Indian, Caucasian (I see I put a question mark after Caucasian.)

Date of birth: April 2, 1979 (which means, for those of you without calculators, that Paco was not quite twenty-four)

Place of birth: Teófilo Otoni, Brazil

Father's name: Unknown

Mother's maiden name: Coehlo, Teresa (deceased)

Marital status: Married

Wife's name: Maria

Children: Elena (age 6), Fernando (age 5—deceased), Gilberto (age 3+), Serita (14 months)

Person to be notified in case of death: Wife, Maria Coehlo

Religion: Roman Catholic

Insurance: Blue Cross/Blue Shield # 014502312 (I invented this number by looking at my own to get the proper number of digits, then making a few alterations. The hospital was so short of beds that I didn't think I could get him admitted without insurance coverage, and he absolutely had to be in the hospital. I figured that by the time Blue Cross started chasing him, he'd either be long gone or I'd have discovered a way to cover his expenses.)

Medical: Mrs. Coehlo (Maria did the talking for Paco who couldn't open his mouth without pain. She didn't speak English then, but we somehow managed to communicate in Spanish.) reports onset of symptoms approximately three weeks ago: stiffness of jaw followed by neck, arms, legs; difficulty swallowing, sore throat; headache, chills, back pain, difficulty urinating, two recent convulsive episodes.

Physical examination discloses moderate fever (39.3), elevated pulse and respiratory rates, exaggerated responses to deep tendon reflex testing. Poorly healed wound (gash, 8 cm. × ca. 1.3 cm. in depth) on lower right arm, sustained late November when patient fell on trash heap. No evidence of IV drug use.

Diagnosis: Tetanus (what you call lockjaw). Patient presents classic symptoms further suggested by wound and *no history of immunization.*

Frankly, this isn't much of a history; I didn't even bother to measure Paco's height and weight because the moment I spotted him in the waiting room I recognized that he was desperately ill. I took him ahead of other patients who had been waiting a long time, and I knew immediately what was wrong with him, so I only looked for clues that would confirm my diagnosis. I honestly didn't think he would make it, but getting him into the hospital and under treatment fast was the only chance he had.

When I announced that Paco had to be admitted, he shook his head and moaned what sounded like "não" through his poor clenched jaw. Maria turned pale and begged for pills. I tried to make her understand that Paco needed a machine to help him breathe, that another machine would have to monitor his heart, that a surgeon would have to debride the wound on his arm.

"Hospitals are factories of death," Maria announced. "If you won't give us any medicine, I'll take care of my husband myself."

No sooner had she spoken than Paco went into convulsions; his breathing became extremely labored, and I knew if it got any worse he might die of asphyxia. I telephoned over to Surgery, and they sent one of the residents who performed an emergency tracheostomy and intubated Paco right there in my office. My secretary had to restrain Maria, and meanwhile all three children were howling which was understandable considering that a strange guy with a knife was cutting their father's throat and shoving a fat tube down his windpipe. Mind you, horrible though it sounds, tracheostomy was about as simple as you could get in surgery in those days—easier than disjointing a chicken—and the fellow who did Paco's was an expert and finished the routine in a couple of minutes.

When Maria saw Paco with that obscene object in his throat, she gave up her fight to keep him out of the hospital. Paco himself started feeling the effects of the shot of diazepam he had been given to relieve his muscle spasms and patted the oldest child, a girl, on the head. He passed out on the examining table while my secretary arranged for a bed.

I'll spare you the details of Paco's treatment except to say that things were touch-and-go with him for almost a week while he was on a respirator. Meanwhile, I got acquainted with Maria.

Maria was . . . well, first of all—and Helen won't mind my saying this, I'm sure—Maria was the most beautiful woman I'd ever seen, on screen or off. No, beautiful isn't the right word; it doesn't tell you anything. *Delicious* is closer to what she was. Maria had ripened to perfection like a plum or a pear or a berry. If you taste a fruit too early the flesh is unyielding and the juice makes your mouth pucker; if you pick it too late the flesh has gone rotten, or mealy and dry; however, if it has grown under the proper conditions and you pluck it at exactly the right moment it releases a whole symphony of tastes and textures. But whereas fruit attains maturity and begins to decline in a few hours, Maria held on to her moment of ripeness for almost twenty years. God alone knows how.

. . .

"What are you giggling at, Helen?" Bertie interrupted himself. "Did I say something funny?"

"Forgive me, dear," she sputtered, "it's . . . it's just the idea of Maria as fruit. I doubt that she'd be amused by the metaphor. She was quite vain, you know. I'm sure she'd prefer to be likened to flowers."

"Flowers are banal. The newspaper columnists worked that one to death. Some guy named her the 'Brazilian Orchid,' as I recall, but as far as I'm concerned she was fruit."

. . .

Bear in mind that the creature I've been describing as perfection was clad in a faded red T-shirt, old jeans, and sneakers which were the only clothes she possessed. She was illiterate. She had three small children, had recently buried a fourth, and her husband was desperately ill. With all that she still looked luscious.

Well, after we got Paco settled in a private room, hooked him up to all the machines, put in IV lines and a catheter and so forth, I finally got back to the rest of the patients in my office. And then I had meetings—I don't remember what, exactly, but I was running later than usual, so I didn't return to Paco until after ten that night. When I entered his room I discovered Maria dozing in a chair in the corner.

"You're not supposed to be here," I whispered. "Visiting hours end at eight o'clock."

"It's okay," she assured me. "The nurse said I could stay. How is my husband?"

I glanced at the monitor and his charts, noted that the wound on his arm had been tended. He was asleep.

"Resting comfortably." I looked around suspiciously. "What have you done with the children?"

She pointed to the bathroom door. I opened it and saw all three kids lying on top of towels on the floor, snuggled against one another in a tangle of arms and legs, sleeping soundly.

"Does the nurse know about them?"

"No."

"She'll find out soon enough, and then you'll all get thrown out."

"I will not leave my husband alone in such a place," Maria said emphatically.

"Then you'll have to find somewhere for the children to stay. Do you have a friend who can take care of them for a while? If not, I can take them home with me tonight, then perhaps I can arrange something more permanent for them."

Maria appeared to consider my offer. "No," she replied politely, "I cannot accept your kindness. Serita, the little one, she needs me. We will stay together and we will stay here."

"Now listen here, Mrs. Coehlo—"

"Please, Doctor, my name is Maria." She smiled.

"Okay, Maria. But this is impossible." I was angry. I meant to point out that I'd already compromised myself for them, that I'd smuggled Paco into the hospital by making up an address and an insurance number, but I didn't know the expression in Spanish and besides, the spectacle of her beauty was turning my brain to mush. What the hell, I decided; let the cops throw them out. So instead of scolding her, I inquired if she had had anything to eat.

"Oh yes." She smiled again. "The nice doctor, the young one who put that thing in Paco's neck, he came back later to look at his arm, and then he left and he came back again with three big hamburgers from the cafeteria"—she wrinkled her nose (she had a wonderful, bony nose; it would have looked awful on any other woman)—"and some ice cream, and a banana and milk for the baby."

I had to laugh.

That's how it went with Paco and Maria. The staff ignored all the rules and hid them from the administration. Four people, including myself, showed up the next morning with blankets and pillows for the kids; the nurses invented huge meal orders for Paco whose nutrition for the first week or so consisted exclusively of fluids dripped into his veins; and people brought in candy bars and toys and used clothing. As rumors of Maria's beauty traveled around the hospital, male doctors from other services found pretexts for visiting Paco—as though tetanus were an exotic disease—just to get a glimpse of her.

In her own way Maria obeyed the rules. She kept the children tidy and quiet. She received the parade of gawkers with dignity. (I'm sure she knew that men were coming to look at her—even enjoyed that fact—because Helen is right, Maria was vain, but she was never a tease.) When formal visiting hours ended at eight o'clock, she closed the door, tucked the children into the bathroom for the night, and denied admission to anyone who wasn't essential to Paco's care. I heard from one of the nurses that sometimes after midnight Maria sat at the foot of the bed and sang songs to her husband in a voice as pure as spring water; when the night staff heard her singing, they would stand in the corridor and listen through the door.

I got into the habit of going up to Paco's room at the end of the day to check on his progress and, I must admit, to see Maria. During our conversations over the next few evenings she told me how Paco had been a worker on the Amazon highway, how she had earned money washing laundry in a stream behind their hut, how the family had left the town on foot and made their way to Belém where she had suffered a miscarriage and had to rest for two weeks; how they had stowed away in an empty hold of a cargo ship they thought was bound for New York but which

landed instead in Caracas where they had been discovered and
set ashore; how they had joined the scavengers on the garbage
heaps outside Caracas, which was where her son Fernando had
died of fever and where Paco had fallen and hurt his arm; how
Paco had heard gossip and, by hanging around the waterfront,
had found a yacht that would take them to Miami if Maria would
cook and Paco would take care of the engine; how Paco had lied
about his mechanical skills and how the owner of the yacht had
also lied because what he really wanted from them was to deliver
cocaine in Miami; how the children had gotten seasick in a storm;
how one night the owner of the yacht had cast them off with
four kilos of cocaine in a small metal boat miles offshore and
ordered them to row; how the sea had stayed calm and they had
landed; how Paco, who was a man of honor, had delivered the
cocaine; how the man who had received it had shaken Paco's
hand and shooed him away; how Paco had been excited to be in
Miami and had started his search for Gregorio Fisher—

"You mean he didn't mind that he wasn't rewarded for de-
livering the cocaine?" I asked in amazement.

"The voyage to the United States was reward enough," Maria
replied. "Besides, Paco would never take money for cocaine which
he hates ever since he was a child and his brother died from it,
and which he knows is dishonest. He does not wish to break the
laws of the country."

To which I muttered something like "hmmm, hmmm," because her story had made plain to me what I had suspected all
along, that the Coehlos were illegal aliens. If we had been in the
1980s or early 1990s, I would have been less concerned about
them because in those days temporary residency and even citizenship could often be arranged by a sponsor; but in the mid-
'90s Congress passed an extremely restrictive law empowering an
enforcement agency, the National Immigration Police, to detain
and deport illegal aliens and to discourage newcomers from trying
to slip into the country. The NIPs, as they were known, had been

criticized for brutality by international human rights agencies, but illegals did not enjoy the protection of citizens under United States law, and the immigration authority periodically trotted out figures showing a decline in illegal aliens to justify the NIPs' "unfortunate but necessary" measures. I shuddered to think what the NIPs might do to Maria.

Not wishing to alarm her, I broached this subject delicately one evening toward the end of the first week, while Paco and the children were sleeping.

"Yes," she replied, "we have heard the stories of your police in Amazonas. They are evil, but like all evil people they are stupid, and they are slow and will not find us because we do not want to stay in the United States. When Paco is better we will go to Pennsylvania, speak with Gregorio Fisher, and then go back home to my mother in Borba."

"To *Pennsylvania?* Why on earth would you want to go to Pennsylvania? *Where* in Pennsylvania?"

"To speak with Gregorio Fisher. He is in Pennsylvania."

"And who is Gregorio? Is he a relative?" I was thinking maybe this Gregorio carried medical insurance.

"No, he is not a relative," answered Maria. "I don't know who he is. Paco believes he has something to do with the television."

"The *television?*"

The conversation had taken a wacky turn. I stared at the lump on the bed, plugged in to its medical paraphernalia, and considered the possibility that Paco was a crackpot.

By way of explanation Maria launched into a story about a whore without teeth whose name I have forgotten, the failure of the only television in the settlement where she lived, a goat named Belita, *macumba* mumbo jumbo, and Paco's obsession with television and Gregorio Fisher. I didn't know what to make of her tale, but for the first time since his convulsions in my office, I was more curious about Paco than I was about Maria.

Paco kept me in suspense a few days longer, but finally the antibiotics began to kick in, his symptoms subsided, and we were able to wean him from the respirator, remove the tube, detach him from the heart monitor, and cut back on the heavy doses of narcotics. I happened to be in the room when the surgeon took out the tube. Maria kissed the bandaged wound on her husband's throat; he whispered into her hair, and she laughed and kissed his right eyelid. Their intimacy embarrassed me, so I started to leave, but Maria stopped me.

"The doctor wants to know who is Gregorio Fisher," she told Paco.

"Gregorio Fisher?" he croaked; his throat was sore from the tube. "You have never heard of Gregorio Fisher?"

"No, I can't say that I have. Who is he?"

"Gregorio Fisher, the astronaut."

"Oohhhh." It finally hit me. "You mean *Greg* Fisher! Yes, of course I've heard of him." Who hadn't? He'd been the legendary Bad Boy of the space program, the renegade astronaut, the one who wouldn't play by the rules and, accordingly, the one pursued by the media. But he had been out of the news for years now. And I couldn't fathom what Paco wanted with him.

"Why must you speak with him?" I asked.

"Because he is the only man who can fix the television!"

Yeah sure, I thought. That does it: Paco's a crackpot.

"And how do you know that?" I asked, humoring him.

Paco shook his head.

"I don't *know* how I know," he admitted. "Sometimes I think I am loco. But I know it is true, and what is more, Gregorio Fisher doesn't know it yet. That is why I must find him. To tell him."

"And how is he supposed to fix the televisions?"

"I don't know that either. He will know what to do." Paco covered his neck with one hand and swallowed; a shadow of pain passed over his expression.

"That's enough for now," I said in my doctor voice. "I can see you're tired. Try to get some rest, especially your vocal cords. I'll leave orders that you're not to be disturbed."

"Doctor," Paco whispered with the remnants of his voice, "may I have some ice cream?"

"Yes, Paco. Of course. Maria knows how to order it for you."

"Chocolate, please. That is my favorite."

When I left the room Maria pursued me into the corridor, closed the door, and grasped my arm.

"I know what you think." Her words came out fiercely, attacking me. "I thought so too for a while. I thought Tanya Mamou had cast a spell on him, but it is not that. I don't know what it is with the televisions, but my Paco was never loco before, and he is not loco now. I beg you to trust him."

Maria took my face between her hands and kissed me lightly on the mouth.

"I thank you for all you have done for him," she said. "Please, believe him."

I believed Paco. The testimony of Maria's kiss made me believe him.

I don't pretend to have behaved rationally with respect to Maria and Paco, nor did my enchantment with Maria really account for my reaction, despite people's willingness to accept infatuation as an excuse for all manner of nonsense. No, now that I've had several years to review the events, I believe I fell for Paco's story because it was so very *strange,* because it was the only story I'd heard that equaled the strangeness of the failure of television itself.

And the longer that went on, the stranger it got. By January 2003 the televisions hadn't been working for seven months, and not one of the special scientific-engineering committees on earth had hatched a credible explanation of what might have happened to them, let alone a solution. Scientific hypotheses had given way

to off-the-wall theories about invisible extraterrestrials, radio
jamming signals from other galaxies, and Lord knows what else.

I recall one particularly farcical episode when members of a
Lebanese terrorist faction seized a Beirut radio station, announced they were holding television reception hostage, and
promised to restore function immediately upon elimination of the
state of Israel. Believe it or not, some people took this ridicu-
lousness seriously, and there followed a learned debate in which
radio talk-show hosts and their callers speculated upon the technology the terrorists might have employed to kidnap reception.
When challenged to back up their claim, the terrorists could not
produce an electron of evidence.

Then Paco, a simple but not simpleminded Brazilian laborer,
showed up with his weird story. I doubt I would have listened to
him if he had been ready with all the answers—what was wrong
with television, why he had to see Fisher, what Fisher was supposed to do. In fact, Paco's own confusion was what attracted
me to him. Which is not to say I had confidence that he could
accomplish anything. I was merely overcome by the feeling that
I must help him do whatever he believed he had to do. And,
since I recognized that people would label me a lunatic, I resolved
to keep my actions secret.

But I have never been able to conceal anything from Helen,
not even Maria's kiss in the corridor, and my resolution came
unglued the same night of the day Paco told me about Greg
Fisher. I blurted out the whole story while Helen and I sat on the
patio drinking gin-and-tonics. She heard me through to the end
without a word, and when I finished speaking we listened to one
or two movements of the tree frogs' concerto.

"What is it you think you have to do?" she finally asked.

"Well, first of all there's the matter of protecting the Coehlos
from the immigration authorities. I don't think they appreciate
what zealots those NIPs are."

"How can you protect them?"

"They're safe as long as they're in the hospital, but as soon as I discharge Paco they're back on the streets, without any money as far as I can see. I don't think they know anybody in Miami, and the NIPs concentrate on the casual labor down here. So their best bet is to find Fisher as fast as they can, let Paco deliver his message, and then get the hell back to Brazil."

"If the NIPs find out you're helping them, you'll wind up in jail. You know that, don't you?"

"Yes. I know. But once in a while you have to get out of your rut and take a real risk."

We caught the last section of the frogs' third movement before Helen spoke again.

"How can I help?"

"Helen," I said, "I love you! Do you think my trolley's gone off the track?"

"I love you too, Bert," she replied.

The next morning Helen got on the telephone to a friend who worked as a computer programmer for the space agency at Cape Canaveral and asked for her help in locating Greg Fisher. Helen told her friend that one of the boys was doing research for a school project and wanted to write Fisher a letter. The friend called back two days later with an address for Fisher in upstate New York, but no telephone number; Fisher, she explained, had an unlisted number that he changed frequently to avoid old girl-friends.

"And tell your son not to be disappointed if Fisher doesn't answer his letter," Helen's friend added. "He's got a reputation for chucking his mail into the fireplace unopened."

When I told the Coehlos that Fisher didn't live in Pennsylvania at all, but in New York, Maria's eyes lit up.

"Not New York *City*," I specified. "New York *State*. Near a place called Poughkeepsie."

"Oh," she said, her light extinguished.

Meanwhile Paco's health improved rapidly, and I had to start thinking about his discharge. One risk I didn't dare take, especially with the hospital overflowing, was to keep him too long and arouse the suspicions of the utilization review committee because if they started nosing into Paco's insurance credentials they would figure out his illegal status. Therefore I decided on a Wednesday that, provided he continued to mend, I would sign him out on Friday—two days earlier than I would have discharged him under normal conditions, but the conditions were hardly normal.

As soon as I had settled on the discharge date, a plan fell into place. I knew it was naive, infantile in its simplicity, but I reminded myself that simplicity was deemed elegant in science. I could only hope that elegance had some operative value when it came to human affairs.

"What if Fisher isn't at home?" asked Helen.

"We'll wait for him," I replied.

"He could be anywhere. Don't you think you should write ahead?"

"You heard what your friend at Cape Canaveral said. The guy doesn't open his mail."

"All right," she sighed. "Let's be optimistic and suppose he's home. What happens then?"

"Paco says whatever he has to say, with me doing the translating in case Fisher doesn't speak Spanish. Then we pile back into the car, take the kids to McDonald's for Big Macs, and drive to New York where I put the Coehlos on a flight to Brazil."

"I'm worried about them. They don't have passports. What will happen at the airport when they see they don't have passports? Won't they call the NIPs?"

"It'll be okay. As long as the Coehlos are flying out on a one-way ticket, nobody will bother them. That's what the immigration authority wants, for these so-called undesirables to go away, although how anybody as desirable as Maria could ever be declared—"

"Bert," Helen cautioned.

The first part of my plan went perfectly. Simpler is better, I always say. Paco, Maria, and the three children left Miami South around noon on Friday. I put them in a taxi, wrote down our address for the driver, gave him a twenty-dollar bill, and went back to the hospital. During the afternoon I had my secretary arrange for other doctors to cover my patients so I could go away for a week; I'd been working long hours since October, and nobody questioned my entitlement to a vacation.

The Coehlos spent the night at our house. Early Saturday morning we got into the old Volvo and started the drive north . . .

. . .

Bertie yawned.

"And then what happened?"

"I think that's enough for now," Bertie said. "The pear brandy must have caught up with me."

"Did the NIPs follow you?"

"No, we didn't see any. They gave the Coehlos some trouble later, though."

"I don't understand," said one of the girls. "Who were these NIPs? Why did we have them?"

"That was an unpleasant time in history. Very nasty, if you ask me. And such things didn't happen only in the United States. All the rich countries in the world were trying to defend themselves against refugees from poor countries—it's a complicated story. Don't they teach you anything in history class these days?"

"Did you ever see Maria again, after she became famous?"

"Indeed I did." Bertie yawned again. "But that's another tale. . . ."

"Uncle Bertie, you promised to explain literary license."

"Shhh," commanded Helen. "Your uncle Bertie's taking a nap."

S u s a n ' s   S t o r y

"What do you want?" Susan inquired through the screen door.

"Hi, I'm Dan Melcher," the stranger announced. "I sent you a letter last month to say I'd be dropping by. I'm working on a book about Gregory Fisher, remember?"

"Ah, yes," Susan grumbled, "and I didn't answer your letter, remember?"

"No, er, you didn't, but I thought I'd take a chance—"

"Go away! I have no intention of telling you anything about Greg Fisher."

"But you can't *do* that," Melcher protested, pressing his nose against the screen. "You have a duty as a member of the older generation!"

"How dare you remind me of my duty! My duty is to tell stories to children, not to submit to the interrogations of writers who quote me out of context and bend my memories out of shape. Parasites! You're all parasites." She withdrew from the doorway and merged with the gloom of the house.

Melcher held fast to his piece of porch. He narrowed his eyes to slits in an effort to see what she was doing.

"I'm not here to feed on your past," he shouted through the screen. "I want to know the truth about Fisher. You——"

"Truth?" Her voice came two inches from his ear, startling him; she must have been hiding right inside the door, against the wall. "Whose truth? *My* truth? Hasn't anyone told you I'm a loony?" she cackled. "That's what people say, you know, that I'm a loony. Personally, I haven't reached a verdict yet. What's your opinion, Mr., um——"

"Melcher. Dan. Melcher. I, er, can't say I've, er . . ."

But she'd retreated again, so he let his stammering response wilt in the afternoon heat. He heard a clinking of glassware.

"How do you take it?" Susan called from within.

"Take what?" he asked. When she didn't answer, he raised his voice a notch and made a wild guess. *"Straight!"*

"You can't drink this stuff straight," she observed as she banged through the screen door balancing a tray laden with a pitcher and two mismatched glasses filled with a poisonous-looking green liquid. "It'll kill you!"

Melcher, whose mother had taught him it was rude to stare, averted his eyes, then dared a peek from under his half-closed lids. Susan stood six feet tall and, despite the weather, had swaddled herself in layers of heavy clothing. Melcher took mental inventory from bottom to top: black rubber boots, pink pants, brown tweed skirt, sweaters (two—one red pullover, the other a gray cardigan spattered with food stains), brown knitted muffler about eight feet long wound twice around her neck, and a knitted beret of a melancholy shade of blue pulled down over the ears, from which a few colorless wisps of hair had escaped.

She set the tray down on the peeling wicker table and turned to face Melcher. Her eyes were concealed behind aviator glasses.

"Sit!" she ordered, pointing to a chair. "The sun comes around soon, and we'll be warm here. So you're looking for Greg Fisher, are you?" She pushed the green concoction toward him. "Here. Drink up."

Melcher lifted the glass, sniffed, dared a sip.

"What *is* this stuff?" He gagged.

"Kool-Aid. But don't worry. I diluted it with alcohol."

"What's Kool-Aid?"

"They don't make it anymore. I bought out the last batch when it was taken off the market. I save it for special occasions," she announced proudly, almost hospitably. "Now, young man, what makes you think I can help you find Greg Fisher?"

"I'm looking for the *truth* about Fisher, of course, not Fisher himself," Melcher corrected her. "I've heard you two were close for a while. Perhaps you could start with how you met him." He switched on his tape recorder.

"I'll start anywhere I damn well please," Susan snapped. "I won't let you turn this into an inquisition. Just pay attention."

This is the tale Susan told.

Greg Fisher was a bastard.

He didn't have to make any effort at all to seduce women. He was born with a God-given talent, amplified in adulthood by fame. All he had to do to cast his magnetic field was saunter into a room, glittering with space dust, and lay on that lopsided smile. Women—or, as he sometimes referred to them, *broads*—forgot about their husbands or lovers or vows to swear off men for the next six months, as though Greg had pushed a brain button that erased their common sense.

The minute I laid eyes on him, I knew he was no good. I wasn't naive. I was a good deal older than Greg and I'd been around long enough to recognize—

· · ·

"Excuse me," Melcher interrupted, "and forgive my asking

an impertinent question, but how old are you? Just for the record."

Susan appeared to consider the question, but since Melcher could not see her eyes, he couldn't have said precisely what she was doing.

"One hundred and forty-one," she replied after some seconds.

"WHAT?"

"I attribute my longevity to Kool-Aid. Green is the most potent flavor, so don't waste it."

Melcher obliged his hostess with another sip.

"Please," he gasped, "go on."

. . .

All in all I reckon an affair with Greg was worth whatever tears a woman shed when he ditched her. I don't intend to draw pictures to make you understand what I mean, because at my age one doesn't encourage one's blood to go galloping around the arteries. Mind you, exquisite lovers, though few and far between as my aunt Katie used to say, nevertheless do turn up from time to time. But in addition to stamina, technique, originality, and concentration, Greg had a most delicious idiosyncrasy: *he glowed in the dark.* When he turned off the lights and stripped off his clothes, he shimmered like a swimmer rising out of phosphorescent waters, like a fairytale prince. He never explained the glow, and one didn't ask about it for fear of breaking the spell.

Until Hsu-ling came along, Greg went through women as though he were eating his way through a box of imported chocolates. As long as a woman pleased him, he was hungry and tender, but once he'd finished he forgot about her and moved on to the next. When you're sinking your teeth into a champagne truffle, you don't think about the raspberry cream you had the day before yesterday.

I don't expect you to take my word for this. I'm sure some of Greg's other women are still alive, since most of them were several years younger than I. You might try Maria Coehlo, the singer. I always thought she had an affair with Greg, before she became famous. She shouldn't be difficult to locate. I know she's living because I recently read something about her in a magazine. The writer claimed she's still quite beautiful.

· · ·

"You don't happen to know anything about Hsu-ling, do you?" Melcher inquired.

"Hsu-ling was said to have gone into seclusion after Greg vanished. I've never heard that she came out. The last time I saw her was when she came to help me close down the house after— well, you know."

"What about Jesse Randolph and Ozzie Elmwood? Do you know anything about them?"

"I think I heard that Jesse died not long ago, but that could be wrong. As for Ozzie, I lost track of him."

"There's another thing. You've been pulling my leg, haven't you, about Fisher glowing in the dark?"

"What a stupid question!" Susan snapped. "I'm warning you, young man: Watch your mouth. Don't afflict me with absurd questions."

"Yes, ma'am," Melcher murmured.

"I see your drink is getting low. Why didn't you say something? Time to fill up." She poured another glass of green.

· · ·

Okay. Now that you know Greg Fisher was a bastard, and you understand why he kept changing his unlisted telephone number and didn't open his mail, I can go back to the beginning.

By his own account Greg had a disgustingly sunny childhood. Unlike most kids of that generation, he grew up surrounded by relatives and dogs and vats of homemade spaghetti sauce and stability. His father was Jewish of Romanian descent, his mother a lapsed Roman Catholic of Italian origin. Father was a hydrologist who operated his own consulting firm out of an office in their remodeled Victorian house in the Philadelphia suburbs; he was somehow involved in that insane plan to save Venice by floating it to cleaner waters in the Mediterranean. Mother, who had studied law at Yale, happily abandoned legal practice during her first pregnancy and chose to manage the household.

Greg arrived rather late in the marriage, nine or ten years after the previous child, and was the only male child, pampered by his parents, much doted upon by three older sisters. He was adored by his Jewish grandmother who lived in his home, and by his Italian grandparents who lived within walking distance, as well as by numerous aunts and uncles. He recalled his childhood as one long holiday filled with crowds of people, pets, games, good things to eat, family arguments flaring up in the kitchen and extinguishing themselves on the living room floor, music, presents, hugs.

"I was spoiled rotten," he sometimes said, "except for television. I wasn't permitted to watch television, not even 'Sesame Street.' But I had my own computer and a room in the basement where I could do science experiments. One summer when I was about thirteen I found an old black-and-white portable TV in a neighbor's trash. I got it working again and spent about ten days watching anything that moved until my father discovered what I was up to and made me get rid of it."

Greg cut a brilliant academic path for himself, carelessly littering its margins with the bruised hearts of coeds, not to mention one susceptible instructor of French literature. He graduated high school at the top of his class, won a scholarship to Stanford where he earned Latin honors in chemistry, and then moved on to MIT for his doctorate in atmospheric chemistry. His thesis adviser pulled political strings in Washington, and Greg went into the space program with expectations of expanding his dissertation in the agency's laboratories in Atlanta. He'd been there a little more than a year when he saw a chance to get himself and his research project aboard one of the space missions. He grabbed at it, and he got it.

I put this background together from bits and pieces of conversation. Maybe Greg made it up, but I doubt it. Still, if I were you, I'd do some careful research. However, his career as an astronaut was well documented by the press.

In any event one day Greg Fisher rode the tiny elevator to the top of a rocket named after an ancient god, climbed into the cabin of an improbable vehicle, strapped himself into a seat, clenched his teeth while fifty thousand tons of fuel ignited under his tail, screamed past the clouds up through the ozone layer, soared into the stratosphere and—weightless—fell heels over head in love with space. It was the ultimate orgasm. When he came back down to earth he wanted to go up again, so he applied to the astronaut program as a mission specialist.

But space travel, like everything else, had a downside which, in this case, took the form of the space agency with its red tape, regulations, training rituals, defense secrets, debriefings, and schoolmarmish efforts to control all aspects of the astronauts' lives. All that drove Greg crazy. The agency frowned upon his promiscuity, his habit of dropping out of sight during leaves, and the time he dyed his hair blue. They especially disapproved of his unsupervised dialogues with the press corps. After he discussed the drug and alcohol problems of former astronauts on a television talk program, the agency nearly fired him in a fit of embarrassment. At the last second, however, they punished him by grounding him for one flight because he was irreplaceable as an atmospheric chemist—

· · ·

"That's not entirely accurate," Melcher interjected, "although that's the story that went around at the time. But three or four other astronauts could have carried out Fisher's experiments. What saved him was his gift for improvisation. If something screwed up during a mission, he could always figure a way to wiggle around or out of the problem. The other astronauts had confidence in him; they all wanted to ride with him. That's one of the reasons he logged so many missions. In fact, when they heard he might be fired—"

"Are you going to tell this story," asked Susan impatiently, "or am I?"

"Sorry, ma'am," said Melcher. "I'll have some more of that green stuff, if you don't mind."

• • •

Whatever the reasons, the agency wouldn't fire Greg, and Greg tolerated the agency's insults to his independence because he was so in love with space. Eventually he stopped talking to the press because his notoriety had achieved critical mass: he couldn't go to the men's room without some reporter tagging along behind, waiting for him to leak a newsworthy item. He convened a farewell press conference and then sealed himself shut like a Trappist monk. The press proved less forgiving than the agency, but Greg didn't care what they wrote about him as long as they stopped following him, which they did when they realized that his silence was more impenetrable than an oak.

He retired from the space agency at the age of thirty-six, having flown eleven missions, and bought the derelict farm north of mine. When asked why he had quit, Greg would mumble something about his semicircular canals. But there was nothing wrong with that man's balance; he clambered around replacing the shingles on his roof like a mountain goat. In my opinion he left the agency because space was pulling on him more strongly than earth, and he sensed himself in danger of tearing away altogether from his moorings. There was definitely something peculiar about Greg's relationship with gravity.

That's why he came to Strangeways and went to work on the wrecked shell of a house which he rebuilt board by board with fanatic attention to authenticity. He dug one garden for antique roses and another for vegetables, adopted a mongrel puppy, and read geology and funny periodicals—all earthbound activities that might reattach him to his proper planet. He was a man filled with helium, trying to find something with enough ballast to keep him down, a commitment more powerful than his love for space.

He went so far as to refuse to set foot inside an airplane. When he had to travel, as he occasionally did because he continued reviewing atmospheric research data, he either drove his ancient Land Rover or took the train. Luckily he could accomplish most of his work in his study on the computer.

A series of women—an *overlapping* series—passed through his life like falling stars in a summer sky, beginning with the girl who arrived with him, a velvet brown Jamaican named Dulcie, on through the third-grade teacher at the local elementary school, myself, an associate professor of Russian literature at Vassar, the veterinarian who treated his dog for ear mites, various neglected wives, and no doubt others unknown to me. None satisfied the need he could not name.

Long after he ceased to be my luminous lover, he shoveled my driveway after snowstorms, fetched my groceries when I hurt my back, helped me put up and take down my storm windows, and repaired whatever broke. He could fix absolutely anything, from a window sash to a microwave; during the four years he lived next door I never had to call a plumber or a carpenter or an appliance serviceman. In return I looked after his dog Benny and watered his garden when he went away and fed him chicken soup when he had the flu. We swapped vegetables, jokes, ideas, and life histories. Yet, though Greg was more reliable as a neighbor than a lover, I didn't dare depend on him because I realized that any morning I might wake up and find him gone just as surely as if I'd dreamed him. No matter how many old roses he planted, Strangeways would never pin him down; he might pause to rest, but he would never *belong*. Sometimes late at night I'd see him out my kitchen window, standing behind his house adoring the sky through his telescope.

That fateful summer of 2002 was a killer. The heat arrived early in May, and it sat on us for more than three months, as though the dynamics of weather had been suspended. Each new day was a Xerox copy of the one before: hot, humid, windless, rainless, suffocating; even the clouds seemed to be yesterday's profitless puffs. The last week in May the gypsy moths hatched in such multitudes that if you stood still in the woods you could hear the sound of munching. The county initiated severe water conservation measures in June, including a ban on watering public parks as well as private gardens.

The next morning I heard Greg's Land Rover pull into my driveway, and his footsteps on the front porch.

"That does it!" he yelled through the screen. "This place is uninhabitable. We're getting out of here."

"We?" I inquired. *"Who* we?"

"Benny and me, that's who we. Poor guy just lies around on the bathroom tiles next to the toilet with his tongue hanging out." Greg grinned. "You didn't think I was going with a broad, did you?"

"Woman, Greg dear. The word is woman."

"Whatever."

"Where are you going?"

"I don't know." He shrugged. "Listen, Susan, don't worry about the garden. It's already half dead. But could you keep an eye on the house? I don't want anyone walking off with my computer. Here are the keys, in case anything looks suspicious. Also, I'd appreciate it if you'd empty my mailbox every couple of days. You can throw away everything except first-class letters from Pennsylvania—that'll be my family—and the magazines. I want to save the magazines."

"Are you coming back?"

"What kind of question is that? Of course we're coming back! This heat won't go on forever." He deposited a fraternal kiss on my cheek and drove away.

I followed his instructions. I let his garden wither and watched his empty house bake in the sun. I collected his mysterious mail—mysterious in that it consisted of a bizarre assortment of magazines (among them, *The Romanian Weekly, Journal of the International Association of Plant Taxonomists, Technology Review, Ad Astra, International Wildlife,* the German edition of *Vogue*); the usual junk mail addressed to "Current Resident"; miscellaneous letters, many in perfumed envelopes which I resisted opening; and no bills, not a one—no telephone bills, no electric bills, no credit card or bank statements, no checks, no evidence of a financial life.

When a man glows in the dark and casts no financial shadow, one begins to wonder what he's made of.

The rains came in August, too late to save the roses or the tomatoes, but just in time to prevent the county from enforcing more draconian restrictions on water consumption and to wash away the heat. One evening in September I saw Greg's Rover sitting under the sugar maple. He called me the next morning to announce his return.

"I never used your keys," I explained. "Is everything okay over there?"

"No problems that can't be solved by a giant feather duster, except the TV's busted. I guess the picture tube died of old age . . . Susan? Are you still there?"

I was there, all right, but I was absolutely stupefied. I couldn't conceive of anyone on earth not knowing the televisions had failed more than two months ago. Where could he have been?

"Where have you been, Greg?"

"Away. Counting my toes."

"So you really don't know."

"Don't know what? Is anything wrong? Are you ill, Susan?"

"No, I'm okay. Your magazines are here." I don't know why,

but I didn't have the energy to tell him about the televisions over the phone. "How's Benny?"

"Benny? He had a great time. He fell desperately in love and got involved, if you know what I mean. It couldn't last, of course, because he'd aspired above his station to a gorgeous pedigreed bitch. He sulked for half a day when they split up, but next thing I knew he was good as new, back chasing rabbits."

"Good old Benny. A regular chip off the old block," I said. "Why don't you come over and collect your magazines? I'll make some Kool-Aid. We have to talk."

That afternoon I gave him a rundown of events during his absence: the caterpillars had chewed the deciduous trees bare; the pond I had been studying for nineteen years had gone dry; birds had toppled out of the trees; Mr. Creekmore's favorite cow Bossie had collapsed in the field and died, and old Mrs. Creekmore had been taken to the hospital with heatstroke. Greg followed my narrative with a fallen face until I got to the televisions, when he laughed. He didn't believe me. He thought I was joking. When he saw I was serious he thought—though he phrased it delicately (I hadn't believed him capable of such tact)—I'd gone crackers. I had to pull out three weeks of magazines and newspapers and show him the articles before he could accept the fact of television failure.

"You said the television quit a week or two after I left?" he asked.

"That's right. It was the twenty-first of June, a Friday."

"What time of day?"

"Early afternoon in this part of the world."

"What were you watching?"

"Why are you asking?"

"I need to know!"

He *needs?* I asked myself. "All right then, I was down at the pond watching bugs, if you must know. I didn't realize anything had gone wrong until evening when I wanted to run a movie and

all I got was a white screen. I read in the papers that a lot of
people on the East Coast were watching baseball games, and out
West it was still kiddie cartoon time. But the main event was the
World Cup match which was being broadcast live all over the
world from Barcelona. Somebody has estimated that half the televisions on earth were tuned to the soccer game."

"Wow!" Greg inhaled deeply, releasing his breath with a
whistle. "Start over again, Susan. Tell me everything you know
about that day, every detail you can remember, I don't care how
trivial you think it is."

"Honestly, Greg, I can't believe you didn't hear about this.
It's all anyone talks about. Where have you been?" He slapped
my question aside as though it were a gnat; I could see it was
squashed, and I'd never discover where he'd been.

June 21 wasn't enough for him. He had to know about the
twenty-second, too, and then the whole week, how people had
behaved, what the president had said, whether the United Nations was looking into the matter (it was). Who had been on
which committees and what they had said. I remembered some,
forgot others. Well, he pressed, had they been discussing the
likelihood of unusual solar activity?

"Yes, indeed," I said. "That's very high on the list of speculations except they don't have any evidence for it unless you
count the televisions themselves."

"Hmmm," said Greg, "curious. And how are people adapting
themselves?"

"*Adapting?* They're angry and impatient with all these windbag politicians and professors. They're not prepared to adapt.
According to Gallup, fifty-two percent of American households
still keep at least one TV set turned on because people don't want
to miss the moment when it starts working again. Why should
people adapt? You make it sound as though TV had gone the way
of the brontosaurus."

"And you don't believe that?"

"Well of course I don't believe that! As soon as they figure out what's gone wrong they'll fix it."

"Really?" Greg arched an eyebrow. "Who are *they*? And what is broken that can be fixed?"

"What are you saying, Greg? Do you think we've been captured by aliens or are you blaming God for this?"

"I don't know. Don't you believe in God, Susan?"

"No." My denial dropped into the September afternoon. I drew an extra breath. "But if I did I'd choose a god who had loftier things to do than play games with manmade widgets!"

"I'm sure you would."

We slipped into separate thoughts and sat on the porch until sunset sipping red Kool-Aid. It was starting to get dark by the time I helped Greg load his magazines into the Land Rover. Benny, who had spent the afternoon dozing in the shade, clambered into the driver's seat, tail thumping against the plastic seat covers.

"If you want the latest information about television," I said as I handed Greg his house keys, "try one hundred point four on FM radio. They broadcast television news and panel discussions twenty-four hours a day now. They call themselves the Television Station, WRTV. How's that for irony?"

"Thank you, Susan." He kissed me on both eyes with a gravity that felt more like a blessing than affection. "My God!" he exclaimed. "Look at that sky!"

I looked. The sun had left off its exaggerated display and given up its claim to the sky; the colors were subtle and deep, in honor of the last few seconds between night and day. I entertained second thoughts about God. Greg, I noticed, was contemplating Venus.

I didn't see much of Greg for the next three or four months. During the fall, I gave a series of lectures at Yale—

. . .

"Really? What was your subject?" Melcher asked.

"Ah. I see you're still awake. Maybe Kool-Aid loses its punch after a while."

"I didn't know you were an academic. What was your field?" Melcher persisted.

"I was trained as a biologist. My field was ecology. My subject is the pond at the bottom of the hill. I've been studying it since I was twenty-six years old."

"Heavens. That's a long time," Melcher observed.

"Yes indeed. And I'll tell you a secret: I still can't predict what will happen next in that pond! It continues to surprise me."

. . .

Anyway, during the fall term I spent four days a week at home preparing my lectures and the other three in New Haven. Greg came over as usual during the first cold snap to help with the storm windows, then after snowstorms to shovel the driveway, and dropped in a few times on a Saturday morning for coffee. The fact that I remember nothing at all about those conversations suggests to me that there was nothing to remember. I assumed from the occasional unfamiliar car that spent the night in his driveway that he didn't lack female company. Maybe I missed a clue I should have noticed, some sign that would have prepared me for Greg Fisher's next incarnation so I could sit here now smugly and tell you "I saw it coming." But I won't lay belated claim to insights I never had.

The last week of January, on a slushy colorless Thursday, an exhausted man knocked on my door and, when I answered, addressed me tentatively as Mrs. Fisher, which made me laugh. The poor fellow got rattled. Wasn't this 475 Daly Road, he asked? No, I replied, it wasn't. Well then, could I kindly point him in the proper direction. Knowing how fastidious Greg was about his privacy, I balked. Listen, the man lashed out in anger, I'm not an ax-murderer, I'm Dr. So-and-so, and I've driven sixteen hundred miles since Saturday and these folks—he jerked his thumb back toward the car—are risking their lives to see Fisher. All we want is an hour of his time, one lousy hour.

I peered around his shoulder at the car, a big green Volvo with Florida plates, loaded with passengers whom I couldn't make out through the steamy windows. You're really a doctor? I asked the man with the bloodshot eyes. Yes, a physician, he sighed, but that's irrelevant. When I pressed him for details about the people in the car, his face closed and he took a step backward. I felt sorry for him. After all, the doctor did have the correct address. Mr. Fisher lives next door, I said, in the white house with the black shutters. Please don't say I told you. The doctor thanked me with a weak smile and stumbled down the steps.

Greg himself called a few hours later, saying he had unexpected guests and asking if he might borrow kitchen paraphernalia; also, could I spare a few blankets and pillows.

"Sure," I said. "What's going on over there?"

"I don't know."

"Is everything okay?"

"Maybe you can pack the dishes and so forth in a box," he suggested, "and fold up the blankets. I have to make a run to the supermarket; I'll drop by on my way back in about forty-five minutes to pick them up."

I tried again later to discover something about the visitors who were obviously preparing to impose on Greg for a good deal longer than the one lousy hour of the doctor's outburst.

"What's up?" I asked breezily. "Family?" I thought it improbable that Greg's relatives would have to risk their lives to see him.

"Susan, if I told you you'd never believe me."

"Try me!"

"Okay. To begin with, there's this big highway being laid in the Amazon by laborers who live in temporary towns. And then there's a toothless whore named Gloria who goes crazy when her television quits, and a guy who falls in love with a goat—or maybe it's the other way round . . . You want more?"

"Never mind." He was right: I didn't believe him.

The green Volvo stood in Greg's driveway all day Friday and Saturday. I saw two small dark children running in the meadow, sometimes with a dark-haired woman, other times with a man— not the doctor, the man in the meadow was smaller and darker than the doctor—often with Benny. When I got up on Sunday, the Volvo was gone. The dark family, however, remained in residence, for I saw the children later in the morning in the meadow again, tossing sticks for Benny.

Greg's call came a few days after that. He needed a favor, he said: could I give him a ride? Usually when they ask for a ride, people say where they want to go, a detail Greg omitted. Well, I thought, never mind; I'll find out soon enough. When do you want to leave? I asked. Now. Right now? Yes. Okay, *now.*

"Where to, your honor?" I asked. He was wearing an expensive camel hair coat over an impeccably tailored pinstriped suit. In the four years he'd lived next door I'd never seen him dressed in a suit, let alone a necktie, and I was surprised how easily he inhabited his city garments, how like an experienced actor he had made modifications of posture and gait in deference to the role implied by the costume.

"Head toward Poughkeepsie," Greg ordered. He tossed a small piece of luggage into the backseat, slid into the front, crossed his legs, and adjusted the crease in his trousers. Seeing that I had caught the gesture, he turned to me and grinned. "Go ahead," he said. "Ask me about the suit."

"You've got to go to a funeral," I snapped. All this mystery was making me nervous, and sometimes when I'm nervous I just have to be a wiseass.

"Well, that would be one explanation," he said.

We drove a few miles in silence. As we passed the service station in Dover Plains I remembered to ask about the car.

"What happened to the Rover?"

"Nothing."

"Then why——?"

"Because I need to talk with you. I need another favor, an important favor." He spoke in a sober, pinstriped voice I hadn't heard before. "The people who are staying in my house——"

"I've seen them in the meadow. Are they——"

"Their name is Coehlo, and they're Brazilians, illegal aliens. You know what that means. The NIPs will be after them. They came from a rotten shanty town in the Amazon, they went through hell to get here, and I don't want them to get shipped back there. The woman sings——she's something special. I think I could find her a job in one of the local bars. The man, Paco, is gifted. Maybe——"

"Gifted? In what respect?"

"He *knows* things," Greg answered inscrutably. "Hang a left at the next light."

I made a left-hand turn.

"I have to go away for a while, and you're the only person I trust to look out for them while I'm gone. I've stocked the freezer and so forth with food which Maria can cook, and I left a full tank in the Rover in case they have to make a dash for it, but Paco doesn't have a license so it's better for him not to drive if he doesn't have to. It would be terrible if he got caught for running a stop sign. Take your next right."

I took the next right. We turned onto a back road unfamiliar to me.

"I think they can manage, but in case anything goes wrong—— say if one of the children gets sick or the house catches fire——I gave them your name. You're the only person around here I trust. And keep an eye out for strange cars. It could be NIPs. Now, bear right at the fork."

"What about the doctor?"

"The doctor?" Greg smiled. "Ah, the doctor. He's gone. You must be the beautiful blond woman who showed him my house."

I let the vintage Fisher charm slide by.

"And what are these Coehlos to you that you should—"

"What's Hecuba to him or he to Hecuba?" replied Greg. "Slow down. You want to stop just beyond that tree up there."

"I do?"

I braked the car beyond the crippled skeleton of an elm. On my right I saw scrub, on my left, beyond a shrub hedge, a clearing bisected by a macadam road the proper function of which made itself known to me by the presence of a small silver aircraft with the beak of an exotic waterfowl.

"Looks like a drug drop," I observed.

"Idiot! That's the Air Force." He opened the door and ducked out of the car.

I guess it was. The lettering on the side read AF plus some numbers I can't recall.

"What's this all about? You don't fly."

"There's been a change in policy."

"Where are you going?" I shouted over the roar of the jet engine.

"Look after the Coehlos," he called back. "I'm going to fix the televisions."

Before I could think of a comeback, a pair of hands had reached down to hoist Greg into the cockpit, and the plane had raced down the runway and leaped into the sky.

Greg's inadequate explanations and our back-road drive to the secret airfield—his skulking around like a second-rate spy— knocked me off balance. I didn't know what to make of his comment about television: on the one hand the guy *was* an ex-astronaut, an atmospheric chemist, and he *did* glow in the dark; on the other he'd as much as said he didn't believe television could be fixed. Still, the U.S. Air Force did not send a private plane for Greg Fisher without reason, so he'd gotten himself involved in something. And what did his mission, whatever it was, have to do with the Brazilians whose materialization on the scene could not be mere coincidence? Where did the Florida doctor fit in? If I'd been younger the layers of mystification might have thrilled me. Instead I was annoyed to have been left holding the bag, so to speak, without having been told what was in it.

Nevertheless, when I got back home from the airport I turned on my television for the first time since the previous June just in case Greg had been telling the truth.

The TV glared back at me, emptied of images. I left it on anyway. I looked out the window toward Greg's house for signs of the Brazilians. Nothing to be seen there either. I waited all afternoon and the next day, and the day after that for a glimpse of them, maybe for a knock on my door, for the dreaded immigration police van. By the third morning I was frittering away so much time and feeling such a fool that I marched over and pounded on Greg's kitchen door. No one answered. Maybe they left, I thought, though Greg's car was still in the barn. But where was Benny? I called out, and then I heard him on his hind legs, scratching at the door and panting.

The door was opened cautiously by a slight young man armed with a baseball bat, who was blindsided by Benny who burst out and jumped up to lick my chin in greeting. Not wishing to alarm the man, I explained who I was and that I had come to inquire if he and his family needed anything.

"No Eeenglish." He shrugged.

"No brazilio," I apologized inanely.

"Ah!" He smiled lamely.

"DO YOU NEED ANYTHING?" I shouted like an idiot, "MAYBE TO EAT?" I mimed eating.

He threw up his hands. "Maria!" he called into the house.

She arrived in the doorway, a little emerald-eyed goddess carrying a baby in one arm, with two giggling children half hiding behind her.

"*Senhora* Susan?" she inquired.

Then she smiled.

As I registered Maria's smile, ten days of mental mist evaporated. So this was what that bastard was up to! He couldn't pass up such a woman—never mind the husband, never mind the kids. What had he said about her? "Something special," that was it! The bastard had probably gone to Washington to arrange for deportation of the husband and the children. And *I* had driven him to meet his plane!

"Yes. Susan," I said. Furious though I was at having been sucked into Greg's rotten little scheme, I managed to mind my manners. "I came to ask if you need something. Food? Diapers?"

"Thank you, no. Everything okay," said Maria. "*Senhor* Fisher, he give everything. He beautiful man."

"Yes, indeed." Has she seen him glowing in the dark? I wondered. "Well, so there is nothing I can do?"

"Nothing, thank you, no."

Benny by now was sitting at Maria's feet reclining against her shins. I'd never seen him quite so smitten.

"I'm sorry if you were alarmed. I know you're worried about the police." As there was nothing I could do for them, I backed down the slate path. "But you mustn't be afraid to let the children out to play as long as they stay in the meadow."

"Excuse, please?"

"The children. It's safe for them to go outside"—I pointed to the meadow—"to play. With the dog. Benny."

"Ah, *sim!*" She smiled that damned smile again. "Thank you."

"And Maria, be careful of *Senhor* Fisher. He screws women."

"Excuse, please?" She leaned into Paco, who had his arm around her. "What is 'screws'?"

Forget it, I thought. It's none of my business.

I went back home and turned off the television. Which only proves, Mr. Miller—

. . .

". . . Um, Melcher."

"—Melcher, that a scientist with a PhD can make a jackass out of herself. Because as you know, I was wrong. I trust that you won't write everything I—"

". . . Um, Melcher."

"You just said that. I'm not deaf, young man." Susan leaned forward and peered through her aviator glasses at the slumped form of her interlocutor.

Melcher snored.

"Young people," Susan reflected. "They don't have any staying power. They don't get the proper nourishment. Too bad. I was going to tell him about the day I saw Greg walk three feet above the tops of the meadow grasses."

She swallowed the last drop of her Kool-Aid and set off for the pond to verify her census of the frog population.

Jesse's Story

Billy Randolph wanted to die. Nothing permanent, mind you: merely a quick, painless, temporary death that would release him from the mortification of the dinner table. Squeezing both eyes shut, he composed a silent prayer with faint hope that it might rise above the din of voices and silverware to enter the ear of God.

"Billy? You got something wrong with you?" The inquiry, which came from Billy's grandmother, didn't reach him through the cacophony.

"Billy"—Tita prodded him softly with an elbow—"your grandmother asked you a question."

"Oh," Billy said, embarrassed. "Yes, Grandma?"

"I said, Billy, you got something wrong with you?"

"No, ma'am."

"Billy?" That was his mother, coming in late on the action. "What's wrong with Billy?"

"Daydreaming," said Grandma, "like always."

"Well, pay attention, Billy, and finish your supper," his mother ordered. "What about you, Tita honey? Can I offer you anything more? I don't want your folks saying I starved you. A little succotash, maybe?"

"No thank you, Mrs. Randolph. That was just right."

"No, George, that's not how it went. . . ." Mother plunged back into her previous discussion, smack into the middle of George's declamation which George continued as though she hadn't spoken, and it started all over again, everybody except Uncle Jesse talking at the same time so that anyone who hadn't been following carefully (like Billy) wouldn't know whether he was hearing several simultaneous conversations or one conversation with simultaneous talkers, a constant chant punctuated by fanfares of "Pass the salt," or "Is there any more iced tea?" or "Pop, while you're up, grab me another beer."

Billy stabbed a lima bean and shoved it around his plate. Tita must think we're jerks, he thought. I should never have let Mom talk me into inviting her over. Dinner in Tita's home is dignified: the mother prepares each plate, the father reads the newspaper, the grandfather directs conversational traffic, the children speak only when spoken to. Almost as much as he loved Tita, Billy loved eating dinner with Tita's family who let him finish his sentences. Tonight, among his kin, he established a lima bean in the center of his plate and deployed corn kernels around it. He felt Uncle Jesse's gaze settle on him and looked up. Jesse rewarded him with a terse smile. Uncle Jesse understands, Billy thought gratefully; he's like me. The only one.

"Billy," Tita whispered, "when are you going to ask him?"

"Huh? Ask who? What?"

"Your uncle Jesse. About what Mr. Stahlberger told us in school today."

"Oh, that," Billy muttered. "There's no point asking him. He won't——"

"Why not?" demanded Tita, crashing into his explanation like a full-blooded Randolph.

"Because he won't say anything," Billy explained. Just his luck: the only member of the family with anything interesting to say wasn't a talker. "He was an astronaut. Astronauts don't talk much, especially about space."

"Did you ever ask him about that?"

"I *told* you! He wouldn't——"

"Mr. Randolph," Tita projected across the table in Uncle Jesse's direction, "today in history class Mr. Stahlberger was telling us about the time the televisions stopped and mentioned a man named Fisher. When Billy asked Mr. Stahlberger a question, he said to ask you because you were an astronaut and know more about Fisher than he does. Is that true?"

"Could be," replied Jesse.

"Would you tell us about him?" Tita asked.

"You kids got homework to do?"

"Some," said Billy. "Not much."

"Better do the homework," said Jesse.

"Please, Mr. Randolph," pleaded Tita, "this *is* homework. Mr. Stahlberger said to ask you."

Jesse said something that got lost in Aunt Aretha's laughter.

"What?" Billy shouted. "I couldn't hear you."

Jesse pushed himself away from the table and came around to the opposite side, posing himself between the two adolescents. "Not here," he said. "Too much racket. You kids want to hear about Gregory Fisher, you eat your succotash and come to my room. Ten minutes, you hear?" He shuffled off down the hallway to his bedroom.

"I don't believe it," Billy exclaimed as he gobbled up his cold corn kernel guards and their captive bean in a single bite. "Uncle Jesse never says anything."

"Did you ever ask him?"
This is the tale Jesse told.

You see this picture? It was taken three days before lift-off, at the Kennedy Space Center in Florida. That's the space shuttle *Inquisitive* on the launchpad there in the background, and that's us, the crew, out in front. This one here is me, which I guess you don't have any trouble recognizing since I'm the only black guy in the group. This guy here, the tall good-looking fella second from the left in the back row, he's Greg Fisher.

· · ·

"Uncle Jesse was the first black astronaut," Billy announced proudly to Tita.

"No, son," Jesse corrected, "you got that wrong. I wasn't the first, not by a long shot. Where'd you get that notion?"

"Grandma."

"Your grandma, she's got a habit of getting her facts screwed into the wrong sockets. Maybe it comes from trying to forget all the bad things that happened back then. Those were hard times for folks like us. I suppose you heard about that."

"Yes," said Tita. "My grandfather tells us stories about the twentieth century."

· · ·

Now this other picture was taken two or three months earlier down at Johnson Space Center outside Houston where the astronauts trained. And you see? There are only six of us. The woman on the left—not the dark one, the one with the blond braids—that's Starr Grodzka. She wasn't one of the astronauts. She was what was called a payload specialist, someone who came along for the ride to launch an experimental photovoltaic solar-power satellite. You don't see Fisher in the group. That's because he only got assigned at the last minute, and I can tell you we weren't crazy about that.

Flying those first-generation space orbiters was like flying a bus; they were clumsy and uncomfortable; also, a lot of things could go wrong with the technology. So each crew used to spend about eight months down in Houston training for a mission so that everybody had the thing down cold. First of all, you had to know your own responsibilities up, down, and sideways. Then you had to have a good handle on what the other people were doing and on the spacecraft itself in case both the commander and the pilot were disabled and you had to fly it. And you had to practice working together so that in the event of a major malf people wouldn't be tripping all over each other trying to correct it.

. . .

"A major malf?" Billy asked. "What's a malf?"

"That's short for malfunction." Jesse chuckled. "Like 'sim' is short for 'simulation.' That's the way astronauts used to talk. I expect they still do. We don't say much, so every syllable has to count double or triple. You can get a lot of mileage out of jargon."

. . .

The space agency had developed a routine whereby the crew worked by itself until five or six months into training, when the payload specialists—in this case there was only supposed to be Starr—came aboard for the last two months. The training was extremely rigorous; it *had* to be rigorous. Man, I can remember nights I went to bed and dreamed checklists. We did different things individually depending on our assignments. On that mission, for instance, I was scheduled for an EVA (that's a space acronym for "extravehicular activity," a space walk) so I had to study the space suit, practice putting it on and taking it off, and wear it in the pool to get an approximation of how to work in a weightless environment. (It's not the same, of course, since you get resistance in water that you don't get in space, but it's the best we can do at one G—that's regular gravity to you.) I also spent a lot of time going over a mock-up of the Hubble telescope with its designers and manufacturers because that's what my space walk was all about, trying to make some repairs on the Hubble which seemed to have gotten hit by a piece of space junk. Meanwhile the other folks were rehearsing their roles.

But the most important part of training was the hundreds of hours we spent together doing sims. By the time you come out of that you're a pretty tight team. You've gone over a dozen times everything you've got to know to carry out the mission and get back home alive, you know how every member of the team will react in such and such a situation, and you've figured out the strong points of the person you don't especially like—because the guy you're riding with doesn't have to be your best friend, he just has to be damn good at what he's supposed to be good at. You've got no time to get bent out of shape on a shuttle flight. You leave your ego on the ground and pick it up when you get back down.

Partly because we have a great commander, a three-flight veteran named Robida—he's the dark-haired little guy in the middle of the front row—the 82-G team gels early, and we hold. We're worried about what might happen when the payload specialist joins us, but Starr makes all the right moves; she understands when to stay out of the way and when to lend a hand. So we're about three and a half weeks to launch, we're doing real well on the integrated sims, and we're feeling pretty good and congratulating ourselves with a beer when a rumor drifts our way that we're going to be carrying another passenger, and it hits us like a ten-ton truck. Imagine: we've got a seamless team, and now they're trying to slip in some joker; it's like trying to fit a right angle into the circumference of a circle. Can't be done. Aside from that, though the *Inquisitive* can carry seven, it's a squeeze, and we've been practicing with six.

Everybody's upset except Robi, who stays cool and orders another beer. There's nothing to get excited about, he says; the rumor can't be true. Nobody ever joined a mission that late. It must be a practical joke. But the rest of us are thinking that folks around Johnson know better than to play games like that. There's an unwritten code here which that joke would violate. And I look at Robi's hands and see that he's cleaning the fingernails of one with the thumbnail of the other which I've noticed him doing when he's tense, such as at press conferences which he hates.

"You're probably right," I say to Robi, "but suppose it were true. What would you do? Hypothetically, of course."

"I'd tell them it wouldn't be safe," Robi replies. "I'd say we'd have to scrap the mission. I'd have your backing on that, wouldn't I? Hypothetically, of course."

Well, my heart does a backflip and lands on its tail bone. Because maybe this is a hypothetical and maybe it isn't. After all those months in sims, reality and pretense get all jumbled up, and suddenly here's Robi talking about canceling the flight, and I see him picking at his fingernails. This is going to be my first time in space. I'm a rookie. I've been dreaming about space since I was knee-high to a cockroach, I've been busting my butt through high school and college and graduate school and astronaut school, and I've finally got myself a mission, and now my commander sits on a barstool with beer foam on his upper lip and says maybe it's got to be canceled. The worst part is that I know he's right. We can't go. It's too dangerous.

So I say, "Sure, Robi, we're behind you. Scrap it." And the rest of the crew chime in, "Right. No choice," and we all stare into our beers.

Right then one of the senior astronauts ambles over and throws his arm around Robi's shoulders and says, "I hear they want to put another passenger on 82-G. Tough break." The guy isn't laughing. If this is a joke, he doesn't think it's funny. "Don't let them get away with it," he says. "We're all counting on you."

Robi by now is green. He's one of those Mediterranean guys with a dark complexion that goes green when he's worried.

"I'll check it out first thing in the morning," he says. "I've had enough of this fucking rumor. Either it flies or dies."

I'm shocked because I've never heard Robi curse before. That's one of the first things you learn as an astronaut, to keep your language clean and lily white.

Well, he checked it out, and the next afternoon before we started the sim he showed up, and he wasn't exactly green anymore, but he wasn't my favorite color for Robi either.

"I've got good news and bad news," he said.

We voted to hear the bad news first.

"Okay. The rumor is true. They want us to take another passenger."

"Yeah?" Steve said in a voice like death—he was the pilot, and this was his first mission, too—"and what's the good news?" He was thinking, like the rest of us, that there couldn't be any room left for good news.

"The good news is," announced Robi, "that the passenger's name is Gregory Fisher."

Gregory Fisher?

"You've got to be kidding," somebody said.

"Nope," said Robi. "It's Fisher all right."

Fisher, you see, was a space-agency legend, the Muhammad Ali of astronauts. He held the world record in number of flights logged. He'd saved two missions—once in midflight, by correcting a problem with the cooling system that nobody else could solve, and another time on the ground by spotting a faulty connection in the aft fuselage of the *Curious* when it was already on the launchpad. He was also famous as the guy who'd solved the orbiter's waste management problems, which probably sounds silly to you until you imagine what it might be like for six or seven people to spend ten days in a tight space that smells like a public urinal. Fisher was rumored to be able to fix anything.

However, in the agency's view he'd been too free and easy with the press, apt to tell tales that didn't jibe with the All-

American image the agency's public relations department worked so diligently to promote. One morning Fisher did a guest appearance on a TV program and speculated about the high incidence of psychological difficulties among former astronauts; he mentioned nervous breakdowns, alcohol abuse, cocaine, and other unfortunate conditions the agency preferred to keep under wraps. The same afternoon the front office decided that, hero or not, Fisher had to go. The other astronauts prevented it by threatening mass resignation if he got fired. He stayed on another couple of years. Then one day he touched down at Edwards Air Force Base after a mission where he'd had a lot of EVA, came out of the spacecraft, announced he was through, and—poof—dropped into a black hole as far as the agency was concerned.

Though Fisher had come and gone before my time, I'd heard stories about him. He had a reputation as a ladykiller, also as an individualist. That certainly didn't fit the agency profile: male astronauts were supposed to be sound family men or, failing that, earnest bachelors, not philanderers; they were supposed to be good team players, not flakes. He'd once shown up on the launchpad, well into the countdown, with his hair dyed blue. I sometimes wondered where he'd found the discipline to be an astronaut.

Besides, he wasn't an astronaut anymore. He was an *ex*-astronaut. He'd been out of training more than four years. That was a long time, even for a legend.

We're all thinking pretty much the same thoughts, I guess, and Robi knows what they are because we've reached the point in training where we can read each other's minds.

"I hadn't counted on Fisher," Robi says. "It's a tough one. I told them I couldn't call it alone, that I wanted to discuss it with my crew."

"Uh huh," we say, because we don't know what to say. We're confused now. Robi's sending us mixed signals, like maybe he's willing to take Fisher if *we're* willing.

"Ordinarily I wouldn't have thought twice about it. I'd have said no to anybody, including Fisher," says Robi, inside our heads again. "But I haven't given you the whole picture yet. Fisher says he knows what's gone wrong with television."

Well, that sure got our attention, because the television failure was driving everybody NUTS! We'd be closing in soon on a whole year without TV; nobody had any idea why they weren't working—not counting the weirdos who blamed it on extraterrestrials—and folks were spooked. War, famine, pollution, racism, terrorism, global warming, drugs, poverty, AIDS—forget 'em: the world's problem was television!

Now you might suppose that astronauts, being pretty narrowly focused characters who didn't log a whole lot of hours in front of the tube, wouldn't care much about television, but that wasn't the case at all. Along with creating who-knows-what problems for the astronauts at home—kids coming down sick, mothers-in-law complaining they couldn't watch the soaps, and so forth—the loss of TV was threatening the space program. As long as there was no TV, communications companies weren't launching or repairing many satellites, which had been a major source of agency income during the 1990s. Furthermore, since most of its funding came from congressional appropriations, the agency depended heavily on popular enthusiasm, and popular enthusiasm in turn depended substantially on television images; people never got bored with turning on the evening news and seeing astronauts floating around the cabin, sucking up balls of orange juice from the air with a straw, or doing two-finger pushups. And as for listening to a launch on the radio—well, that was about as exciting as reading about July Fourth fireworks in the newspaper. There was plenty of gloom-and-doom talk down in Houston about scrapping a couple of scheduled missions, maybe about cutting back the whole program.

Now I'll tell you something funny that I bet isn't in your history books. A lot of people who weren't scientists or engineers, but lay people such as politicians and journalists, thought the space agency might be able to fix television, and the front office was getting bombarded with calls. The agency's official line was sorry, no, we don't see what we can do. Meanwhile on the sly, we were using every piece of technology we had, both in space and on the ground, to see if someone hadn't slipped some evil gizmo into orbit when we weren't watching. We were making this search even though no one could conceive of any instrument that could cause a worldwide TV malf. Owing to my background in astrophysics, I was sent down to our tracking station in the Atacama Desert in Chile to work with the search team, and after I got my assignment I remember asking what I was supposed to look for. "I don't know," the team leader answered. "Anything you've never seen before, I guess. Anything that's not supposed to be there."

But that's not all. Two shuttle crews before ours had tried to fix the televisions by checking out major satellites. The reason it's funny is because sending an astronaut out in space with a screwdriver made about as much sense as checking the basement fuse box when the Western Hemisphere has a power failure. Never mind that the plan wasn't quite so simpleminded, everybody in the agency knew it was illogical, but they went ahead and did it anyway because, well, why not? The failure of television was itself illogical. Naturally, no mysterious objects were observed in the sky, and nothing was wrong with the satellites. And the reason you don't find any of this in history books is because the agency never told anyone for fear of being laughed right out of the federal budget.

Now here comes Fisher claiming he can fix TV, and after our failures you'd think we'd take a long, hard look at what he has in mind. But do we? Nah! All of a sudden we forget that the guy only has a few weeks to train, that we may all end up drifting out to Jupiter or on the floor of the Indian Ocean. ALL WE CAN THINK OF IS THE STUPID TELEVISION!

"Fisher's the one who fixed the toilets, isn't he?" asks Steve.

"Yup," says Robi.

"Isn't he an atmospheric chemist?" somebody asks.

"Yup," says Robi again. He was a great yupper, that Robi.

"Well," I say—I'll never forget my words, I should have them engraved on my tombstone—"could be there's something in that . . . funny chemistry."

You bet. Could be. Funny chemistry! We're all enthusiastic.

"So it's a go?" Robi asks. "Fisher comes along for the ride?"

"It's a go!" we sing in unison. "We're going to be heroes!"

"I hear Fisher glows in the dark," Starr says.

We stare at her.

"Huh?" says Robi.

"Never mind," says Starr.

"In that case," Robi says, "let's go meet Greg Fisher. He's over at Mission Control."

Fisher was not what I expected. Here was this guy with a reputation as a hotdogger, and he was all business, very professional. Right away he apologized for getting into the act so late, said he understood how that could throw off the teamwork, said his old routines were probably out of date, said he knew how to stay out of the way if things got dicey during a flight. The next morning he started working with the training team, for a few days on his own as a refresher, and then with us in sims. In between he did a few practice sessions with me in the pool because he was going to be coming along on my space walk to do chemical experiments that I didn't really understand and didn't have time to ask about.

In my whole career I never saw anybody, no matter how experienced, plug into a team so smoothly. Fisher was a natural astronaut, a born star-child. When he got into space he was like a man returning home after a long exile, like a fish thrown back into the sea. What really knocked me out was that he always had a sense of where he was in space—not the fancy set of coordinates that came out of the computers, but a sense of *place* the way you'd refer to the newspaper stand on the corner of Washington and Twenty-third streets. No two stars in the sky looked the same to him. He knew them like women, intimately, by age, by color, by distance, by position. He'd even given nicknames to some the astronomers hadn't gotten around to.

Okay, we're just about ready for lift-off now. *Inquisitive* is on the launchpad, we've finished up in Houston, and we've flown to Cape Canaveral. Everybody feels relaxed about the team. Robi is back to his regular color, Steve has quit grinding his molars. Day before lift-off the PR officer poses us for a bunch of pictures. There's no regular press coverage, by the way, because first of all the press has other things on its mind and second, even if it were interested, the agency has declared this mission off-limits on the grounds of "national security." In reality, they're keeping Fisher under wraps because they don't want it getting out that he's going to try to fix television, just in case he fails. The only photographs the agency released to the press was this one here, where we're moving into the orbiter and you can't see anyone's face, and another of Robi. Later on, there was one of me out in space, except you couldn't tell who it was because of the space suit; so your grandma, Billy, I don't think she ever believed I was on that flight. When I called her from Edwards after we touched down, she said, "Prove it."

Getting back to the group pictures here, you see? We're all smiles, and they're genuine—not those fake cheese photographer's smiles. We're smiling because Robi told a joke. But check out this shot here: see how Starr's making goo-goo eyes at Fisher? I get the impression that Starr, who has developed a case of the hots for Fisher, is moderately miffed that he hasn't made a pass at her, but maybe I'm misreading the situation, and even if I'm right, I can trust her to keep her hormones in neutral. Also, according to the legend, Fisher never messes around with crew or other astronauts' wives.

In the evening we eat early and hit the sack around six P.M. because they've been moving our sleeping schedule up one hour a day for a while now so we can get a good sleep and be up at 2 A.M. to get suited up for a 6:30 lift-off. This being my first flight, I'm so excited I sleep like the princess on the pea, but I play it cool and pretend I was out cold. Fisher slices me in half with a sharp look, and I know he knows I'm faking, but then he gives me this savvy smile that lets me know that only a corpse could sleep soundly the night before the first mission, and at that moment I love him almost as much as Starr does.

. . .

"Were you scared?" asked Tita.

"Of course I was scared. That's what I've been trying to tell you."

"Did you think you could die?" Billy asked.

"Yeah," said Jesse, "though that wasn't the uppermost thought in my mind. I was more scared of not coming down again, just sort of sailing off into empty space, than I was of death. All that nowhere, beyond time. That's one reason Fisher got to me. Space had a real physical presence for him, he could locate himself there. If he'd put his mind to it, he could have tap danced in space."

"You mean it?" asked Billy.

"Sure do," Jesse replied.

. . .

Here we are boarding the shuttle: this is the photograph that made the newspapers, the one Grandma didn't believe I was in. We strap ourselves into our seats and listen for what seems like forever to the countdown, and then it happens, the breath of God carries us through the atmosphere, and we're UP! And for an hour or so it's fantastic, but after I get used to it it's pretty much like the sims, and sometimes I forget I'm not at Johnson, that if something screws up we can't back up and do it over again.

Now 82-G is a six-day mission with a number of complicated tasks, including the launching of Starr's solar-power satellite, and the EVA coming up on the fourth day. Everything slides along like satin, just like training in Houston plus the customary minor mishaps. Everybody except Fisher feels a little queasy in the weightless environment for a couple of days; they've given us too much to do, so we get slightly behind schedule, but never so far that we can't catch up with ourselves; we have a few glitches which we handle routinely. Fisher, I notice, lives up to his promise and fades way into the background whenever there's a problem. Only once, when one of the alarm systems misbehaves, does he offer a suggestion, and then it's the right one. Otherwise he keeps his mouth shut and waits for a turn in the cockpit, to look out the window into space. But he doesn't use his time to take research pictures the way the others do. When he gets the window he glues his eyeballs to the binoculars like a birdwatcher. Once when I wake up from sleep, which is also when he's supposed to be sleeping, I see him at the window again.

"Hey, Greg," I ask him. "What are you looking for?"

"Can't say until I find it, Jesse." He shrugs.

Day four: my big act is coming up. Three hours before the EVA Fisher and I climb into our underwear and start our prebreathing which means we inhale pure oxygen to get the nitrogen out of our systems so we won't get the bends. Then the crew helps us on with our space suits and straps the jet power packs to our backs: we're not going to be tethered to the orbiter, we're going to be flying free in space, propelled by the gas jets. This way we get more mobility around the telescope.

Well, they let us out the hatch and when I don't fall down but float into space, I get an incredible rush. And you want to know the crazy thing I'm thinking? It comes to me how my brother Luther, the one who OD'd on crack and broke our mama's heart, used to talk about how great it was to be high, and now here I am three hundred and eighty miles high off the sidewalks of Detroit and I wish he could be with me. I look back at the earth—it's beautiful and huge—to see if I can make out Detroit where Luther's buried, but I'm looking at the wrong hemisphere. North America won't be coming 'round again for another hour or so. But for a few seconds there, I get the feeling of Luther floating alongside, in his jeans and his Lions sweatshirt.

Somehow I shake Luther out of my brain cells. Then Fisher comes flying by, and from the way he's moving I can tell he's clowning around, so for a few minutes we just tumble in space like a pair of dolphins until Robi, who's watching us from the orbiter, says okay, that's enough play period, time to get serious. Originally, of course, I was supposed to work on the Hubble myself, but when Fisher joined the crew it was decided, since he'd had a lot of EVA experience and was Mr. Fixit himself, that he should back me up and then I'd stand by to help with his experiments.

Fisher, seeing that I haven't quite gotten the hang of the jet pack, leads the way to the Hubble. It's a big mother, and we spend about an hour going over it inch by inch before I locate the damage which turns out not to be where the engineers on the ground predicted. Though it's not a repair I've rehearsed back in Houston, Fisher agrees it can probably be accomplished in a couple of hours with the tools we're carrying. We report the situation to Robi and Mission Control who gives us the go-ahead. So I pull out my pliers. Man, do I feel clumsy! The gloves are much stiffer in space than they were in the pool at Johnson. If you want an idea what it's like to handle tools in a space suit, you might try playing a guitar with hockey gloves. Consequently, I'm being extra careful, taking it real slow. Fisher, meanwhile, hangs alongside of me out there below heaven, like an angel designed by NASA, snapping pictures of the injury for the folks back home.

It takes me quite a while to expose the wiring. Fisher takes a

close-up look at it and suggests a procedure to fix it—so simple
and elegant that I can see how he became a legend. I go back to
work. I don't want to make a mistake, so I'm concentrating so
hard I've more or less lost sight of the fact that I'm out in space,
when I suddenly hear Robi's voice asking me where Fisher's gotten to. I look around to where he was the last time I'd noticed,
and he's gone. I look up, down—or what passes for up and down
in space—in back of me, and I don't see him anywhere. I try to
make voice contact with him, but I don't get any response. I
figure maybe he's gone to take a second look at the other side of
the Hubble, that's why I can't see him, and I ask Robi if I should
make my way around and check it out. First he says yes, and then
he says wait a minute no, it's okay, I've picked Fisher up on the
screen, stay with the Hubble, finish it up. Which, because I've
been trained to follow orders, is what I do. It takes another forty
or fifty minutes, I guess, and I'm screwing in the next-to-the-last
screw when Fisher sails over the telescope and gives me a smart-
ass salute, like he's been at the beach or something.

"What did you do?" I ask him, "take another survey of the
other side?" Robi, of course, can hear us, as well as Mission Control, because of the way we're linked up.

"I figured you had things under control here," Fisher doesn't
explain, "I didn't want to be in your way."

I don't ask him why he didn't make radio contact. "No problem," I say, tightening the last screw. "It's your turn now. Let's
get on with it."

"Let's go home. I've done what I needed to do."

"You mean—"

"Not now!"

We make our jet-propelled flight back to the *Inquisitive*. On
the way I remember Luther again and get another glimpse of the
earth; it looks strange, and I can't recognize the land masses,
which bothers me until I realize that I'm probably suffering from

eyestrain after all that close work on the Hubble and also there are lots of clouds. You'd be surprised how many clouds there are floating around the earth.

We're back in the orbiter, getting out of our space suits. Instead of the usual excitement after an EVA, everybody's *real* quiet. All you can hear is Steve talking astronaut talk to Houston. When I'm all out of my suit, Robi gives me a pat on the shoulder and says good work, Jesse, you did it. But he's that green color again, and I don't like the way the muscles stand out like ropes on the back of Steve's neck. Fisher looks a little dazed.

"When do we go off the air?" he asks Robi. He's asking when we'll be out of contact with Houston, when Mission Control won't be eavesdropping on us.

"At eighteen hundred," Robi answers, "and believe me, you'll be the first to know!"

When eighteen hundred rolls around a while later, Robi explodes. I've never seen a man so angry and not throw a punch.

"You sonofabitch," he screams at Fisher (excuse my language, Tita), "what the fuck did you think you were doing out there? You came about *that* close"—he holds his thumb and forefinger a quarter of an inch apart under Fisher's nose—"*that* close to screwing up the whole—"

"Did you guys see that?" Fisher asks, absent-like, as though Robi's been reciting the phone book.

"See what?"

"The tree."

"What tree?" Robi snaps. "What kind of crap are you pulling, Fisher?"

"I have too much experience in this business to play stupid pranks in orbit, Commander," Fisher replies soberly. "I saw a tree during my EVA. Obviously you missed it or you wouldn't be asking what tree."

It's so quiet now I can hear the stars burning themselves out light-years away.

Robi rubs a speck out of the corner of his eye. "Yup," he
says slowly, "I guess we musta missed it. Why don't you tell us
about it."

Everybody has collected around Fisher by now, including Steve
who's letting Houston do the flying. He's eyeing Fisher like a
mailman eyes a pit bull.

Fisher catches the look. "Okay," he says calmly, "I know it
sounds crazy, but I saw a giant tree growing out of the Sahara
Desert, I'd guess somewhere around the border between Libya
and Chad, but I could make out what looked like a tap root
extending all the way south to Lake Chad."

"Um," hums Steve, "you mind if I ask what you mean by
'giant'?"

"Well." Fisher takes a deep breath. "Hold on to your socks,
now. I can only make an estimate, of course, but I'd say twenty
or thirty miles tall and twice the spread."

"Thirty MILES?"

"Like I said, that's a guess."

"Seems like somebody might have noticed it before," Steve
remarks sourly. "Should've made a few commercial pilots wet
their pants, f'rinstance."

"That'll be enough, Steve," Robi orders. "I'll handle this."
It's the first time I've heard him pull rank. "Greg, where were
you when you saw the tree?"

"Initially I was earthside of the *Inquisitive*," says Fisher, meaning what you might call underneath the orbiter which was at the
time flying upside down. "If you're trying to find an optical illusion to explain what I saw, you'll come up dry. I changed my location three or four times, and the tree was still there. I——" All
of a sudden he remembers me. "Jesse, you must have seen it."

"Sorry," and I really am sorry; somehow I want to see what
Fisher saw. "Can't say as I did. I was too busy with the Hubble."

"I'm sorry, too," Fisher says. "When is our next pass over
North Africa? Let's take a look at it."

Steve consults his watch. "Should be about now." He rushes for the cockpit window as fast as you can rush in zero gravity. "Take a look for yourself, Fisher. Not a cloud over the Sahara. A naughty African boy chopped down your cherry tree."

Fisher squeezes out a tight smile. "I'm not surprised." He turns to Robi, who is picking at his fingernails, and faces him squarely. "Let me tell you what's on your mind, Commander. You're considering an abort. You've got this fruitcake on board, and you don't know what he's going to do next. In your place I'd be thinking the same thing. I know what Houston would do: if they knew what was going on up here they'd bring us down faster than a falling star. Why do you think I waited until we were out of contact to tell you about the tree? Believe me, the last thing I want to do is spoil your mission. If you decide to go home early, the press will be all over the agency with embarrassing questions. You've got another thirty-three hours to go. You can trust me that long. I give you my guarantee. I may turn out to be a fruitcake after all, but I'll never be the kind of fruitcake that kills you."

Robi, whose commander's insignia hides the heart of a democrat, polls the crew.

"What do you say?" he asks.

Steve shrugs. I wait for the others.

Starr, who is still loyal to Fisher, says, "I say we complete the mission."

Which is how we decided to keep quiet about Fisher's tree and complete the mission.

"By the way, Fisher," Robi asked, "what about television?" Funny how the television had slipped our minds.

"I've got what I need," Fisher said. And not a word more.

By this time we were dead tired. We finished off the prescribed routines, reestablished contact with Mission Control, grabbed some lousy space food, and turned in. I slept deeply for the first time since two days before lift-off. At one point, though, somebody shook me by the shoulder. I opened an eye. It was Fisher.

"Jesse," he whispered, "were you telling the truth? You really didn't see the tree?"

"I don't know what I saw out there," I admitted. "For a minute I thought I saw my dead brother Luther. But no, I didn't see any giant tree. Wish I had."

"Okay, buddy," he said. "Go back to sleep. It doesn't matter. I took pictures. I got it on film."

"Uh huh."

"You don't believe me, do you, Jesse?"

"I believe *you,* it's the *tree* that's giving me the problem, if you see what I mean," I explained. "I believe you think you saw a tree, and I don't believe you're crazy. And I know your tree isn't like Luther. I mean, I knew all along I was imagining Luther; my imagination surprised me, is what happened. So I guess you saw something, but maybe it wasn't a tree. Whatever it was, the photographs ought to clear it up."

"Hope so," Fisher said without conviction.

"Did you discover anything about the television failure?"

"Seems to me I did. But I expect it's going to take me a while to figure out what it was."

"You mean lab work?"

"Not exactly." Fisher paused and frowned as if he had an argument going on in his head. I thought he was going to tell me more about television, but instead he sent me back to sleep. "By the way," he added, "I wouldn't mention Luther to the others, if I were you."

The rest of the mission went by the book, though folks were pretty quiet, and every now and again someone would sneak a peek at Fisher to see if he had changed into a toad. He stayed down on mid deck; I think he was trying to keep out of Steve's way because he knew he was making Steve nervous. And I could see he—Fisher, that is—was thinking about that damn tree.

We were supposed to land in Florida but the weather was bad so they diverted us to Edwards. Otherwise the reentry was ordinary. Here, that's the *Inquisitive* at Edwards, a couple of seconds before touchdown. It may look like any old orbiter to you, but I know for a fact she's the *Inquisitive,* and I'm inside it. And so is Greg Fisher.

. . .

"Don't you kids have homework?" asked Jesse.

"Nah," said Billy.

"Don't you go telling me tall tales, William. Your math teacher always gives you homework. I see you do it every week night. It's about time you got started on it."

"But what about the pictures, Mr. Randolph?" asked Tita. "Did they show the giant tree?"

Jesse smiled. "I'm about all talked out now, honey. I don't think I've said so much since 2006."

"What happened in 2006?" asked Billy.

Jesse chuckled.

"You remind me someday when you're a few years older," he said, "and maybe I'll tell you."

Z e k e ' s   S t o r y

"Watch it, Grand——"
"God *damn!*"

Lucy's warning, the dog's yelp, and Zeke's oath stumbled over each other as Zeke lurched into the upholstered arm of the sofa and landed with a thump on the carpet.

"Are you all right?" cried Lucy, racing to his side.

"No thanks to that clumsy animal," Zeke grumbled. "Who let her in, anyway?" Rosie, an aged English setter, licked the old man's nose apologetically.

"I did," said Lucy. "She can't be out in this weather. It's bad for her arthritis."

Lucy hoisted her grandfather off the floor and eased him onto the sofa, noticing that he weighed almost nothing, as though his bones had turned to balsa wood.

"Grandad," she said gently, "you wouldn't have accidents if you wouldn't be so stubborn about using your cane."

"I don't need a stupid cane to find my way around my own house!"

"Maybe so, but I don't think poor old Rosie's gotten used to the fact that you're blind."

"Well, then," Zeke remarked crossly, "that makes two of us, doesn't it?"

Lucy, having long ago exhausted her supply of platitudes, gave her grandfather's bony hand a squeeze.

"Unless you need something, I'll get back to my book now," she said. "Would you like me to read to you?"

"Depends on the book," said Zeke suspiciously. "What sort of trash are you reading?"

"Trash, is it? Listen to this: 'Japanese billionaire pachinko tycoon Akiro Takahito yesterday sent shock waves through the international art market by revealing his intentions to put his entire collection up for sale. Takahito's holdings, acquired over the past quarter century at a cost estimated at close to a billion dollars, consist primarily of late-twentieth-century American and European paintings, along with a dozen or more exceptional examples of French Post-Impressionism including a Van Gogh, and are considered among the finest two or three private collections in the world.' "

Zeke smiled in spite of himself. "Hmmph! That was my very first real assignment. I had a hell of a good time with it. You really enjoy reading that old stuff? It's ancient history."

"You bet," said Lucy, "and there's more. Listen: 'Takahito, who is visiting New York on a business trip, made his announcement during a press conference, and it hit the art world with the force of a major earthquake. New York representatives of Christie's and Sotheby's, the two principal auction galleries, declined to comment, but several experienced dealers expressed off-the-record opinions that the Takahito sale would have disastrous consequences for the art market.

" ' "We've been worried for a long time something like this would happen," said one expert who asked that her name be held in confidence. "People tend to unload their soft investments in times of economic chaos. When a collector as important as Takahito does a dump, prices fall faster than hog bellies in Haifa." ' "

"Yeah," Zeke chuckled, "I remember her. Colorful woman who had a way with language."

"You really loved your work, didn't you?"

"A newspaper reporter was all I ever wanted to be."

"And you were. Lucky man!"

"Lucky? You don't know the half of it, child."

This is the tale Zeke told.

I was the only happy man on earth on June 21, 2002, when the televisions went blank.

No — that's not accurate, because at the time I was watching the World Cup match and was just as annoyed as anyone else at the loss of transmission. But as soon as I understood the dimensions of the failure, I realized I'd finally gotten the break I needed.

I'd dreamed of being a newspaper reporter ever since I was seven years old and my father had taken me down to his paper and shown me the giant printing presses. I wanted to be a foreign correspondent and to win a Pulitzer Prize just like he had, though I planned to skip the part about getting knifed in a Singapore alley.

I guess journalism was in my genes. I published my first article in the elementary school paper when I was eleven. Five weeks before he died my father read it and said, "Zeke, it's a good start. You've got all the facts here. Next time, though, put your imagination in gear. Imagination is the glue that holds the facts together. Otherwise, they're just so many pieces lying around on the floor. That's Jakobovsky's Second Law of Journalism."

"Yes," I replied sturdily, trying to conceal my ignorance of the geographical boundaries between imagination and lies, "and what's the First Law?"

"Jakobovsky's First Law," my father intoned sagely and sadly, "is that society values notoriety over virtue and wisdom."

"Who is this Jakobovsky dude?"

"A reflective man," said my father. "You may choose to disregard his First Law, but always bear in mind what he said about imagination."

That's when I got the first clue that news, which I had presumed to be an accurate representation of reality, might be as whimsical as fiction—that it might, in fact, constitute a separate class of fiction, that it was even more fun than I'd suspected.

"Does Jakobovsky have any other laws?" I inquired.

"Indeed he does," replied my father. " 'Don't trust those guys with the blow-dried hair on television. They're actors, not journalists.' "

I edited the high school paper under the baleful eye of Ms. Brady, a long-legged teacher of English composition with a talent for the deployment of semicolons, a suspicion of sloppy metaphors, an eye for the football coach, and who helped me apprehend, if not conquer, the permissible ranges of imagination. In college I became a minor celebrity by writing an exposé of the hypocrisy of the admissions process for the university paper. Instead of going to graduate school to study journalism, I took a job as a waiter in a fancy French restaurant and volunteered for a weekly community handout newspaper for which I produced a column concerning such topics as playground maintenance and zoning violations.

After a year on the provincial beat, convinced that I'd paid my initiation fee to the brotherhood of journalists, I applied for a job on the same downtown daily that had once employed my father. Harry Monahan, the weathered managing editor who had known my father, drew me aside and laid out the facts of twenty-first-century life.

"You've come about fifteen years late, Zeke," he said. "Maybe you don't know anything about the publishing history around here. Back in 1946, in the grand old days of the press wars, this city supported four daily newspapers; two of them had folded by 1975, leaving the battlefield to us and the old *Post* which, though a second-rate tabloid, nevertheless kept us more or less honest. Well, I suppose you noticed that the *Post* went belly-up five years ago, so we're a one-newspaper town now. But the truth is, this isn't much of a newspaper anymore. Our news staff consists of one reporter assigned to City Hall, a second to Police Headquarters, and a third to the State Capitol. The rest we take off the wires or steal from TV broadcasts. Of course we've got seven people on the sports beat, but I don't suppose you want to be a sports writer, or you'd have said so in the first place."

"No," I murmured dully, "I don't think so."

"Plus there's Freddie who writes the obituaries; they say he's been here since the nineteenth century. We dropped the evening edition last year. Anyone who wants the closing stocks can use a computer. The paper hits the streets at 5:30 A.M., a pound of advertising, four ounces of sports and comics, and maybe half a teaspoon of news." Harry sighed. "Such is the pitiful condition of the newspaper industry. The world's going to hell in a handbasket as they used to say, but people can't be bothered to read about it. You can be grateful your old man didn't live to see us sink this low, Zeke. He was a great guy. We sure had some good times together. I guess we belonged to the last generation of hard-nosed hard-copy reporters. Won't be long now before the species is deader than the dodo bird."

"But it's all I ever wanted to be," I protested.

"Then have a go at television journalism. That's where the action is these days."

"Never! I'm afraid I inherited my father's opinion of TV reporters."

"Right," Harry laughed. "Jakobovsky's Third Law, wasn't it?
Your old man was jealous because he had a face like a warthog.
Don't believe a word of it, son. Along with all that cotton candy
disguised as news, you see some solid stuff on TV. Don't pass
judgment too swiftly."

But right or wrong, I couldn't shake my father's prejudice. I
went back to waiting tables at Le Cochon d'Or and—because I
couldn't bear not to be writing—to my dinky column in the
community paper while I pondered the abrupt change in my
existential condition. I wasn't making any progress along those
lines, when the television quit and one by one newspapers rose
out of their graves. I moved to New York on a tip from Harry
who put in a good word for me with a former colleague who'd
been hired to jump start the old *Herald.*

Most of the people at the *Herald* were recently unemployed
television reporters or newswriters who—much as I hated to
admit it—were polished professionals and made the transition
to hard copy reasonably smoothly; I guess deep down they were
news hounds like me, though sometimes I got the feeling they
were pining for their vanished medium. I was the proverbial
greenhorn, and in the proverbial way I started at the bottom,
running out for pizza, checking facts, answering other folks' telephones.

One day, after I had spent three months as an errand boy,
the city editor sent me uptown to Takahito's press conference.
When Takahito turned out to be livelier copy than the editor had
reckoned, I was allowed to stay on the story over the art editor's
objections. My next assignment was an interview with the fellow
who claimed to have developed a no-fart farm feed—

• • •

"Excuse me?" interrupted Lucy. "What is that?"

"Ruminant animals like goats and cattle are, as you ought to know, gassy critters," Zeke explained, "and on their customary diet they produce large quantities of methane which is one of the gases implicated in global warming. This character promised that if a farmer used his feed, the animals wouldn't be flatulent. He sent announcements of his press conference to all the newspapers and radio stations in town, saying he would be demonstrating Frank's No-Fart Farm Feed. Who could resist? The *Herald* got an exclusive, my interview, which sold one hell of a lot of newspapers. That's one of the facts of life I discovered: people still love a good laugh, no matter how bad things get."

"Did the feed work?"

"Yes, but the Agriculture Department wouldn't allow it on the market because it was loaded with chemicals that might be bad for the livestock. So Frank's No-Fart Farm Feed fizzled out in a frenzy of frightful funnies."

"Grandad!" Lucy giggled.

• • •

After my big start I got assigned to more stories—nothing important enough to include in the anthology you're reading, because no matter how hard you try there are some events you can't invest with any more significance than meets the eye. When I submitted fifteen hundred words on the new traffic signals on Third Avenue, the city editor amputated the last twelve hundred and left a message in my computer reading: "Zeke: After you've covered who, what, when, where, and why, kindly pause and ask yourself *so what?*"

So I made mistakes, but I was a quick study and impatient for real action—something in the South American jungles maybe, or one of the Middle East wars, or environmental terrorism in Bulgaria. That I had been born in the golden age of journalism, into a world imploding with disasters, and was condemned to writing about information systems in the public libraries was an irony I failed to appreciate.

I was heading out of the newsroom after another ho-hum

day, when the managing editor, who had never so much as grunted in my direction before, waved me over.

"Hey, junior, are you old enough to remember Greg Fisher?"

"Greg Fisher the astronaut?" I acted as though I hadn't heard the "junior."

"The same. How would you like to take a ride upstate and have a talk with him?"

"Sure. What's up?"

"I'll be honest with you, kid," said the managing editor, "I don't know. A man identifying himself as Fisher telephoned the paper this afternoon and conned his way through the switchboard to me. He claimed he'd been on the last shuttle mission, and that he'd discovered something important about the television failure that NASA was holding back."

"Sounds like a crank," I observed. "Fisher's been out of the astronaut corps for some time now, hasn't he?"

"My thoughts exactly, son, but he gave me a list of names I could call to check on his story. Wendy's been on the phone to Houston all afternoon, and it turns out that a) his list of the 82-G shuttle crew matches the agency's except that the agency denies Fisher was aboard; and b) four crew members confirm Fisher's presence during the flight. The first is a woman, Starr Grodzka, a physicist with Solargen who went along as a payload specialist. The second is an astronaut, Jesse Randolph, who seems to know more than he's revealing. Then there's the pilot, Steve Ortolani, who's convinced Fisher's bananas and doesn't hesitate to say so provided he's off the record. The fourth is Robida, the commander, who said flatly, 'No, Fisher was not officially on board,' with emphasis on the *officially*—which, of course, means he *was*. Are you taking all this down?"

"How do you spell the woman's name?"

"Starr with two *rr*'s, G-R-O-D-Z-K-A. Here, it's on the list." He pushed a sheet of paper across his desk. "A bright boy like you can see that the situation raises questions, so I think we have a duty to look into it. Fisher probably *is* a crank, but at least he's a crank who was on the last shuttle flight, a crank NASA doesn't want to acknowledge, and I want to know why. Don't get your hopes up too high: we're not talking Woodward and Bernstein here. This television business is bringing all the crazies out of their attics. Every day we get a dozen calls from people who either confess to murdering television or propose wacko schemes to fix it. Your job is to get up to Strangeways, have a careful conversation with Fisher, and let me know if there's a story somewhere. That's a good lad."

"My name's Zeke!" I said. "I'd better dig up some background on Fisher."

"Attaboy." The managing editor grinned encouragingly.

I left the city at sunrise the next morning, driving north against the traffic, parallel to the Hudson River so thick with debris that it reminded me of old minestrone. I hit the Taconic Parkway and made Strangeways by 8:30, which was earlier than I'd counted on so I dropped by the singular eatery in the single-street town for coffee and a doughnut. The fat lady behind the cash register obliged me with directions to Fisher's place and the observation that it was "high time the law looked into the goings-on over there." When I asked for specifics, she muttered, "Mighty peculiar, if you ask me."

Though midmornings aren't meant for mystery, this one grew more mysterious by the minute. Fisher waylaid me in his driveway, demanded to see my press credentials, and asked if anyone had followed me. Having reassured himself that I had indeed been sent by the *Herald* and had no one on my trail, he dragged me out for a walk in the meadow behind his house. And then he told me the wildest story I ever heard, either before or since, namely that while he'd been on a space walk during the shuttle mission, he'd seen a giant tree growing out of the Sahara Desert. He'd taken photographs, he explained, which the space agency insisted hadn't come out, but he'd managed to acquire one print—never mind how. At that point he reached inside his shirt and pulled out a manila envelope from which he withdrew an eight-by-ten color picture. I could see it was a shot of the earth taken from space and, sure enough, smack in the middle of the Sahara was this tree, two hundred times larger than life.

Naturally I recognized the picture as a phony. Anybody with a knowledge of photography and the proper equipment could have faked the illusion by superimposing one image on the other. I'd seen equally convincing photographs documenting Martians and Elvis sightings. For the moment, however, I withheld my doubts. Okay, so Fisher was a fruitcake which would explain why NASA was denying him—although not why he'd been along on the shuttle flight in the first place. I hadn't driven a hundred and ten miles for a ten-minute chat. I remembered the managing editor's instructions about a careful conversation; maybe I was missing something. I figured I ought to string Fisher along for a while longer and then get my tail back to New York.

"Just how big would you say this tree is?" I inquired gingerly.

By way of reply, Fisher said, "You think I faked the picture, don't you?"

"No," I lied. I hadn't yet learned to be a good liar, how to sneak the lie past the censor of conscience and bring it out as ruthless and newborn as truth.

"Never mind," Fisher consoled. "If I were in your place, I'd think it was a fake, too. But maybe I can change your mind. Just stay where you are and keep your eyes on me."

By that time we'd walked well into the meadow—it wasn't much of a meadow, really, more like an old farm field that hadn't been plowed for years. Fisher paced off three or four yards, took a funny soft jump off his right foot, rose up off the ground until he was a foot or two above the tops of the weeds, *and didn't come back down!* He hung in midair for several seconds, and then did a little Fred Astaire–style dance against the sky. Meanwhile his dog, who had followed us, was leaping along on the ground, snapping at his heels and barking like crazy.

"Knock it off," Fisher shouted at the dog. "Sit, Benny." The dog obeyed, trembling, ears flat against his head.

Fisher made an expert landing at my side. "How's that for special effects?" he asked. "You okay? You look a little pale." He grabbed my arm. "You'd better sit down before you fall."

On the way down I fainted. I wasn't out for more than half a minute. Fisher was on one knee, bending over me when I came to. "Don't get up too fast," he advised. "Take a few deep breaths. I probably should have warned you."

"I just saw you walk on air, is that right?"

"I suppose that's what most people would call it."

"Would you mind doing it again?"

"Why?"

"For the sake of my sanity."

"Oh, all right," said Fisher like a prima donna coerced into one rehearsal too many, "but only once more, so pay attention." He drew back a step, jumped off his right foot, and sailed up three feet in front of me. Benny howled like a coyote. Fisher took a dozen no-nonsense steps on his ethereal platform and then punctuated his performance by turning himself upside down and balancing on one finger. He righted himself and dropped to the ground.

"Satisfied?" he asked.

"How do you *do* that?"

"It's a matter of fine-tuning the relationship between mass and gravity."

"Yes, I guess I see that in principle, but *how* do you do it?"

"It's an art form," Fisher replied glibly. "You might as well ask Picasso how he painted pictures. Anyway, it's beside the point. You're not going to write about it."

"I beg your pardon," I said slowly.

"Well, you could write a story, but I'd deny every word. You see, Zeke, I've never demonstrated this particular talent to anyone else. You're the only witness on earth—not counting Benny and a few birds and bees. Let's say you run back to your word processor or, better yet, phone in your copy to the editor so it can make the evening edition. D'you suppose he's going to take your word for it that Gregory Fisher walks on air? Not on your life, my young friend. He's going to send a squadron of reporters and photographers whom I'm going to receive with the utmost courtesy. I'll offer them a drink and tell them I have no idea how you came by the misguided impression that I can outwit the laws of God and Newton. Your career, I imagine—"

"All right, all right, all right," I said. "I get the point."

"No, I think you've forgotten the point. The point is the tree."

The tree! Fisher was right. I'd forgotten the goddamn tree.

"I thought if I showed you my parlor trick," he continued, "I might be able to convince you that I actually saw the tree. Believe me. I saw it. I wasn't hallucinating out there."

"Wait a minute. You've been running strange stuff by me so fast I almost forgot why I came. I'm confused. My boss said you told him you'd discovered something about television."

"That's right," Fisher said. "I did. I discovered the tree."

"I don't get it. What's the connection?"

"I don't know."

"Well then, what makes you think there *is* a connection?"

"Can you stay for lunch?" Fisher asked. "I'd like you to meet Paco and Maria, my friends from Brazil. They're part of the explanation of the connection."

"I'd be delighted." I scratched at my ankles and stood up. "Can I ask you one more question about what you did back there—off the record, of course, just to satisfy my own curiosity?"

"Shoot!"

. "How high can you go? I mean, could you go all the way into space if you wanted to?"

"Hey, give me a break. It's brand new to me, too. I'm just getting the hang of it."

Fisher's deliberate strides carried him well ahead of me, foreclosing further discussion of the subject of walking on air. I trotted to catch up with him.

"Another question, different topic," I ventured. "Why did you ask if I'd been followed? Who's after you?"

"Nobody's after me as far as I know, but the NIPs may be looking for my Brazilian friends. I'm trusting you on this one, Zeke."

"No problem," I replied truthfully. "The NIPs are fascists."

Okay. After that we went inside for lunch which was a memorable meal in more ways than one. First off, Fisher served feijoada. More precisely, he *ate* feijoada prepared by Maria and dished up ceremoniously by Paco who, Fisher informed me, was practicing to be a waiter. In case you're not familiar with it, feijoada is a Brazilian dish meant to be washed down by liberal quantities of native beer; it's made with black beans, rice, pork, sausages, oranges, spices, and so on, and tastes very good but does not rest lightly on the digestive system on a hot day. I was treated as the guest of honor, seated at the head of the table, and presented with a huge plateful of steaming black beans.

In addition to myself and Fisher, the company consisted of Paco, Maria, and their three small children who were all staying with Fisher. The woman Maria, who later became a famous singer, was so dangerously beautiful a man could lose himself in the green of her eyes, and more than once I had to pry my own away from her. She seemed to me imperfectly paired with her husband, a wiry and intense young man about my own age, to whom she nevertheless deferred with affection. (I'll be the first to admit, however, that I've never understood the mating habits of humans, which is perhaps why I made such a mess out of both my own

marriages.) I knew from the previous day's research that Fisher
played around with women, and I wondered if he had anything
going with Maria.

Paco finished serving the meal and joined us at the table. At
Fisher's request and in hesitant English, Maria launched into a
long story that began in the Amazon, then shifted to Venezuela
and thence to Miami where Paco nearly died of lockjaw; it was
populated by an exotic cast of characters including a toothless
whore, a sex-starved goat, drug dealers, and a heroic doctor.
Somewhere along the way I lost the thread—maybe because of
all the beans and beer I had consumed or because of the distraction of Maria's cleavage—and started wondering what I was going
to report to the managing editor, how out of the brain-scram-
bling events of the day I could produce an article that anyone
would believe. And then I heard Fisher saying, "So now that you
see the connection between the tree and television, what do you
think?"

Groping for a polite response, I took inventory of my thoughts.
What I thought was that Fisher imagined a connection between
the tree and television, a connection based on the obsession of an
illiterate Brazilian laborer who had risked his own life as well as
his family's to get here. What I thought was that these charming
people were mad and that I was in danger of being sucked into
their madness by the woman with the green eyes and the man
who walked on air.

"Killing. Everything is killing. First killing is of the *imagina-
ción*—how you call it in English?"

The grown-ups at the table turned as one in perplexity toward
Paco who had made this chilling pronouncement. Serita, the baby,
started to whimper, prompting Maria to gather her onto her lap.

"Imagination," Fisher translated. "We use the same word in
English. What made you say that?"

Paco and Maria lapsed into Portuguese. While they were

conferring, Fisher leaned toward me and murmured, "It never pays to ignore Paco. She is gorgeous, but he *knows* things."

"What makes you so sure?" I asked.

"He knows that I can walk on air, though he hasn't seen me do it. More importantly, he knows what he doesn't know. And——"

"Excuse, please," Maria intervened. "We have been speaking with my husband. I will try to explain what he means to say. He tells how the imagination becomes so small, like so"——her hands described an object the size of a walnut——"like a tiny box, and very timid. Always, he says, terrible things happened on the earth, things which the people could not understand and which caused them to fright. But there were the storytellers and the makers of legends who explained where the sun god slept at night and that when he was angry he hid behind the moon. These stories helped the people to be less afraid, to know their places in the world."

Paco, who had been laboring to follow his wife's explanation, let loose in Portuguese again. Maria listened gravely and then resumed her English.

"Paco speaks of an ancient Tupinamba legend, about a great flood. It is a story about two brothers who quarreled, and one stamped the earth with such violence that he brought forth a great stream of water that rose higher than the mountains. The brothers and their wives saved themselves by climbing trees. The Tupinambas also believe in a spirit named Kurupira who protects the creatures of the forest. Kurupira is a funny little fellow with his feet on backward; he does not like humans and must get presents.

"Paco asks how, if men who walked barefoot in the jungles before the time of Christ could imagine such things, men who wear shoes and have the power to fly like birds even as far as the moon no longer know how to tell stories to their children and cannot imagine that a great tree can grow in the African desert."

Having carried Paco's speculation to its conclusion, Maria gazed down at the child who had fallen asleep in her lap. "Sometimes my husband says things I do not understand," she said, "but I think they must be wise. Would you like to take some coffee now?—the strong Brazilian coffee, not the North American brown juice."

"Maria," said Fisher, "ask Paco if he believes the tree in the desert means there is going to be a great flood."

Paco, who had understood the question, answered it himself. "I do not know. What I know of the tree is that you have seen it. This is a truth. If the imagination is great enough, it will find the meaning."

"I still don't understand what this has to do with television," I said.

"Come on, man, *think!*" Fisher said impatiently. "If it hadn't been for the television failure, I would never have gone back into space and therefore I would never have seen the tree."

After coffee I excused myself from the table and, with the intention of clearing my head, went outside for a walk with the dog. I wandered into the meadow and arrived at the approximate spot where Fisher had danced above the wild mustard. Believing myself to be unobserved, I took a few paces and made a soft jump off my right foot only to return rudely and immediately to the ground on top of a sharp stone that caused me to twist my ankle and fall down in pain. There I was, on my butt in the grass again, feeling stupid and kneading my ankle, when the unmistakable sound of a woman's laughter further insulted the shreds of my pride. Or maybe not. Maybe a bird had cried. I was a city boy: what did I know about birds?

Fisher's keen-eared dog, however, took off to the far edge of the field in the direction of the sound. I followed him with my eyes and saw emerge from the woods a long, tall, braided blond woman improbably garbed in a T-shirt, very short shorts, and fisherman's wading boots and bag. She had a trout net slung over one shoulder. Benny the dog greeted her as a friend.

"Are you okay?" she called as she strode into the meadow.

"I think so," I shouted back.

"Here." She approached and extended a muscular arm. "Let me give you a hand."

I accepted her help and stood up on my left leg; the transfer of weight to my right foot made me wince, but I thought I could walk on it.

"Who are you?" the woman demanded. "And what are you doing here?"

"My name's Zeke Kramer. I'm a—uh, friend of Greg Fisher's. Who are you?"

"I'm Susan. I live next door." She laughed again, a laugh no bird could imitate. "What did you think you were doing before? Did you suppose you could walk on air like Greg?"

"What makes you think he can walk on air?" I asked with what I hoped was an air of innocence.

"Empirical evidence. I saw the two of you cavorting around out here from my window this morning."

"And you didn't think there was anything, er, *peculiar* about what happened?"

"My dear boy, the man glows in the dark and exists without bank accounts or credit cards. Why should I find it peculiar that he levitates?"

"Huh?" said I.

"Is the bastard still screwing that Brazilian woman?"

"Maria? No, I don't think so. She appears sincerely attached to her husband."

"That's *your* version," Susan snorted. She knelt down and felt my ankle with expert hands. "You're starting to swell up," she announced. "Come with me. I'll give you some Kool-Aid. That ought to do the trick."

"No thank you, I'll be fine." My stomach lurched at the

threat of Kool-Aid on top of beans and beer. But Susan unfolded
again to her full height and nailed me with a look of savage
determination. I let her support me to her porch where she fed
me two glasses of purple Kool-Aid and an earful of Greg Fisher
stories. By the time I left I knew a little more about Fisher and I
had a stomachache, but the swelling on my ankle had gone down.

I crossed the meadow again—no stunts this time—and found
Fisher in his study. I asked him why he had been aboard the
shuttle flight. It was easy, he explained. When he heard Paco's
story about television, he realized he couldn't accomplish anything on the ground; he had to get back into space. He had
connections in Washington and, though he didn't mean to sound
immodest, a certain reputation as an astronaut and a scientist.
He'd put in a call to a senator indicating he might have a solution
to the television problem. Television being the top priority item
on everyone's list—and every politician aching to have a hand in
fixing it—she, in turn, had called a man on the National Security
Council and set off a chain reaction in government. Next thing
Fisher knew, the Air Force sent a jet to whisk him off to Washington. He'd met with a high-powered committee, advanced sophisticated theories about permutations of atmospheric gases and
deflections of radio waves.

"You mean you bluffed them," I said.

"Not exactly. The theory was improbable, I admit, but it
wasn't any more improbable than what had happened to television. At any rate, it played well enough to get me onto 82-G.
Then, as soon as I saw the tree, my theory went out the window.
I knew the tree had to be the link. Unfortunately, though, I'm
the only one who saw it, and the officials at the agency don't
trust my photographs. But by the way, just to keep myself honest,
I took some samples of the atmosphere during the shuttle trip.
Nothing unusual. The tree is the clue, I'm positive about it. I just
don't know what it means."

"So what do you want from the *Herald*?"

"What everybody wants from the press," he said, "publicity. I want this story to get into the newspapers. Maybe somebody will read it and make some sense out of it."

"For a guy who wants exposure, calling a single newspaper is a mighty funny way to go about getting it," I pointed out. "Like you said, you've still got a reputation—name recognition as we call it. Why not arrange a press conference, let the wire services and radio stations in on your story?"

"What? And have to walk on air to prove my picture isn't a fake? The press would make me into a circus performer, and that's the last thing I want. I'm not the story. I'm only the messenger. Even though I can't decipher the message, I still have to deliver it. That's where you come in, Zeke."

· · ·

"And that's how I signed on as the messenger's messenger. It was dumb luck. Of course, Fisher didn't make life easy for me," Zeke concluded. "I talked my vocal cords raw convincing the managing editor that I had a story, and somehow made him believe me. I had to fly down to Houston and extract a confirmation that Fisher had been on the shuttle mission, talk to a couple of the astronauts, and so forth. I interviewed the Grodzka woman who had a crush on Fisher. But my first story got printed, every blessed word of it, and because of the way events unfolded—not to mention what my series did for the circulation of the Herald—the paper kept me on Fisher right through the assassination, and I wound up with my first Pulitzer. I like to think my old man would have been proud of the way I took advantage of Jakobovsky's Second Law. Most of the articles are in that book you're reading, as I recall."

"Yes, I glanced at a few of them," said Lucy. "You never wrote about Fisher walking on air, did you?"

"Are you kidding? I did better than that. Read on and you'll see. Funny thing, though. Since my eyes went bad, I've given a lot of thought to the sense of sight, how the brain filters out what's obnoxious or irrelevant to it and apprehends only what it's inclined to see. Where one person sees rosebuds, the second sees aphids, and the third the center of the universe. Sometimes I wonder what really caused Fisher to see his tree, and me to see Fisher play his tricks with gravity."

Isabelle's Story

"Once upon a time, owing to a vast dense fog muffling the Northeast, a small airplane had to make an emergency landing in Poughkeepsie," Isabelle began. "Among the—"

Isabelle's nephew David groaned. "I hate stories about places like Poughkeepsie. C'mon, Izzie, you've been all over the world. You can improve on the location. Don't tell us a story that starts with Poughkeepsie!"

"I never did take kindly to critics," Isabelle commented severely. "They're inclined to be lapsed artists, people with withered imaginations. And I especially disapprove of critics who write their reviews before seeing the show. What do you know about Poughkeepsie? Have you ever been there?"

"No, but it—"

"Then button your lip, young man!"

This is the tale Isabelle told.

One foggy evening several years ago two friends of mine, let's call them Bernice and Nicky, got stranded in Poughkeepsie. Their flight was canceled at about five but the airline dithered as usual, so by the time they checked into a hotel it was past eight, and Bernice—who was inclined to excesses of temperament even when her life ran on schedule—was cranky. All she desired in the world was to crawl between crisp sheets, call down to room service for a club sandwich, and watch the tube. Then she remembered that the televisions weren't working.

Funny how even after a year she hadn't accustomed herself to the absence of TV. Quite apart from the financial difficulties the loss of television posed for the talent agency she and Nicky operated, Bernice still missed flipping the channels back and forth so she could watch three programs simultaneously and let the muscles of her mind hang loose. Maybe funnier was that hotels she stayed in had left the television sets in the guest rooms where platoons of hotel maids continued to wipe the dust from them every day. Probably, Bernice reasoned, no one wanted to be caught off guard in case the reception resumed as mysteriously as it had vanished. Although, as I once pointed out to her, this was absurdist logic: even if the reception did suddenly start to function again, there wouldn't be anything to see because no programs were being broadcast.

Extracting a half-read paperback potboiler from her suitcase, Bernice was about to resign herself to an evening of high cholesterol prose when Nicky telephoned from across the corridor and suggested they hit the hot spots.

"Hot spots?" hooted Bernice whose concept of Poughkeepsie, like David's, was based on the fact that she couldn't spell it. "You've gotta be kidding."

"I'm not gonna spend the next three hours staring at speckled brown wallpaper, Bernice. You wanna stay, you stay. Me, I'm gonna check out this town and get something to eat. I'd like it a lot better, though, if I had you along for company and a couple of yuks."

"Oh well," she relented.

• • •

"Bernice is really you, isn't she?" interrupted David, "and Nicky is Uncle Nate, so why don't you say so?"

"Since the line between historical fact and fiction has always been fuzzy in my mind," Isabelle commented, "I prefer fiction because it liberates the imagination. I can tell all the lies I want without being accused of falsifying memories. So be careful how much of me and Nate you read into Bernice and Nicky."

• • •

Together Bernice and Nicky exited the hotel into the warm soft foggy noxious night. They turned right past the movie house where people were standing in line for tickets to the next show, past a burger joint, then a pizza palace, next a narrow beery barroom followed by an all-night drugstore, and at the corner a discount shoe store shut tight and barred against predators. Four days' worth of fast food and newspaper litter lay decomposing on the sidewalk. Three punks on motorcycles raced down the street, weaving through traffic, and ran a red light.

"Hot spots, you promised," Bernice reminded Nicky tartly.

"Hold yer water," said Nicky, using her elbow as a rudder and steering her across the street. "Now, waddya think about this?" He paused at the corner next to a remodeled brick building bearing a painted sign of a chef ladling out spaghetti and the name "Enzo's."

"I think overcooked pasta and accordian music," replied Bernice grouchily. "C'mon, Nicky, face it: Poughkeepsie is a dump. Let's give it up and go back to the hotel."

"I'll make you a deal. Three more blocks, and if nothing turns up we go home. Maybe if we head toward the river."

Bernice wrinkled her nose. "The great grey green greasy Limpopo," she muttered.

"Huh?"

"Didn't your mother ever read you bedtime stories?"

"My old lady's idea of bedtime didn't include me," Nicky observed.

Midway into the third block, along a lazy commercial street sloping down to the Hudson River, they arrived in front of an establishment with a red and blue neon sign in the window advertising "Moose's Place." A hand-lettered announcement stuck to the glass with scotch tape promised "Honest food, fairly priced booze, & live entertainment. Every night: Jimmy Williams. This week: Maria! (Closed Mondays)."

"I like Moose's pitch," Nicky commented. "Let's see what he has to offer. When was the last time you had food that didn't lie?"

Bernice and Nicky found Moose's Place crowded and all the tables occupied. Having been instantly won over by the aroma of baking bread and the sound of a smoothly played jazz piano, they made their way to the bar which ran the entire length of the mirrored side wall of the large dining room. Nicky spotted a single empty stool which he promptly appropriated for Bernice.

"Nice crowd," said Nicky, scanning the room. "Mixed. A little bit of everything agewise, racewise. You don't see that much these days. Plus which, the guy on piano knows his stuff. Reminds me of somebody, I can't think who."

Bernice swiveled around and conducted her own survey. Not much you could say for the interior decorator, she observed. Emptied of people, the room would be ashamed of itself; it borrowed its color from the variegated patrons most of whom were sipping drinks or polishing off their honest desserts and, if not concentrating on the cool intelligent music, speaking low enough not to insult it. The black piano player bent over his keyboard, smiled a private smile, and executed an elegant passage from minor to major key.

The figure of a man seated at a table against the opposite wall stopped the sweep of Bernice's gaze. She fumbled in her handbag for her eyeglasses. She took another look and frowned.

"Hey!" She elbowed Nicky in the ribs. "Who's that tall good-looking guy sitting by himself across the room? I recognize him, don't you? I'm sure he's somebody."

Nicky studied the man through narrowed eyes. "Looks kinda familiar," he said, "but I can't place the face. Probably he's a nobody who just looks like a somebody."

"Excuse me," said a raspy voice behind them, "may I help you folks?"

Nicky and Bernice turned toward the source of the voice. Its owner proved to be a Goliath of a man with a battered face enlightened by a pair of humorous blue eyes.

"Don't tell me!" Bernice exclaimed. "You're Moose."

"None other," the man acknowledged. "Can I get you something to drink?"

"Well, the lady will have a white wine cooler and you can draw a beer for me, but to tell the truth," said Nicky, "we're kinda hungry. Our plane got grounded here for the night on account of the weather, and the last meal we had was crummy airline food. You think maybe one of those tables is gonna empty soon and we could grab some dinner?"

Moose consulted his watch and shook his huge balding head. "Not likely. Everybody will stay for Maria's first set in about half an hour. If you want, though, I can serve you at the bar. I don't say it's comfortable, but the food's good. The special tonight is Peruvian chicken."

"Peruvian chicken?" Bernice raised an eyebrow. "You call that honest food?"

"Damn right! My brother-in-law raises the chickens ten miles out of town. He feeds them corn he grows in his own fields, and they run around like regular chickens the way God intended. Plus which, I happen to have a Peruvian couple in the kitchen these days. They can turn out a mean old-fashioned meatloaf if you insist, but you won't find better chicken north of the equator."

"Where's the equator?" asked Bernice.

"Sounds great," Nicky said. "We'll try the chicken."

With the wave of a giant arm, Moose summoned one of the waiters, a small worried man whom he called Paco, and told him to bring two orders of chicken to the bar. Paco scurried off to the kitchen. Moose served up the drinks.

"Say, Moose," Nicky inquired, "who's the guy on piano?"

"That's Jimmy Williams. Maybe you remember, he used to return punts for the Dolphins. He got laid off when the owners canceled the season because of the television thing. He's been playing here since before Christmas."

"Of course! *That* Jimmy Williams! I *knew* I knew him from somewhere! Guy had great hands. Hey, the old brain's beginning to click again. You're not Moose, uh, whatshisname—the Moose that used to be on the Pats line the year they won the Super Bowl, when was it? 'Ninety-six or something? Moose, Moose, wait a minute, don't tell me, it'll come to me, Moose *Stickles!* That's it. Stickles. Number seventy-seven, wasn't it? Are you him?"

"The same." Moose grinned.

"Well, I'll be damned. That was one great game. I still—"

"Excuse me," Bernice interrupted, "but while we're playing who's who, Moose, do you happen to know the name of that guy across the room, the one talking with our waiter? Is he anybody?"

"You bet! That's Greg Fisher. Don't tell him I told you, though. He doesn't like to be bothered."

"The astronaut?" she asked. "The one who sees giant trees? What's he doing here?"

"Beats me," Moose replied with a blank expression. "I expect he likes good music and honest food."

Moose excused himself to attend to other customers. Jimmy Williams finished off his set and joined some people at a table.

Paco delivered the Peruvian chicken which Nicky pronounced "the best goddamn meal I've had since mother's milk." Bernice and Nicky stumbled into a conversation with the man on a neighboring barstool who gave them a condensed history of Moose's Place.

Moose, the stranger explained, was a living legend in Poughkeepsie—maybe the *only* living legend not counting Vassar College—the oversized kid who'd led Poughkeepsie High to two straight Class B championships, who'd won (now get this!) an *academic* scholarship to Cornell and played Varsity all four years (not that he did Cornell any good; though the line had been solid as a concrete wall, Cornell had never recruited a decent quarterback to pass behind it), and made a name for himself in the pros. Moose was smart. He'd quit at the top of his career, after the Pats won the Super Bowl and he'd made a killing on endorsements—before professional football wrecked his body—and opened Moose's Place as a sports bar—giant TV screen over there, back of where the piano is now. The restaurant part had developed accidentally, a Topsy-like progression from sandwiches to occasional hot specials and before he knew it to full-course meals, because Moose appreciated good food and so, it seemed, did his customers.

Lucky accident, too, since the sports-bar end of the operation died with television, but as Moose said, people still love an honest meal. Next thing you know—around Christmastime—Williams turns up and starts playing piano. It's not like he needs the money: hell, he made 8.6 million his last full season. But he can't stand the notion of spending the rest of his life on the phone with his broker. A man's got to use his hands. Then about a month ago Moose took on this Brazilian girl, Maria. Business is better than ever. The crowd's changed a little, but there's more of 'em.

"Williams could do better than this joint," Nicky observed undiplomatically. "I'm pretty sure my partner here and I could fix him up in a good club in New York."

"No way!" said the stranger. "Jimmy wouldn't go to New York. He lives in a house out in the country. Breeds llamas. He hates cities. Poughkeepsie's about his limit."

"I can't believe that," said Bernice. "There isn't a performer alive who——"

"Shhhhhhhh," hissed the stranger. "Maria's coming on."

As the customers shushed each other and rearranged their chairs so they could watch the show, a dark and delicious woman dressed in white seated herself on a stool that had been placed next to the piano and started tuning her guitar. When all the strings satisfied her ear, she raised her head and, without a word but with the absolute authority of the born performer, commanded the room to stillness. In Bernice's opinion that gesture alone—the set of the head, the serene green gaze—made up for Poughkeepsie.

Maria sang. She didn't use a microphone. There was just Maria's guitar and Maria's sure voice reaching back beyond the farthest table into the smoky recesses of Moose's Place. She sang nine or ten songs, passing from one mood and rhythm to another, migrating from sad to sexy to bright to bold to plaintive with self-confidence. Though she sang in Portuguese, she carried the audience with her the entire distance. After the last number, she climbed down from her stool and bowed her head, causing her long black hair to cascade over her face.

The standing cheering whistling clapping crowd shouted for more. Maria tossed back her head and, for the first time, turned her smile up to full power. The audience roared.

Maria raised her arms, palms out, signaling quiet.

"I sing more songs for you at eleven," she said. "And tomorrow, or maybe after tomorrow, I sing a new song, in Engleesh." She smiled another thousand-watt smile, then stepped away from the stool and made her way past outstretched hands to Greg Fisher's table where she sat down.

"Holy shit!" Nicky exploded.

"Are you thinking what I'm thinking?" asked Bernice.

"You better believe it. That babe is worth millions, and she's up for grabs. Ergo, she's ours."

"Maybe she already has an agent."

"C'mon, Bernice. What kind of an agent would book her into a joint in the boonies? If she's got an agent, he's an idiot and we can buy him out with petty cash."

"You folks ready for another round?" rasped Moose from behind the bar.

"Why not?" Nicky leaned confidentially on the bar. "So what's the scoop on Maria?"

"She's good, isn't she?"

"Good doesn't begin to describe her. She's fantastic! How did you find her?"

"Got lucky," said Moose inscrutably. "She sings such beautiful songs."

"I was wondering about that," said Bernice. "Do you know where she gets them? Are they popular in Brazil?"

"No, no. Maria writes some herself. Her husband writes the rest."

"She has a husband?" asked Nicky.

"Paco, your waiter, he's her husband."

Bernice laughed. "You're kidding! The little guy with the worried puss is her husband? I had it all wrong. I figured her for the astronaut's girlfriend. Before he started seeing things, Fisher used to have a well-known weakness for pretty women."

"Maybe he still does. Maybe that's why the little guy looks so worried," observed Nicky. "What kind of a deal d'you have with her, Moose? You got a contract or something?"

Moose scowled the way he used to, back when he was on the Patriots line. "You sure do ask a lot of questions, mister."

"Hey, Moose, don't get sore, buddy." Nicky grinned, backing off a foot or two from the bar. "It's a straight deal. We don't want to steal Maria out from under you. You got a contract, we'll buy it out, maybe even throw in a little extra if you're not over-paying her, which I presume you're not or else the worried little guy wouldn't be hauling trays."

"You lost me, mister," said Moose. "What are you talking about?"

"Let me introduce myself," said Nicky, reaching his right hand across the bar. "My name's Nicky, and this here's my partner Bernice. Here's our card. We're in the entertainment business, got offices in New York and out on the Coast." Never mind that the West Coast branch consisted of a post office box in East Irvine; Nicky was determined to make a big impression.

Moose gathered Nicky's hand into his own great paw and shook it tentatively. "In other words, you're agents. Correct?"

"You got it, Moose! I expect in your former line of work you knew all about agents."

"Parasites. They make a living off other people's talent." Moose scowled and polished a wineglass with a white towel. "Sorry. I guess I saw too many guys get burned by their agents. You seem like decent folks. I don't mean to sound offensive."

"But you do!" exclaimed Bernice.

"Jeezus, Bernice——," Nicky objected.

"Oh shut up, Nicky. I'm asking you, why should we sit here and take insults when we're paying for dinner? You may be in the mood for punishment, but I'm not! I've had a rotten day." Bernice turned on Moose who was still wiping glasses. "Now you listen to me, Giant Jock! If it weren't for agents, you and the rest of the overgrown pea-brained adults who call kids' games work would have been lucky to get minimum wage. Think about it. How many football players did you know with enough smarts to negotiate themselves a decent contract? Half those guys are functional illiterates, and you know it!"

"Bernice——," Nicky wailed.

"The lady may have a point there," Moose observed. "Go ahead, Bernice. Don't mind Nicky."

"Which brings me to Maria. You think Maria's pretty good, don't you? Well, you're wrong. She's one of those rare performers who have everything it takes to be a great star. So who's gonna help her, huh? Who's gonna put up the money to cut a demo and schlepp it around to the right people? Who's gonna make sure she gets booked into the top clubs. You? The little waiter who hardly speaks the language? The astronaut who hallucinates in space? God forbid she should have an *agent!* Or maybe I've got it all backwards: maybe Maria really wants to spend the rest of her life singing in a chicken restaurant in Poughkeepsie, New York. Maybe we should ask her. How about it?"

"Is she always like this?" Moose inquired of Nicky with a grin.

"And don't patronize me!" Bernice ordered.

"Sorry," Moose apologized. "You're serious, aren't you? About Maria being a star, I mean."

"Moose," said Nicky, "ninety-nine outta a hundred people come into our office who wanna be stars, they're running high on dreams, low on talent, and absolute zero on charisma. Bernice and me, we've been around and even though it's gonna cost us, I'll be honest with you: I've never seen a singer as good as Maria unless they was already at the top of the heap, and half the people on top don't have what Maria's got."

"C'mon, Moose," Bernice urged. "You see what she does to this room. Give her a mike and half a dozen loudspeakers and she'll put Yankee Stadium in orbit, which is more than you can say for the Yankees. You want a piece of the action, we'll arrange it, because there's going to be plenty of action to go around."

Moose hunched his huge shoulders around his earlobes in a shrug. "Be my guest. I don't want a cut. There isn't any contract. I pay her by the week. As long as people keep coming in, she gets paid. Talk to her, talk to Paco. You might want to talk to Fisher, too, since he's the one who brought her to me. But there might be a problem"—Moose leaned over the bar and dropped his voice—"I guess I should tell you. She's an illegal."

"Never mind. We can fix it," said Nicky.

"Then you've got to fix Paco, too," added Moose, "plus three cute kids who hang out in the kitchen while their folks are working."

"No sweat."

"Nicky," Bernice warned, "we're not talking parking tickets here, we're talking illegal aliens, and that means NIPs! They've got a reputation—"

"So they got a reputation. Big deal! I'll letcha in on a little secret, babe: it's the decent guys, the ones who're trying to make the world a better place, that can't be bought. The mean ones like the NIPs, they're dumb. They're greedy. All you got to do is flash your cash."

Jimmy Williams started to warm up for his next set. Bernice glanced over at Fisher's table where he and Maria had been joined by a tall, stunning blond woman, also a young man who seemed to be her boyfriend. Paco had his tray tucked under his arm and was hovering next to Maria's chair.

"Nicky," Bernice observed, "we got no cash to flash. At any rate, not the kind that buys off cops."

"Maria's money in the bank."

"Not until we've signed her, she isn't. I say we talk to her now and make our deal."

Bernice slid off her barstool and threaded her way among the tables. Nicky followed close behind and, when he reached Fisher's table, pulled out a business card and cut loose with his spiel, talking into Maria's face. Maria's emerald eyes widened and she appealed to Fisher. The astronaut stretched out his long legs and arched an eyebrow, which made Bernice go wobbly at the knees because she'd never seen such a sexy man in the flesh. The young guy started scribbling in a notebook. The blond Amazon sipped an indecently green drink from a tall glass. Paco's eyes darted desperately back and forth between Nicky and Fisher. Nicky, caught in the current of his sales pitch, rushed on. Bernice tugged at his sleeve to make him shut up.

"Boliss?" Paco whispered hoarsely.

"Huh?"

"No, Paco, not police," Fisher said reassuringly. "Maria, do you understand what these people want?"

"I think a little," said Maria. "Not all maybe."

"Zeke, translate for them."

The man with the notebook, who spoke some Spanish, explained the gist of Nicky's proposition to Maria, whereupon she and Paco fell into Portuguese while Nicky and Bernice anxiously observed their conversation. Nicky didn't like the expression on Paco's face or the way he was shaking his head.

"Hey," Nicky whispered to the man named Zeke, "tell them we know all about them being illegals. No problem. We can fix it for them to stay in the States."

"Don't make promises you can't keep, man," warned Zeke.

Nicky looked insulted. "What I promise, I deliver. Just tell them what I said."

While Zeke was translating, the blond woman with the green drink leaned across the table. "If I were you folks," she said in a confidential tone, "I'd try to sign Mr. Fisher. He walks on air."

Nicky made a face like a prune. "Lady, if I was you, I wouldn't drink any more of that stuff!"

Bernice, however, looked sharply at Fisher whose own eyes were trained on the plastic philodendron at the far end of the bar. "Is that true, Mr. Fisher?" she asked.

"Is *what* true? Sorry, I haven't been paying attention."

"What she says—that you walk on air?"

"Could be," Fisher mused. "It never pays to argue with Susan."

This was when Maria reported that she and Paco had decided she couldn't become a famous singer until the televisions were fixed. Nicky tried to explain to Maria how she could be a big star without television, bigger even than Julio Iglesias. Susan started to laugh. Maria kept shaking her head and saying no, no, no. Zeke tried to tell Nicky he was missing the point—without saying what the point was. Bernice's handbag spilled its contents onto the floor, and Bernice crawled under the table to retrieve them.

Then Paco spoke: "Most important is first I help Gregorio Fisher fix the television."

"You're kidding!" said Nicky.

"No, he isn't," said Zeke and Susan, Greek-chorus style.

"Paco isn't much of a kidder," said Fisher.

"What is a kidder, please?" asked Maria.

Nicky caught Bernice's elbow and dragged her out from under the table to the rear of the restaurant, back by the restrooms and the kitchen.

"These people are all *nuts!*" he exclaimed. "You think they've been snorting something?"

"Fisher can walk on air, I'm sure of it."

"Come off it, Bernice. You're starting to sound like them. I just knew there had to be something wrong with that broad Maria. She was too good to be true."

"The trouble with you, Nicky, is you don't pay attention to the right things."

"What's that gotta do with Fisher walking on air?"

"He isn't wearing any socks, is what, and his ankles glow in the dark."

"Come off it—"

"You think I'm seeing things, wise guy, you drop a dime and check it out for yourself."

Upon rejoining the company at Fisher's table and on the pretext of paying for the last round of drinks, Nicky contrived to empty the contents of his wallet on the floor. He dove under the table on all fours to retrieve them; almost a minute passed before he resumed a two-legged stance.

"Bernice and me, we're pretty bushed," he announced, to

the surprise of Bernice who wasn't bushed at all. "Maybe the best thing is we go back to our hotel, catch a few zees, and give Maria a chance to think about our offer. You folks got any questions, you can reach us at the Hotel Hudson tomorrow during the day. Otherwise we'll see you here tomorrow night, okay?"

Nicky didn't wait for answers. He laid an arm firmly across Bernice's shoulders. "C'mon, babe. You look ready to keel over. Let's take you home and tuck you in bed."

The blond woman with the green drink smirked.

Bernice pouted. "I'm not anybody's babe," she said. She shook hands around the table, saving Fisher for last and half expecting sparks to fly when her hand touched his; the ordinary sensation of his cool, dry palm disappointed her.

After Nicky settled the bill with Moose, he and the reluctant Bernice exited the restaurant into the still foggy night. No freshening wind had stirred Poughkeepsie's air, and new, pungent odors joined the stale smells already trapped in the errant cloud.

"I don't get it," said Bernice, who had never known Nicky to back off a hot deal no matter how tired he was.

"You were right. Fisher's ankles glow in the dark, as far up his shins as I could make out," said Nicky by way of explanation. "I gotta think."

Knowing that thinking in Nicky's case customarily took the form of a monologue, Bernice braced herself against his words.

"I thought you said you were thinking," she remarked after three blocks of silence.

"I am," said Nicky. "In here!" He tapped his head.

"Hmmph. Well, I suppose it's never too late to try something new!"

Nicky either affected not to hear or had, indeed, withdrawn into thought.

Nicky propped himself up on the pillows and lay in bed staring at the TV set that he had absentmindedly switched on and left running because the luminous screen presented itself to him as a corral wherein the wild, racing contents of his mind might be tamed. When fatigue and confusion overcame him some hours later, he mumbled "Oh shit" and went to sleep. Therefore he was startled upon awakening at dawn to find himself refreshed and with his thoughts in a pleasing order.

Nicky rang the front desk to cancel his and Bernice's seats on the interrupted flight to New York and to extend their hotel reservations "indefinitely." Then he rang room service to order coffee for himself as well as breakfast to be delivered to Bernice's room—poached eggs on English muffins, her favorite—"and stick a red rose on the tray, okay?" After he'd drunk his coffee and flipped his way through the newsless pages of the local paper, he padded into the bathroom. Twenty minutes later, encountering his showered, shaved image in the mirror, he gave it a thumbs-up salute. Thus fortified, he marched across the hall and banged on Bernice's door.

"Point number one," Nicky outlined to his groggy partner as she brushed muffin crumbs from her bathrobe, "is that it's no accident we got stuck here in the fog. Point B is that the dame, Maria, can make us rich. Plus which, point C is that, like you said, Fisher's ankles glow in the dark which means maybe he can do what the blond broad says, namely walk on air, and it's all got something to do with the televisions. Somehow Fisher's the key to the televisions, and we're part of the solution. Which brings me to point number three which is that I canceled our flight."

"That's point number four, Nicky. Or maybe D. In either case, I don't follow your logic," said Bernice.

"It's what I said at the top, namely there's some reason we got grounded here. We can't run out. There's something we're supposed to do."

"Like what, Mr. Deep Thinker?"

"Don't go sarcastic on me. All I know is, it's got something to do with the televisions, and we got to hang in with these

people—Maria and the little waiter and the astronaut who sees
giant trees." Nicky paused and cleared his throat; he didn't want
Bernice to see he was choking up. "I never felt anything so strong
before, Bernice. We get on that plane, then nothing changes:
Maria stays in the chicken joint, the TVs stay dead, and we spend
the rest of our lives booking ventriloquists into bar mitzvahs. You
gotta trust me on this one. I can't even promise there's a buck in
it for us, but just this once I'm begging you to stick with me.
Everybody needs you. Don't ask me how I know it, but I do!"

"You're a pussycat, Nicky," Bernice said softly. "Always were."

"Wipe your chin, babe. You got egg on your face."

That's how it happened that Nicky and Bernice stayed another day in Poughkeepsie, and then another and another and
another and another. While Nicky spent his days on the phone
trying to drum up work for their clients, Bernice finished her
potboiler as well as three biographies of film stars. In the evenings
Bernice and Nicky walked the grimy streets over to Moose's Place
to listen to Maria, to eat Peruvian food, and to wait for the sign
that would point them in a new direction, that would reveal to
them the purpose of their waiting. At least, that's what Nicky
was waiting for. Bernice, whose entire life, as she once said, seemed
to her to have consisted of an unsystematic series of accidents
and who was accordingly ill disposed to look for meaning in
events, was waiting for Nicky to get back to his normal self.
Though impatient to return to New York, she remained in
Poughkeepsie, held there by her fear that Nicky would let Maria
slip away and—more powerfully, perhaps—by Greg Fisher's
magnetic field.

Bernice noticed that the incongruities in the geometry of
Nicky's logic escaped Fisher and his entourage—Nicky spelled
out his case to them, Points One, B, C, and Three—and they
actually welcomed him. The young man Zeke, who turned out to
be a reporter for the *New York Herald,* interviewed Nicky for his
newspaper, which got the agency several inches of free publicity,

a fact appreciated by Bernice who understood that even negative publicity (and you had to face it, Nicky came off as a flake in the article) was better than no publicity at all. Maria related an improbable story about Paco's determination to find Gregorio Fisher and the Coehlo family's hair-raising journey from the Amazon basin to Poughkeepsie, New York. Paco wrote a new song about Nicky and Bernice which Maria performed in Portuguese. The tall sardonic blond woman named Susan wasn't Zeke's date after all but a neighbor of Fisher's; she consumed gallons of gin mixed with Kool-Aid of a different color every night.

"What are you doing here?" Bernice once asked of Susan.

"Same thing you are."

"What's that?" Bernice persisted hopefully.

"Waiting."

"What for?"

"To see what happens next."

But for four days nothing much happened except that the Peruvian couple in Moose's kitchen produced a velvety avocado-chicken soup and Maria sang her first song in English, a ballad about a man who walked through a field of stars and called each one by name.

On the fifth evening, between Maria's sets when Jimmy Williams was improvising on an ancient Little Richard number, a woman appeared at the table—a young black-haired woman, tall and delicately boned, with the blood of many races in her veins.

"My name is Hsu-ling Hu," she introduced herself. "Which one of you is Mr. Gregory Fisher?"

"That's me," said Fisher. "What can I do for you?"

"You're a very elusive man, Mr. Fisher. I wrote you three letters you never answered."

Susan, the blond woman, smirked.

"Yes, I'm afraid I didn't read them," Fisher admitted. "I'm very embarrassed, but perhaps I can correct my mistake now. How can I help you?"

"I'm not sure. Maybe we can help each other. You see, I didn't have any ideas about the television failure until I read about you in the newspaper, about the extraordinary tree you had seen from space. Then I——"

"You believe the part about the tree?" Zeke interrupted.

"Of course," replied Hsu-ling. "I knew immediately that it was what Christian scriptures call the Tree of Life, but the same tree appears in the legends of many cultures as a symbol of life and spiritual renewal. In Chinese mythology, for instance, immortality is represented by the peach tree."

Paco, who by this time had come over to the table, was listening to the strange woman intently and asking Zeke for translation. When Zeke converted "tree of life" into Spanish, Paco nodded his head excitedly and said, *"Sim, sim, leyendas."*

"What I couldn't understand," Hsu-ling continued, "was the connection you made between the tree and the television failure. The truth is, I still don't understand it—though I believe there *is* a connection——"

"You *do?*" asked the astonished Bernice.

"Shut up, Bernice," ordered Nicky. "Let the lady say her piece. Go ahead, miss. Don't mind my partner here. She wouldn't believe in the sun, either, if it didn't come up every morning and slap her in the kisser."

"But then, Mr. Fisher," Hsu-ling went on, "it came to me quite suddenly what we must do next. . . ."

Everyone at the table, including Bernice, leaned toward Hsu-ling, waiting for words that might release them from their waiting. They didn't see Moose's huge hulk hastening across the floor in their direction.

"Everybody stay cool," Moose whispered hoarsely, "and don't look at the bar. Two guys are standing there who look like NIPs. In fact, I know they're NIPs. I expect they want to have a look in my kitchen. I've got a buzzer under the bar to signal the Peruvians so they can skedaddle out the back, but I don't know what to do about your kids, Maria, and once they get them you and Paco are history. So if I were you folks, I'd collect the children and make a very calm exit out the back." Moose executed a casual wave at the patrons of an adjoining table and lumbered over to greet them.

"*Boliss?*" inquired Paco in a panic.

"Yes, Paco," said Zeke. "This time it's the police."

Paco dropped his tray with a clatter. Maria covered her mouth with her hand to hold back a scream. Fisher rubbed his temples. It was Nicky, of all people, who took charge. He ordered Paco to pick up his tray and clear tables as though nothing were wrong. He commanded Hsu-ling and Bernice to slip into the kitchen, act like cooks, and conceal the Coehlo children until someone came to collect them. He deployed Zeke to distract the NIPs. ("Distract them? How?" demanded the flustered Zeke. "Use your imagination, kid," snapped Nicky. "Ask 'em questions. Tell 'em you're working on a human interest story. People love to talk about themselves.") Then Nicky invited Susan for a drink at the bar.

"Which leaves you two," Nicky hissed at Maria and Fisher. "Make like you're crazy about each other."

Fisher reached awkwardly for Maria's hand.

"Come off it, lover boy!" Nicky objected in disgust. "You call that crazy? Show 'em your stuff, Fisher. You remember necking, don't you?"

Nicky patted the blond woman's heavenly rounded ass and propelled her toward the bar. Playing her part like a veteran, Susan poised one foot on the bar rail and hitched up her miniskirt, exposing another two or three inches of ripe thigh which distracted the NIPs from the distraction of Zeke's interview. Nicky ordered a double Scotch for himself and a gin and grape Kool-Aid for Susan, this being one of her purple nights.

Nicky swallowed a mouthful of Scotch. "I gotta take a leak," he announced loudly to Susan. "Don't forget who you came in with, doll."

Bernice later described how Nicky charged into Moose's kitchen. The Peruvian couple had already escaped along with the Haitian kid who washed dishes. Hsu-ling, who had donned a chef's hat and an apron, was expertly filling late orders for strawberry shortcake and other honest desserts while Bernice—whose culinary experience consisted of transferring take-out meals from styrofoam containers to paper plates—stood next to the dishwasher noisily scraping dirty dishes into the garbage.

"Where'd you stash the kids?" Nicky demanded.

"Behind the garbage pails," replied Bernice.

"Time to come out and play," Nicky called to the garbage. Accustomed as they were to desperate escapes, the children emerged and stood obediently at attention like little soldiers, even the smallest one. Nicky hoisted the baby, Serita, into his arms. "Okay, you two," he challenged Elena and Gilberto, "I bet I can run faster than you can."

Using the alley exit, Nicky and the children ran to the Hotel Hudson where he locked them into his room and instructed them to wait for an adult. Ten minutes later he reentered Moose's Place and swaggered back to the bar where Susan was now flirting with Zeke and the NIPs.

"Hey," Nicky said belligerently, "didn't the lady tell you she was engaged?"

"You were gone so long she thought you'd fallen in," remarked one of the NIPs, a runt of a guy with a squashed nose. "Like to tell us what you were doing?"

"Geez, Nicky, you're such a slob," said Susan, reading Nicky's signal perfectly. "Didn't your mommy ever teach you to zip up your pants after you go potty?"

The NIPs and Zeke laughed. Nicky's eyes flew to his crotch. He managed to look embarrassed as he turned away to zip his fly. A glance in the bar mirror told him Paco was taking orders for drinks; back against the wall, Maria was curled in Fisher's lap nibbling on his left ear.

Nicky decided to make himself obnoxious, which in his case wasn't a major effort. Within minutes, the NIPs remembered why they had come into Moose's Place to begin with and hot-footed it for the kitchen. There, according to Bernice, Hsu-ling confounded them by responding to their questions in one of the several languages in her repertoire; the NIPs, suspicious of her exotic appearance and her apparent ignorance of English, de-manded to see her papers. She baffled them by producing impec-cable documents and switching from Urdu into unaccented English. When the skinny one with the squashed nose asked her what she was up to, Hsu-ling responded in a neutral tone, "I don't approve of your agency. Making your task more complicated satisfies my sense of justice." The runt snarled and raised his arm to strike her. "Don't you touch her, you little creep," yelled Bernice. "I'm a witness. One good scream from me, and Moose himself will be back here in two seconds and personally reach down your throat and rip out your lungs." The commotion in the kitchen gave Nicky time to pass his hotel room key to Zeke who fetched Paco and left with him through the front door.

Nicky was back feeling up Susan at the bar behind which Moose was calmly polishing beer glasses, and Jimmy Williams was winding down his set with Fats Waller's "Black and Blue," when the NIPs came back from the kitchen. Nicky could see by their faces they weren't in a sociable frame of mind.

"Hey you, Moose," growled the runt, "you tell those bitches in the back to treat us polite next time, or we take 'em in on general principles, you hear?"

"I run a restaurant here," Moose observed, "not a charm school."

"You wanna keep running it, you watch your step. There's rumors you've been using illegals here instead of regular Americans. Air smells funny, like people don't wash right. You aren't off the hook yet, pal."

"Relax, Roy," advised the taller NIP, a chinless individual who played the role of Nice Guy to Roy's Heavy. "Hey, Moose, how about the house offers us one for the road?"

"The sign says cheap booze, not *free* booze," replied Moose.

"We're leaving, but just because you can't see us don't mean we can't see you," said Roy darkly. "So don't make no fast moves, Moose."

"You mean you don't want to stay for Maria?" asked Moose. "There's no cover charge."

"Who's Maria?" asked Chinless.

"She sings."

"In a joint like this? You gotta be kidding."

Susan fluttered her fingers at the NIPs as they passed her on the way out, but their mood was ugly and they didn't respond.

It was Nicky's idea that the rest of the night should proceed as usual, just in case the NIPs decided to take a second look. So Bernice and Hsu-ling cleaned up the kitchen while Maria performed her eleven o'clock show. When it was over and people were paying their checks, she went over to Moose, stood on her tiptoes, and kissed his mouth.

She never sang in Poughkeepsie again.

• • •

Isabelle sighed.

"You mean that's *it?*" David demanded. "What a crummy ending."

"I beg your pardon," huffed the offended Isabelle.

"You've left a lot of loose ends, Izzie."

"Name one!"

"Well, for instance, what happened to Maria and Paco after that night? Did the NIPs ever catch up with them again?"

"Nicky had a cousin in Brooklyn who knew a guy named Lenny who forged citizenship documents. Even the NIPs with all their fancy equipment couldn't tell them from the real thing. One look at Maria, and Lenny knocked fifty percent off his price. Nicky borrowed the balance from his brother-in-law."

"And then?"

"What do you mean, 'and then'?" Isabelle demanded. "Maria went on to be a big star—"

"So you and Uncle Nate got rich?"

"*Bernice and Nicky* got rich enough to pay back Nicky's brother-in-law with interest, and then some. But they weren't clever about managing money, so eventually they got poor again. Even so, they had a good time."

"Another thing," David continued, "did you—or rather Bernice and Nicky—ever find out what Hsu-ling wanted to say before Moose interrupted her?"

"Yes. She said *we must ask the children.* I, er, Bernice couldn't make any sense of it."

"You see?" David crowed. "I knew Bernice was you all along, Izzie. I knew it was all true! But that stuff about Fisher's ankles glowing in the dark, you made that up, didn't you?"

"Maybe I did." Isabelle smiled. "And maybe I didn't."

Timothy's Story

Timothy entered his grandson's bedroom without announcing himself and caught Eddie unawares.

"How come everybody in this house rates privacy except me?" the boy demanded, his face gone blotchy with guilt. He was lying belly-down on his bed, fully dressed in jeans, sweatshirt, and basketball sneakers. One hand darted under his pillow in the act of concealing what Timothy registered as a suspiciously book-like object.

"Forgive me, kid. I supposed you weren't at home. It's Friday, isn't it? Or am I losing it? Don't you usually go to Arthur's after school?"

"Arthur had a dentist appointment."

"Dear me. Well, I'm sorry I barged in on you," Timothy apologized. "No excuse for my not knocking."

"Why should you? Nobody else bothers," Eddie remarked. "What did you want, anyway?"

"To use your computer. I dropped into the software library this morning and borrowed a program to help me brush up my Russian so I can read Chekhov in the original."

"Oh, yeah," said Eddie suavely, as though he actually knew who (or maybe what?) Chekhov was and why Timothy would bother reading something in Russian when the computer could be programmed to translate it into plain English. Someday, next week maybe, he'd ask his grandfather about that. But not now. Now he had More Important Things on his mind.

"I see this isn't a good time," said Timothy, edging out the door. "I'll let you get back to whatever it was you were doing."

"Homework," Eddie lied. If he'd only kept his mouth shut his grandfather would have left; instead, the lie pulled the old man back into the room.

"Really?" Timothy asked with surprise. "I thought I saw you with a book. Do you mean to tell me a teacher asked you to read a real book?"

Ever since first grade, Eddie's computer had been linked to the school's mainframe so he could access his assignments, plus any texts he needed, electronically. He could even browse through the school library without leaving his terminal. Which, Timothy conceded, was all fine, possibly edifying, except that children didn't acquire the habit of books, and no one had yet come up with a computer you could take to the beach or read in the bathtub. So if Eddie was doing homework from a book, Timothy wanted to hear about it. "Let's have a look."

"It wasn't exactly an assignment." Eddie flushed. "I just wanted to . . ." His voice trailed off. He kneaded an incipient pimple on his jawline.

"Never mind," said Timothy gently, seeing the boy's embarrassment. "I'll just——"

"It's actually yours." Eddie retrieved the volume from its hiding place and handed it to his grandfather. "I borrowed it. I hope you don't mind."

Timothy's eyebrows shot up. The book was Baudelaire, the Francis Duke translation, surely not standard ninth-grade fare. Must have some connection to that new French teacher Eddie was always talking about, the one he said was sexy and painted her fingernails pink and white. "Of course I don't mind," Timothy said, observing his grandson more carefully now. "How do you like Baudelaire?"

"I dunno. He's okay. I guess." Eddie sighed and rolled over on his back to ponder the ceiling. "Grandad?"

"Yes?"

"Never mind."

"You're sure?"

"Yes . . . um, no," said Eddie. "If I ask you a question, will you promise not to tell anyone?"

"You don't have to ask, kid. You should know that by now."

"And you won't laugh?"

"Of course not."

"Well, then, here's the question: before you married Grandma, were you ever in love with a woman who was older than you?"

"Hmm, that's going back a ways." He cast the net of his mind back half a century and snared a scrapbook of past girl-friends, some of whose faces were faded and whose names he had forgotten, others who resided in memory with distracting detail. "Yes," he admitted, "there were one or two."

"I mean somebody a *lot* older," Eddie specified, "not like you were fourteen and she was fifteen, but like she was maybe ten years older. Even more."

"Ah!" said Timothy, who was beginning to develop a hunch about what might be bothering his grandson. "I was in love with a teacher once. Would that count?"

Eddie brightened. "Why not? What happened?"

"It didn't work out."

"How come?"

"You promise you won't laugh?"

"Promise!"

This is the tale Timothy told.

Whichever way you said it — whether in the American manner, or pronouncing the last name first as the Chinese do — her
name had the sound of wind chimes: Hsu-ling Hu, Hu Hsu-ling.
We of course called her Ms. Hu and made juvenile puns on her
name to give ourselves another excuse to talk about her outside
the classroom. We all adored her except, perhaps, Mary Beth
O'Connor who was crazy about horses. But —

• • •

"You mean the girls were in love with her, too?" Eddie inquired.

"Sure," said Timothy. "Before sex enters the picture, girls
get crushes on women teachers just like boys, and vice versa.
You'll see what I mean later on. Didn't you ever have a crush on
a male teacher? A coach maybe?"

"No!" denied Timothy emphatically. "That's stupid! What
grade were you in anyway?"

"Fifth. Ms. Hu taught fifth grade."

Eddie giggled. "No wonder the girls got their signals crossed.
You were just little kids!"

"You promised not to laugh," Timothy reminded his grandson sternly.

"Okay. I won't laugh. Promise."

• • •

Nobody loved Ms. Hu as much as I did. In fact I doubt that
I have ever loved any woman with greater intensity than I did
Ms. Hu in the fifth grade. I lay in bed at night spinning elaborate
fantasies in which I rescued her from all manner of demons and
catastrophes. I stole marigolds for her from the neighbor's gar-

den. I volunteered to stay after school to wash the blackboards. I
did extra homework to gain her approval.

Love, as you may know, is terrible for your health. I came
down with vegetative symptoms: dizziness, rebellions of appetite,
hiccups, hyperventilation, and an embarrassing urge to pee at
inappropriate moments. Every time Ms. Hu displayed to one of
my classmates what seemed to me excessive favor, my heart con-
stricted with jealousy. Nevertheless, I was almost certain that she
loved me. Sometimes I'd look up from whatever I was supposed
to be doing and find her watching me with a tenderness I was
positive she reserved for me. Plus which, I had a more significant
piece of evidence, for there came a time when I could no longer
manage my passion. One day I hung around for two hours after
school in the teachers' parking lot. When I saw her heading for
her car, I ran over and blurted, "Ms. Hu, I love you," to which
she replied, "Why, Timmy, I'm flattered. I love you, too. I love
all my children. But I do think you ought to hurry home before
your mother calls the police."

Although some people might not have dignified that as a
declaration of romantic love, my stricken self saw through Ms.
Hu's feeble attempt to disguise her true feelings for me by pre-
tending to spread her adoration thin over the entire class. No
doubt about it: we were in love.

• • •

Eddie let loose a hoot of laughter. "I'm sorry, Grandad," he
apologized, "but I get this picture of this little kid mooning around
over a grown-up lady and meanwhile trying not to wet his pants."

"And you find that amusing?" Timothy asked. "What about
a little compassion here? I was in agony, dear boy! Obviously you
have no experience of true love."

"Says who!" Eddie replied indignantly.

"You want to talk about it?"

"No, I want to hear more about the fabulous Ms. Hu. What
did she look like? Did she have big boobies?"

. . .

Big boobies? I don't remember. Perhaps I wasn't interested in boobies yet. She was willowy and tall, a fact that sometimes tripped me up in my fantasies because I couldn't fathom a way of taking her in my arms and deploying a manly kiss without standing on a chair. She was also considered eccentrically beautiful. She wasn't the type of woman who attracted wolf whistles or "Hey, babes" from construction crews, but as my mother once remarked after a PTA meeting, "She grows on you. She's actually a fascinating-looking woman—quite exotic."

"Not my type," observed my father.

But she was *my* type!

Despite her pure Chinese name, Hsu-ling Hu was a racial mixture. She once began a social studies lesson by explaining to us, her fifth-graders, that her father was half Chinese and half Polish-American whereas her mother, who had been born in Trinidad, counted Africans, East and West Indians, and an Englishman among her ancestors. Imagine all those microscopic chromosomes battling for dominance! In retrospect, I have the impression that the Chinese and Caucasian genes combined to create the substructure of a long-boned, delicate skeleton and high cheekbones; whereas the external cladding—hair, mouth, eyes, and skin which was a mellow coffee color—revealed the influences of the darker races.

Although she was beautiful, it was Ms. Hu's voice that enchanted me. In ordinary conversation she spoke in pleasant, clear, and unremarkable tones. But when she told a story, her voice became a magical instrument capable of reproducing bird calls, animal cries, engine noises, music, and many variations of laughter and despair. She could sound like a Frenchman or a field of corn according to the requirements of her story. Ms. Hu told her fifth-graders a story every day.

I see the "big deal" expression on your face, Eddie, but before you protest, hear me out. Unlike you, I wasn't brought up with stories. During my own childhood the oral tradition had declined into a condition of neglect. Even the African griots were entering obsolescence. My mother who was a hardworking woman—she had a full-time job as a biomedical technician—plunked me down in front of the television at an early age, which was the way she had been raised by *her* mother back in the 1970s. I don't mean to imply that my mother ignored me, because she did play games with me and ask me about school and help me with my homework. She just never told me stories. I suspect it never occurred to her that a story could compete for a child's attention with the Roadrunner and Wile E. Coyote.

My father, by contrast, often began tales that never got anywhere owing to his weakness for free association. He'd start off talking about a sailboat race, and before the first tack he'd meander off into a discussion of international banking which in turn would remind him of something that had happened to him during the war in Vietnam. Mind you, once you got the hang of them Father's monologues could be fun; my mother, my uncle Robert, and I used to make side bets as to which subject would pop up next. He had a weirdly wired brain, my father; I've often wondered how he got to be a professor of economics. He was kind and funny, but he was incapable of holding on to a thread of narrative thought long enough to weave it into a story.

Furthermore, by the time I entered Ms. Hu's fifth grade, the televisions had been out of whack for more than a year. I've told you about how they all quit on June 21, 2002, while my father and I were watching the Baltimore-Yankees game. Well, when fifth grade got under way in September 2003, there still wasn't any television. Frankly, I don't remember much about the year in between except that I hated my fourth-grade teacher, I stayed home sick a lot, Mother took up knitting and canasta, and we didn't go to the seashore during the summer owing to an outbreak of cholera. I wasn't looking forward to going back to school: I remember *that!* I'd heard a rumor that the old fifth-grade teacher had quit, and the person who'd been hired as a replacement was a dork.

But as you already know, Ms. Hu was definitely no dork. Around ten o'clock on the first day of school she told us a story. It was an ancient Chinese legend she'd heard from her father's father, about K'uei-hsing, the god of examinations, who was famous as one of the ugliest of all the Chinese gods—by way of demonstration, Ms. Hu contorted her pretty features into a fearsome grimace. During his life on earth K'uei-hsing had been an excellent student and placed first in his examinations; but when the emperor saw the young man's ugliness, he refused to accept the results of the tests. In his despair K'uei-hsing jumped into the sea and tried to drown himself. Instead he fell upon the back of a turtle who carried him back to land.

And so forth and so on. It was a charming legend, appropriate to the first day of school, and I can still picture Ms. Hu standing in front of the class, producing the voices of the wrathful emperor and the aggrieved student, the splash into the water, and the melancholic speech of the turtle. She used no props, no sound systems, no script, no supporting cast, no technological chicanery; it was a performance of naked imagination. We children were spellbound. And by lunchtime I was in love.

Ms. Hu devoted almost an hour every day to telling stories and discussing the art of storytelling. She showed us how the most ordinary objects or events—a ticket stub, say, or a trip to the supermarket—might be transformed by imagination into a story, how stories could make the opaque transparent and expose the soul of a rock, how great stories matured into legends passed down from one generation to the next. Soon she began to encourage us to invent stories of our own—one kid, I remember, made up a tale about the integer four getting lost by a careless student in a long division problem and wandering around until it found a home for itself in the denominator of a fraction. In my eagerness to please Ms. Hu, I began to peruse my surroundings, to ask myself questions about what I perceived, and to make up stories which I tried out at home before taking them to school. I seem to recall monopolizing the dinner table for a week with my rehearsals of a romance I called "The Carrot and the Pea," which drove Mother bananas and made Father laugh.

So there we were, three and a half or four weeks into fifth grade, and everything was going along dandy. I earned better marks than usual on the first few tests. I was in love. I had declared myself to my beloved, she had indirectly declared herself to me, and I was figuring on proposing before Christmas vacation. I had braced myself for the ordeal of a long engagement. Since I realized it might be awkward for Ms. Hu to have her husband in her own classroom, I was prepared to postpone the wedding until June when I would be promoted to sixth grade. And then—

• • •

"The doo-doo hit the fan," Eddie interpolated with a grin.

"You must learn that you can't tell another person's story," said Timothy. "Contrary to your intuition, things got even better for a while. Though slightly strange, I admit."

• • •

Our fifth grade had a primitive version of the global telecommunications system that you have now, which linked up our class with kids all over the world to do math and science projects such as water-quality and greenhouse-effect experiments. Not that the information we accumulated made any impact on government policy, mind you, even though we passed it on to research agencies; it merely lay lifeless in invisible data banks. But at least we had fun learning how to do statistical analyses and scientific experiments while believing we were actually accomplishing something.

One day—it must have been around the end of September, because it was hot and muggy, a regular Indian Summer—in the middle of a geography session, two grown-up men knocked on the classroom door and were admitted by Ms. Hu. They weren't people we recognized like other teachers or the principal or the janitor.

"I'd like to introduce you to my friends. This," said Ms. Hu, indicating a skinny redheaded fellow, "is a journalist from New York whose name is Mr. Ezekiel Kramer. He writes newspaper articles for the *Herald*. And this gentleman"—she smiled at a tall, good-looking guy—"is Mr. Gregory Fisher, the astronaut. Perhaps you've heard something about him."

You bet I'd heard something about him! My mother and father talked about him all the time. He was the freaky astronaut who claimed to have seen a forty-mile-high tree growing out of the African desert. In Mother's opinion Fisher was a schizophrenic or victim of some other genetic anomaly; Father disagreed, though I never could quite make out the gist of his argument.

What was Gregory Fisher doing in the fifth grade?

Ms. Hu was reading my mind. "Mr. Fisher," she told us, "has a problem he's been trying to solve, and he thinks you may be able to help him. Why don't you tell the class about the problem, Mr. Fisher."

Fisher, who didn't have a schoolteacher's knack for preparing young minds by easing into an important question, flung his problem at us like a major-league fastball: "I'm trying to figure out what happened to the television reception."

Nobody breathed. Even that big show-off Judy Wackenhut, who thought she had the answer to everything and was always the first one to raise her hand, kept her mouth shut for a change.

"Well," suggested Ms. Hu, "let's talk about Mr. Fisher's problem for a while and see what we already know about it."

As often happened when Ms. Hu got us talking about a new problem, we knew more than we thought we knew, though even that wasn't much. We knew that all the televisions in the world had stopped broadcasting at the same time; we knew that all the big-shot committees studying the problem hadn't solved it; and we knew, mostly from our parents, various crackbrain theories about what had gone wrong.

"I think this is a silly discussion," announced show-off Judy Wackenhut who had recovered her wits and was jumping out of her seat and waving her hand for several minutes before Ms. Hu called on her. "My father says there's nothing to worry about because any day now the Japanese will come out with another kind of television that's different from the old one so we can see the same shows."

"I see," said Ms. Hu neutrally. "Ozzie?"

"Yes, Ms. Hu?" That was Fat Ozzie Elmwood who never volunteered for anything. Ozzie was built like a beachball, which is how we, his mean and leaner peers, treated him.

"I thought I saw you start to raise your hand. Did you want to say something?"

"Not really, but, well," Ozzie mumbled, "everybody has these ideas, see? But I think maybe nobody really knows what's wrong with the televisions. Because if they really knew they'd fix it, wouldn't they? Or they'd say they couldn't fix it and it was broken for good. But they wouldn't keep talking about it in conferences and everything. Isn't that right?"

"That's a good observation, Ozzie," said Ms. Hu. "What do you think, Mr. Fisher?"

"Not bad at all. Ozzie's right: nobody knows why the televisions don't work."

Ms. Hu rewarded Fat Ozzie Elmwood with an expression of approval so affectionate that I wanted to kill him!

"Maybe people haven't been asking the right questions," ventured the emboldened Ozzie.

"*Very* good, Ozzie!" Ms. Hu beamed at him. She had never beamed at me in quite that way.

Ooh, that Ozzie! I hated how he was sucking up to Ms. Hu, even worse how she was falling for it! Who did he think he was, anyway? When we got out on the playground, I'd give him a geography lesson of my own—let him know he was trespassing on private property.

The class continued to discuss the television problem, but I was so busy plotting how I was going to handle Ozzie that I didn't hear what was said. Then my bladder started acting up and I had to ask to go to the boys' room, where two older boys who were smoking cigarettes barricaded my stall; so that by the time I got back to the classroom, the rest of the kids had gone to lunch, and I was in a vengeful mood.

Fat Ozzie Elmwood usually hung out by himself near the barberry bushes at the edge of the parking lot, as far away from the playground action as he could get without violating any rules.

"Hey, Ozzie." I saluted as I approached, "What's up?"

"Hi, Timmy," Ozzie replied, extending a plastic bag. "Nothing. Want a carrot?" Ozzie's mother had him on a perpetual diet of carrot and celery sticks; probably she didn't know he used to sneak across the street for Double Whoppers and fries after school.

"Yuk!" I bit savagely into my bologna sandwich.

"I'll trade my apple for half a sandwich."

"Get a life!"

"What's that mean?"

"My mom says it. It means—never mind what it means." I wasn't about to let on that I didn't exactly understand what it meant either. "The *point,* Ozzie, is that I love Ms. Hu."

"You do?" asked Ozzie. "Me too!"

I hadn't counted on that.

"Well," I announced after reflection, "you can't."

"Why not?"

I didn't want to disclose intimate secrets, such as the fact that Ms. Hu and I were getting engaged around Christmas, so I reasoned, "Because it isn't fair. I loved her first. Besides, you're fat. Ms. Hu could never love such a fatso."

"I can't help it if I'm fat," sniffled Ozzie, his face crumbling. "My father says it's gen-gen-gen——"

"Oh stop blubbering, blubberball. Don't be such a fat cry-baby ..." While I unleashed every fat insult in my vocabulary, Ozzie, his round body quivering with sobs, turned his back on me and hurled himself down the path between the barberry bushes and into the parking lot, scratching both arms along the way.

I've never been secure in my own mind as to what happened next. I was watching over the tops of the bushes as Ozzie's heaving form stumbled among the cars on its way across the parking lot. Then a blue van careened into my frame of vision, and it struck me in a flash that Ozzie and the driver hadn't seen each other, and that Ozzie Elmwood was going to get squashed and bleed all over the parking lot. But before my heart could take another beat, this guy comes right over the tops of about ten cars without touching them——I could have sworn he was *flying*——and he plucks Fat Ozzie off the pavement and goes up in the air again over another row of cars. And then I heard a crash as the van plowed into the rear end of a stationary school bus.

Unharmed but angry, the driver slammed out of his van and ran toward the traffic island where Fat Ozzie Elmwood was standing with his rescuer whom I now recognized as Mr. Fisher. Fisher waited quietly while the driver flapped his arms and cursed. I was too far away to catch Fisher's response, but whatever he said silenced the driver who shrugged and walked back frowning to the van, pausing once to cast a glance back over his shoulder at Fisher. Fisher, I saw, was talking with Ozzie who kept nodding his head; then Ozzie said something that caused Fisher to shake *his* head. When their conversation ended, Fisher shook Ozzie's hand very formally; Ozzie smiled a fat smile. Then Fisher took off in the opposite direction while Ozzie retraced his steps across the parking lot, this time keeping an eye out for moving vehicles.

You know that feeling you get when you make a mistake and

barge into the bathroom while somebody is sitting on the toilet? Well, something told me I shouldn't have seen what I'd just seen, and that I shouldn't let on I'd seen it. I ducked down behind the bushes and fished around in my lunchbox. By the time Ozzie returned, I was casually unwrapping a double-chocolate candy bar. He seemed startled to find me still in his spot, and his face turned pink.

"Where'd you go?" I quizzed him.

"Nowhere."

"Did you see that crash?"

"What crash?"

"You want half a candy bar?" I offered.

"Sure! Thanks."

I divided the candy in two and gave Ozzie the smaller piece. He bit into it with a blissful, locked-up expression that told me my bribe was going to waste down his gullet. He wasn't going to tell about Fisher and the parking lot. Or maybe he was, because now he got another, smirky look on his face.

"Timmy," he said, "I've been thinking. If you want to love Ms. Hu, then I won't. It's okay with me."

The next day I discovered that while I'd been worrying about Ozzie and Ms. Hu and getting myself trapped in the boys' room, the class had decided to attack the television problem by using the telecommunications system. Unbeknownst to me, Ms. Hu had assigned us the task of thinking what questions we might most profitably pose about this problem. The plan was for our class to feed questions into the network and then act as a research center, gathering all the responses and analyzing them to see what, if any, sense they made.

Fisher came in while Ms. Hu was taking attendance; he propped himself against the edge of her desk, surveying the classroom. I caught the quick look that passed between him and Fat Ozzie

Elmwood like a laser beam, and I made a big show of staring out the window as though I hadn't noticed anything. The other fellow, Fisher's friend the journalist, was also there; he found a vacant seat in the back of the room and started writing in a notebook.

I was leaning into the aisle, trying to get a peek at Fisher's feet in case he was wearing magic shoes that might explain what I thought I'd seen yesterday, when Ms. Hu called my name.

"Yes'm?"

"Why don't you tell us the question you'd like to ask about the televisions?"

"Um . . ." I had to improvise here. "Well, how about 'Why aren't the televisions working?' "

Ms. Hu wrote my question on the blackboard. She called on two or three other kids who advanced similar, if not identical, suggestions, such as "What went wrong with the televisions?" or "How can we fix the TVs?" which she also listed on the blackboard.

When Judy Wackenhut's turn came, she trashed the questions. "Whenever we do a science project we start by collecting data, right?" she complained. "Isn't that what we decided to do about the television problem? But if we ask these questions, all we'll get is a lot of dumb ideas. We need a hypo, hypoph—a watchmacallit."

"Hypothesis, Judy," supplied Ms. Hu, adding the word to the list already on the blackboard and underlining it twice. "Yes, Timmy?"

"Maybe one of those dumb ideas will turn out to be right," I protested in defense of my question.

"No way!" sneered Judy.

Fisher, who up to that moment had been looking limp, snapped to attention. "The kid has a good point," he said. "Those aren't sound scientific questions. In fact, they're the same kinds of questions the committees have been asking which may be why they haven't produced any results. I like the drift of your thinking, Judy."

Judy honored me with one of her stuck-up I-told-you-so looks.

Ms. Hu delivered a short lecture reminding us what a hypothesis was, how we shouldn't confuse it with a hypo*tenuse,* and about how we should take care to formulate our questions the way adult scientists did, as if she believed her fifth-graders might turn into miniature Einsteins if only they could snatch the problem by the tail. As she was talking I noticed out of the corner of my eye Fat Ozzie Elmwood's flabby scabby arm laboriously lifting itself off his desk and over his head. He was volunteering again, twice in two days! Incredible!

"Ozzie?" That was Fisher calling on Ozzie, not Ms. Hu.

"I guess this is going to sound stupid, but I thought real hard last night," Ozzie huffed and puffed, "and what I thought was this: everybody keeps asking questions about the television, as though it did something bad. But a television is just a thing, um—a machine. It can't really *do* anything but be a television. It can't even turn itself on and off. It needs people to do that. So I was thinking what if what happened to the televisions is something *a person or people* did?"

"Wow!" exclaimed Fisher. "That has the makings of what I'd call one hell—er, heck—of a hypothesis."

Ms. Hu beamed at Ozzie.

• • •

"You're beginning to sound like your own father, Grandad," Eddie complained.

"I gather you aren't paying me a compliment." Timothy pursed his lips.

"Well, you started off in love with the teacher, and next thing I knew you were talking about this television thing. What happened to the romance?"

"Don't worry. I'll get back to that in a minute. Aren't you the least bit curious about Gregory Fisher flying around the parking lot?"

"I figured you threw that in for color," said Eddie. "What's it called? Poetic license or something?"

"In other words you're accusing me of a flight of fancy?"

"Either that or funny mayonnaise in the bologna sandwich!"

"It's curious how each person has different criteria for discriminating between fact and fiction," Timothy sighed. "Well, on with the story and my sad romantic saga."

• • •

Much to my consternation—because my jealous heart didn't trust his vow to lay off Ms. Hu—after some intellectual tidying, Ozzie's musings became the premise of our inquiry into the television problem. We spent the rest of the morning refining a message to send over the networks. When the draft finally pleased everybody (including Fisher who wouldn't allow his name to appear on it), Ms. Hu designated Ozzie to enter the text into the computer. We collected around the monitor and watched while he typed:

> OUR CLASS, GRADE 5, DAN QUAYLE ELEMEN-
> TARY SCHOOL, POUGHKEEPSIE, NEW YORK, USA,
> IS BEGINNING A NEW DATA COLECTION PROJ-
> ECT, AND WE NEED YOUR HELP. HERE IS OUR
> QUESTION: WHAT HAPPENED IN THE PLACE
> WHERE YOU LIVE (CITY, TOWN, SETTELMENT,
> COMMUNITY, FARM, ETC.) BEGINNING THURS-
> DAY, JUNE 20, 2002, UP UNTIL FRIDAY, JUNE 21,
> 2002, WHEN THE TELEVISIONS STOPPED WORK-
> ING?

"Okay?" asked Ozzie after he'd had the computer correct his spelling errors. "Can I send it?"

"It's perfect," said Fisher. "Go ahead."

Ozzie blushed and hit the network button, transmitting our

quixotic query to terminals in more than six thousand classrooms, grades four through nine, around the world. Those were huge numbers at the time, more kids than we'd ever tried to contact before, and I remember getting a physical thrill when Ozzie pressed the TRANSMIT key. I guess what I was feeling was a jolt of power.

"How many answers do you think we'll get, Ms. Hu?" inquired one of the girls.

"Normally I wouldn't have much confidence in a question that wasn't specified in the curriculum. Most teachers don't think they have time for extras. But"—she smiled as though she had a secret—"maybe this isn't a normal situation."

The bell clanged, signaling lunch. Ozzie deliberately dawdled at the computer in what I viewed as an obvious ploy to stay behind so he could have a private meeting with Ms. Hu. I retaliated by rethreading the laces on my sneakers.

"Ozzie, Timmy, stop fussing. Out with you!" commanded Ms. Hu. Ozzie grabbed his lunch and hustled out the door. I managed to lag behind. On my way out I sidled up to Fisher.

"Sir," I asked cagily, "do you know anybody who can fly all by himself?"

"Could be," said the astronaut.

"That'll be enough," said Ms. Hu. "Mr. Fisher's hungry, too. We must let him eat his lunch."

"Yes'm."

I exited the room into the hallway and pressed myself hard against the wall next to the doorjamb in a position where I wouldn't be seen from within.

"I thought only the fat kid knew about the flying," I heard the journalist say. "Could he have tattled?"

"Who? Ozzie Elmwood? I doubt it," said Ms. Hu. "And I'll thank you not to refer to one of my best pupils as 'the fat kid,' Zeke. He gets quite enough verbal abuse from his classmates and his mother without your contribution. Poor Ozzie. He's really very sweet."

"Sorry. But what do you think the other kid meant by his question? Maybe he saw something."

"And what if he did?" demanded Fisher. "I know what you're up to, Zeke, but I'm not changing my position. You can write whatever you please, but don't expect me to corroborate your claims."

"How many people know already? A dozen maybe?" Zeke queried. "Word's bound to leak out, and you'll wind up in the tabloids with the two-headed babies."

"So what?" countered Fisher. "Must be a thousand folks who claim to have eaten pork chops with Martians, and the rest of the world laughs at them. Who cares what the tabloids print?"

"Besides," added Ms. Hu, "I wouldn't read too much into Timmy's question. He's an exceptionally curious child."

My eyes smarted as I quit my listening post and trudged down the hall toward the cafeteria. My mother had always warned me nothing good could come of eavesdropping, and experience had proven her right: Ms. Hu considered Fat Ozzie Elmwood a "best" student, not to mention "very sweet"; worse, she'd referred to me as a "child."

Apart from that, the fact of having more or less validated my impression that Fisher could fly gave me the heebie-jeebies. In all my ten and three-quarters years, I'd never heard of such a human!

Four or five fretful days passed, with a weekend mixed in there somewhere, without any replies to the message we'd sent out over the network. Ms. Hu tried to console us with stories about the virtue of patience, but when you're ten, tomorrow is as far off as Jupiter, and we would not be consoled.

One morning when we'd reached the bottom of our collective emotional pit, we arrived in class to find the printer wheezing away and a heap of paper on the floor, answers from kids in distant time zones. A computer check revealed the electronic mail seriously backed up. Ms. Hu went down to the principal's office to telephone Fisher who hadn't been in class since we sent the message; he appeared an hour later with his own computer and printer which he hooked up to ours to handle the overload. Even then the two systems labored nonstop for the next several days.

Our question had tapped into an underground river of historical consciousness; responses poured in with such force that the fifth grade was drowning in data, and it wasn't immediately obvious how we might convert the raw information into knowledge. However, after a couple of days of reading and discussion, we began to discern patterns that suggested certain organizational principles, and so on. I won't go into the methodological details.

Looking back I reckon that October, November, and December of the fifth grade were the best three months of education I ever had, including Harvard. Ms. Hu made the television problem into a full-time experience: when we got to school in the morning we found a pile of responses on every desk which we read, analyzed, and recorded on our individual charts; during the afternoon we met as a group, comparing the morning's results and raising such questions as had come up in our reading — "What is a Buddhist?" "What makes the Dead Sea dead?" "What's ozone?" "Why do people fight wars?" — which generated pretty sophisticated conversations about religion, geography, science, ethics, and so forth.

Near the end of the day Ms. Hu would ask one of the kids to choose one of the answers and make up a story about it. And finally she would select another response as a basis for her own story. Our homework consisted of maintaining journals. Ms. Hu said we could put anything we wanted in them — drawings, charts, stories, questions, whatever — anything that might constitute a personal record of the project.

Guess what! My mother let slip in front of me that Ms. Hu got into trouble with the school board. I imagine a parent or another teacher complained that she wasn't teaching the curriculum; also, given his current reputation as a flake, there may have been rumblings about Fisher's participation. My mother, who was visibly upset, didn't get to the particulars because Father intervened and started to grill me about what I'd been doing in school. I told my parents about Fisher's television problem and about Fat Ozzie Elmwood's hypothesis and how we'd put a question out over the networks and how we were managing the responses. I left out the part about Fisher swooping over the parking lot because it demanded too much explaining and, besides, it had been a decidedly extracurricular phenomenon. But I did show them my half-finished journal of the project.

"Wow!" said my mother. "That's wild." (Imagine if I'd told about the parking lot!)

"That's terrific!" said my father. "First sensible television idea I've heard. Your Ms. Hu is a woman of uncommon imagination. I bet you like her, huh?"

"Yeah. She's okay." I pulled a bored face. "The school board won't do anything bad to her, will they?"

"Over my dead body," thundered my father.

No doubt activist parents like my father defended Ms. Hu's unconventional approach to teaching against the bubble-headed bureaucrats on the school board. To tell the truth, since our project proceeded unmolested, I forgot about the school board because I had a more important problem to contend with, namely my romantic situation.

One morning, after I'd finished reading the alarming testimony of a sixth-grade class in Madras, India, I happened to glance up from my desk: there was Ozzie standing next to Fisher asking a question which made Fisher and Ms. Hu look at each other and laugh. Something about their respective expressions made my stomach do a backflop. In one horrible instant of lucidity, I saw what a fool I'd been: I had everybody screwed up! Ozzie wasn't in love with Ms. Hu; he'd fallen in love with Fisher. Ms. Hu didn't love Ozzie or, for that matter, *me;* she loved Fisher. And Fisher, as far as I could make out, loved Ms. Hu.

It was like the last act of one of those ridiculous Mozart operas where the characters who have been dressing up in one another's clothing finally strip off their masks and reveal their true identities while exposing various follies. Except that Mozart usually contrived an ending with everybody happily paired off, whereas in this case Ozzie and I were stranded. Not that I grieved for Ozzie. He was fat: no doubt he had built up an immunity to rejection. I, on the other hand, having been chucked under the chin and deemed "cute as a button" for as long as I could remember, had no useful experience of failure.

I guess I should have seen it coming, Ms. Hu and Fisher, I mean. They'd been staying after school together, along with Zeke — who knew *how* late? — to work on the television problem. I bet they dumped Zeke, ate dinner at her house, and went out to the movies. I couldn't take Ms. Hu to the movies: I had to be in bed by 8:30 on school nights. In every respect Fisher was an unfair rival. He was a grown-up. He was an astronaut. He was tall. Oh yeah, and he could fly. I couldn't compete with a man who could fly and who was so tall he'd have to bend his knees to kiss Ms. Hu on the lips. The only advantage I could claim was the ferocity of my love for her.

I had to pee. When I submitted my request Ms. Hu did something uncharacteristic: she said "Again, Timmy?" in front of the whole class, which prompted a few snickers. She might as well have spelled it out in neon lights. She might as well have hammered a nail into my heart. I hated her!

When I got to the boys' room I slunk into one of the stalls and cried. Ozzie showed up while I was washing my hands.

"Hey, Timmy, it's okay. She didn't mean it. Everybody knows you've gotta go a lot."

"Beat it, Fatso," I bawled. Just what I needed, Fat Ozzie Elmwood, Great Humanitarian, explaining that the whole class was aware of the foibles of my bladder while I was dying of heartbreak. "I hate her!"

Ozzie let my incivility bounce off his feelings. He waited until I'd blown my nose and escorted me back to the classroom so I wouldn't have to face humiliation by myself.

Somehow the energy of my hatred for Ms. Hu propelled me through the rest of the day. The next day I faked a stomachache and stayed home sick. But I couldn't stand not knowing what was happening with the television problem, so the day after that I proclaimed myself cured and returned to school.

Young hearts heal. Without my noticing, my anger at Hsu-ling Hu wore off. I didn't hate her anymore, but I didn't love her either, or so I convinced myself. She was just Ms. Hu, the fifth-grade teacher who told wonderful stories. I accepted Fisher's presence in the classroom, and their flirtation, as an unhappy condition of existence, like the federal deficit my father was always sounding off about.

The day before Christmas vacation, the day I had marked on my calendar as the day I would propose, Ms. Hu announced we would have a new teacher after the New Year. She said her departure had something to do with what we had learned about the television problem, that she had to help Mr. Fisher and Zeke and the others (*Others?* I wondered.) explain what we had discovered.

I'm afraid the significance of our research escaped me at the time. I was too immature to grasp it. All I understood was that the first woman I'd ever loved not counting my mother, and the best teacher I'd ever known, was abandoning me.

My heart broke a second time. I cried. Know-it-all Judy Wackenhut, who prided herself on the sharpness of her tongue, cried. Everybody cried except Fat Ozzie Elmwood, which was funny.

. . .

"That's *it?*" cried Eddie. "Your Ms. Hu ran away with Fisher in the middle of the school year?"

"More or less," said Timothy.

"What a bummer."

"Indeed. I was crushed. I didn't fall in love again for at least three weeks."

"She couldn't have been such a great teacher after all if she could just up and elope like that. I don't get it."

"Oh, no. I guess I didn't make myself clear. I found out later that the school board had fired her. But I imagine she would have left anyway because of what we'd found out about the televisions. I think she knew she had to help Fisher make people understand what had happened."

"And what was that?" asked Eddie.

"You really don't know?"

"Never heard of it. Should I?"

"I assumed your history teacher must have told you. I frankly don't see how you can understand the contemporary world without studying the television crisis."

"We're stuck back with the Greeks and Romans now," said Eddie. "I don't think we get into modern history until the tenth grade."

"In that case, I'll tell you now. What we'd turned up was, um, . . . wait a minute. Let me see if I can remember the precise wording. . . ." Timothy floundered. "Well, I can look it up. I've got it in my bookcase, the whole report, including the responses from all over the world, the results we compiled from our individual charts, and the conclusions. It's a fascinating document.

I've reread it a few times over the years and made some annotations. Maybe you'd like to take a look at it."

"Sure. Would you mind?"

"Of course not. But before you read it, I must point out that although we fifth-graders did most of the sifting of data from the children's responses to our query, there was a second element of comparative research accomplished by Ms. Hu, Fisher, Zeke, and some friends of theirs. All by ourselves, we kids couldn't have made much out of the statistics. That goes for the commentaries at the end, too."

"Gotcha," said Eddie.

"Okay. Let me see if I can find the report."

"By the way, Grandad, what ever happened to Ms. Hu and Fisher? Do you know?"

"My mother and father followed them in the newspapers, usually in articles written by Zeke Kramer which they read aloud to me. It's a long story. There were other people involved, including Maria Coehlo, the famous singer. Even Fat Ozzie Elmwood got back into the act, never mind how. But it wound up sadly. The official version is that Fisher was assassinated, though I've heard rumors to the contrary. Immediately after that, Hsuling Hu dropped out of sight. I like to think she went back to teaching and telling stories to other children."

Timothy started for the door. "By the way," he added, "have you had enough of Baudelaire, or do you plan to read more?"

"It's pretty hot stuff," said Eddie with a blush. "I'd like to keep it for a while."

Readings from
The Book of Follies

BIBLIOGRAPHIC NOTE:
The following texts have been selected
from Timothy P. Lee's copy of *The Book
of Follies: A Congregation of Worldwide Happenings, June 20–21, 2002,
Preceding the General Failure of Television, Compiled by Students of the
Fifth Grade, Dan Quayle Elementary School, Poughkeepsie, New York,
USA; with Conclusions and Reflections.*

Lee's "book" consists of 946 photocopied pages, standard
letter size (8.5 by 11 inches), stapled into five paper-covered vol-
umes. Volume I contains the three-page introduction, by Hsu-
ling Hu, which outlines the premises and methodology, and lists
the names of the fifth-graders who undertook the research project. Messages from school children begin on page 4 and continue
through page 935 in volume V. The section entitled "Conclusions" occupies pages 936–942 (plus one world map and tables

A – D) and is signed by Hsu-ling Hu, MEd.; Gregory Fisher, PhD; Susan R. Heim, PhD; and Jesse Randolph, PhD. Pages 943 – 946 are devoted to "Reflections," signed by the above authors. A final unnumbered page bears a quotation from Homer's *Odyssey:* "Look now how mortals are blaming the gods, for they say that evils come from us, but in fact they themselves have woes beyond their share because of their own follies."

Lee's copy is marred by his numerous annotations and underscorings in pencil as well as in red and blue ink which, while reducing its monetary value to serious collectors of historical memorabilia, supply helpful insights. One of TPL's most arresting comments appears on the title page and reads as follows: "Thanks to a financial contribution by G. Fisher, 200 copies of this report were reproduced and bound in December 2003. Members of the fifth-grade class (26) each received one copy; one copy was deposited in the school library. It was my understanding that the remaining reports were distributed to government leaders and institutions throughout the world. Unfortunately, nearly all the original copies have disappeared. At this time (2032) the only other known to me is in the possession of Mr. Osgood Elmwood who also owns the floppy disks containing the responses of the children, but neither the conclusions nor the recommendations.

FROM THE INTRODUCTION, BY HSU-LING HU

. . . We did not disclose the objective of our research project because we did not wish to prejudice the responses. For the same reason we deliberately cast our request for assistance in the vaguest of terms so as to allow the children themselves to establish the relative significance of phenomena. We did, however, introduce a time limitation by specifying the twenty-four-hour period preceding the failure of television. . . .

. . . The number of responses to the query so far exceeded expectations, as well as the capacity of the fifth-graders to manage the quantity of information, that I and other interested adults, including those who joined to write the last two sections of this report, became active participants in the project. We provided English translations from various languages when necessary. We further assisted the children in distilling and representing the data graphically. When that data began to reveal suggestive patterns, we initiated comparative studies in the libraries of universities, and searches of data banks. (See pp. 940–42 for bibliography.)

EXCERPTS FROM THE MESSAGES OF SCHOOLCHILDREN:

JÄRPEN, SWEDEN
Dear Friends in the Dan Quayle School, Poughkeepsie, New York, United States:

Our seventh-grade class received your message and would like to help with your project. Our school is located in Järpen, a town of approximately five thousand inhabitants, situated on the Indals River about 750 kilometers northwest of Stockholm. This is a quiet place without great events, but the day you are interested in is always special because we prepare for the summer solstice which, as you know, arrives on June 21 and is an occasion for celebration in all the countries of Scandinavia. The boys were also excited about the football game, so it was a festive time.

One sad thing happened that day. A man from our town, whose name was Gunnar, died. You may not know it, but for many, many years there was no death penalty in Sweden. Our Parliament voted it back in April 2001 because of all the social disturbances. A jury in Östersund convicted Gunnar of shooting the proprietor of a state liquor store and sentenced him to death. The citizens of Järpen who knew him believed he was innocent, but on the morning of June 20 a doctor injected poison into his veins and ended his life.

Do you also wish to know what happened when the televisions stopped working? We can tell you many stories about that. [*Marginal note by TPL: "Not relevant to research problem."*]

KYOTO, JAPAN

Dear Students of Grade Five,

We have received your most interesting question. It is very curious that, although all of us remember very well where we were and what we were doing when the televisions stopped, we could not recall the events of the previous day. *[TPL note: "Almost half the respondents remarked on this phenomenon."]* We therefore consulted the newspaper and municipal records to help us collect your information.

Here are some of the things that happened in Kyoto on the day in question: There were 8 homicides and 5 suicides. There were 9 traffic accidents, only one serious. The police arrested 84 people (37 for drunken misbehavior). Two wooden buildings in the Pontocho district caught fire when an alcohol-burning stove for the preparation of sukiyaki was accidentally upset in a restaurant. The hospitals reported 91 live births and 82 deaths. Doctors say the number of deaths was abnormal and that many elder people died from a combination of heat and air pollution which was very bad that day. The Prince and Princess of Wales visited the Imperial Villa of Katsura. The new thirty-two-story Modori Hotel opened on the east bank of the Kano River. The municipal government voted to increase the property taxes by .07 percent to pay for more police.

There was one mysterious event. On June 20 at a very early hour in the morning, many explosions were heard at Daitoku-ji, the Zen temple complex in the northern section of the city. The monks who were awakened from their sleep discovered that several ancient trees and gardens, including the beautiful grove of maples at Koto-in, had been destroyed. The police, who found remains of plastic explosives and timing devices, believe the bombs were placed by a deranged visitor, probably a Korean, during the day. Since then, all the temple gardens in Kyoto have been closed to the public. This is perhaps of no interest to your research.

Sincerely, Eighth Grade, Rakuhoku Middle School, Kyoto, Japan.

[Note by TPL: "Last para. = most important. Also, why did they say 'probably a Korean'?"]

MADRAS, INDIA

[Editor's note: The following is part of a much longer message from a sixth-grade class.]

. . . The failure of the televisions came at the time of the monsoon in Madras, and the day after the great lying down of women. . . . One of the women of our city had died in a kitchen accident some time earlier. The father of the woman, who had delivered her to the husband with a large dowry less than a year before, accused the husband of murdering her by dousing her with kerosene, putting a match to her sari, and locking her into the kitchen. The husband's case came before the courts, and hundreds of women attended the trial. When the man was set free, some women demonstrated against the judge and jury and were detained by the police. The next day thousands of women came to the vicinity of the state bus station and lay down on the Netaji Subhash Bose Road, one of the busiest streets in the city, thereby halting traffic. Each time the constables removed a woman by throwing her into a police van, another lay down in her place; nor would the women be moved when the firemen turned their hoses upon them. One very old woman shook her fist at a policeman and shouted, "If Gandhi were alive, he would be lying on the pavement with us. You, an Indian man, should be ashamed of yourself! You are as bad as the British colonialists."

At first the drivers of the vehicles that were stalled on the road laughed about the women and made jokes. However, after several hours these men became impatient and angry. One driver who needed to deliver his load to the port lost his head; he jumped into his lorry and drove over three women lying in his path, crushing them. Then a riot broke out and many people were killed. The police say officially only fifty-eight persons died but we believe many hundred. Two children in our class lost their mothers, and one boy lost his sister, a girl of twelve years. . . . *[TPL note at end of message: "When I read this at the age of ten I thought the Indian students had made up the incident concerning the incineration of the young wife in the kitchen. Ms. Hu assured me that such 'accidents' were quite common in India, thus introducing me to the concept of murder for profit. A loss of innocence!"]*

LARGEAU, CHAD

    . . . At the time you ask about, several of the boys in our class were on a nature tour of the desert with our science teacher and two Bedouin guides. We followed the ancient trade route north to Ounianga-Kébir and went almost as far as the border with Libya. It was a very exciting trip. We rode camels and slept in tents for four nights. Our teacher told us the names of the insects, animals, and plants, and also about the stars when they came out in the night, and how to look for water in the desert.

    One day we saw a tree almost two meters high. This tree surprised our guides who had never seen it before although they passed on the same track twice each year. Our science teacher said it was different from any desert plant and he could not tell us its name. He picked a small branch so he could look up the name in his books. Our camels wanted to eat the leaves of the tree, but the Bedouins said no, it must be a very special tree because it grows in a place where there is no water. Our science teacher says this was the day the televisions stopped, which we only found out when we returned home. *[TPL note: "Fisher got very agitated when he saw this. He succeeded in contacting the science teacher over the network. The latter confirmed the story, also that he was unable to identify the genus of the tree in his botany books. Unfortunately he could not provide a record of the specimen he had taken. On the evening he planned to draw it he carelessly left it on his desk while he went out for coffee; when he returned the leaves and bark had been devoured by beetles, leaving only a bare twig of no taxonomic value. He made one attempt several months later to revisit the site in the company of the same Bedouin guides, but the sands had shifted and obscured the old track, and the party lost themselves in the desert. Zeke Kramer published the children's message, along with the science teacher's testimony in a long article in the NY Herald. I think (though I'm not positive) it was because of this article that Jesse Randolph, the astronaut, came to Poughkeepsie to see Fisher and to visit our fifth-grade class."]*

————, CAMBODIA

Alas, the children of my village are unable to respond directly to your question. As you no doubt know (but probably have forgotten) our country has been at war for the past three and a half years. For almost two years of that time, the children lived in an underground bunker to protect them against the enemy's bombs and poison gas. I was their teacher. Nine months ago the enemy raided the village, burned all the dwellings, and looted the rice caches. The children in the bunker escaped injury, but many of their relatives were killed. Some of the children are now in orphanages across the border; those with parents have fled to other villages or to refugee camps. I am currently hiding in a safe place which I dare not name. My computer is my only connection to the outside world.

I do not know what happened in the village the day before the televisions stopped because I was in the bunker. I presume it was a day like most others during the war — punctuated by work, hunger, death, fear, rumor, and betrayal. The government radio station blamed the television failure on the enemy, and the enemy blamed the government. Several weeks passed before we were told that the whole world was without television. Many people still do not believe it, and others do not care.

TULCEA, ROMANIA

. . . Because June 20 was the last day of school, our teacher wanted to take us on a picnic in the bird sanctuary in the delta of the Danube River. The government would not give her an entrance permit, but she said it was all right to go anyway because she is a teacher, and if we were quiet and did not disturb the birds, nobody would dare to arrest a teacher and her students. When we got to the place where the birds were supposed to be, we found a barbed-wire fence without a gate. Two guards with machine guns chased us away. It smelled very bad, and all the birds were gone. *[TPL query: "Toxic waste disposal site? Romania, Bulgaria, etc., presumably outlawed dumping by W. European countries in 1993!"]*

LOWELL, MASSACHUSETTS, USA

Hey Grade Five: What are you kidlets up to? Day before the TVs quit slipped our minds until somebody remembered it was a real scorcher. Everybody came home from school or work, turned on the air-conditioning, and knocked out the power. After that things got kind of ugly. Some gang members smashed the window of a store owned by a Vietnamese, and before you could say Ho Chi Minh every gang in town was out on the streets—you name it, they were there screaming in ten or fifteen languages, waving guns and knives. Eight killed, seventeen wounded before the police arrived on the scene and shot four more in the process of restoring "law and order." (We've had a curfew since then. It's a real bummer, especially without TV.)

Keep in touch. We're curious to hear what else you find.

Grade Nine, Lowell Middle School

(P.S. Who was Dan Quayle?)

[TPL note: "See also Waterbury, CT, New York City, Baltimore, Detroit, Chicago (USA) as well as Montreal, Birmingham, Leeds, Marseilles, Milan, Timisoara (Romania), Jericho, Pretoria, Malakal (Sudan), Santos (Brazil), Kingston (Jamaica), Djakarta, Lan-chou (China), for other outbreaks of ethnic violence, June 20–21, 2002."]

BANICA, DOMINICAN REPUBLIC

Dear Friends,

Our town is in the mountains, close to the border with Haiti. Sometimes Haitians try to escape the international quarantine in their country by crossing the mountains into Banica. They hope to go from here to Santo Domingo and then to South America or Canada or maybe the United States even though the U.S. Immigration Police are so strict.

On June 20, 2002, one of the teachers in our school discovered a Haitian family (mother, father, sister, and two children) hiding in the supply room. This teacher was very clever and brave. She told the Haitians to stay in the room and that she would bring them some food. Then she ran quickly to tell the border patrol who came in their special suits and took the Haitians away to a place far from the town, eliminated them, and burned the bodies so AIDS doesn't come here. The whole school gave a party for the teacher who protected us. We hope she doesn't get sick and die with AIDS!

We miss the televisions very much, especially "Miami Vice" and "The Cosby Show". . . .

VENICE, ITALY

. . . The bugs came early this year, perhaps because the spring was unusually warm. They are criminals, these insects. If you eat out of doors they fly into your Coca-Cola and your pasta and your father's Campari and your grandmother's ear. Sometimes it is funny, but mostly it is terrible. In August 2001 there were so many the gondoliers went on strike, and they got into the engines of the airplanes. Also the televisions took many pictures and made a scandal with the tourists.

On June 21, 2002, was a big meeting of all the people in the Piazza San Marco because the mayor wanted to spray the lagoon and kill the bugs with DDT but the farmers said they cannot sell their rice and the Greens (who come from everywhere) say DDT will poison everything and the hotel owners and the waiters say the tourists will not come and Venice will die without money and one of the contessas talks about Tintoretto and the city *in-gegnere* says the lagoon is rising all the time. Then the leader of the Socialist Party calls the wife of the mayor a bad name. Everyone is shouting and waving their arms because they are angry and also because of the insects who are flying everywhere. Nothing is decided. Everybody goes inside to watch the preparations for the football match on the televisions.

We hope our English is correct. . . . [TPL note: "We didn't say which language to respond in. Eighty percent wrote in English. Ms. Hu who could speak several languages translated many of the others; experts from Vassar and Yale did the rest."]

CAMP 83, ETHIOPIA (via Rome, Italy)
New Arrivals: 78 (18 men, 23 women, 37 children age 12 or under)
Live Births: 11
Stillborns: 10
Deaths: 212
Total Population: 1048
Food Supplies: 8–10 days (2 of 4 promised truckloads "detained." One-third of grain in delivery received infested with maggots.)
Medical Supplies: 21–28 days. (Plasma: 5–7 *days!*)
Dear Children,

The day you asked about, June 20–21, 2002, was not an especially eventful one by our standards, but even so it seemed to us that a narrative account of any day in the life of Camp 83 might be difficult for fifth-graders in the United States to comprehend. Accordingly, we have sent you a few salient statistics from our records. Perhaps your teacher knows something about the relief stations in Central Africa and can explain what these numbers mean. There was one small, special event: Dr. Olga

Savinkov, who had worked with us for more than five years, returned to her home in St. Petersburg; Dr. Gerard Mercier arrived from France the same day.

Our computer is not on your network. We are linked to relief agencies via FAO in Rome. One of our Rome contacts told us about your research project, and we wanted to be included because if you are trying to paint a picture of the world on one day, Camp 83 and the other relief stations ought not be forgotten.

We used to have a portable television but the batteries died about two weeks before the general failure, and by the time we received new ones there was no television to be seen. The children miss it very much. More importantly, we fear that because people of the developed countries no longer see the images of famine on their television screens, we will weigh lighter than an eyelash on the conscience of the world. Maybe the children of your class will speak to their parents and will exchange messages with some of the children in our camp through the Rome network. [TPL note: "Ms. Hu told us about the African famine and relief efforts, and we did exchange one or two messages with kids there. Ms. Hu's successor, however, taught by the book, and the correspondence lapsed."]

FROM THE "CONCLUSIONS," BY HSU-LING HU, ET AL.

As noted in the introduction, the fifth-graders anchored their research project in the simple premise that the general failure of television reception might be attributable to human activity rather than to mechanical error. The careful reader will recall young Osgood Elmwood's elementary hypothesis that "something a person or people did" could account for the condition. As a group the children held no preconceptions about the results of their inquiry; although some among them initially pursued the notion of a singular catastrophic event, and two had fanciful ideas about extraterrestrial intervention, these ideas lost currency as the students began to collate the data. . . .

. . . The following map shows the locations of schools that

responded to the survey. The higher representation among the developed nations corresponds to their participation in the Global Laboratory Network as well as to the worldwide distribution of computers and telecommunications systems in schools; nevertheless, the less developed countries are adequately represented.

. . . Table A illustrates estimates of the loss of *human* life on the most violent days of the two world wars (1914 – 1918, 1939 – 1945). (Environmental statistics for this period, though imaginable, are unavailable.)

Table B illustrates estimates of the loss of human and *other biological* life on a daily basis, December 2001 through May 2002. . . .

Table C is a reproduction of the graph drawn by Grade Five, Dan Quayle Elementary School, based on the foregoing responses.

. . . Table D illustrates the authors' extrapolation based on the combined figures of tables B and C. . . .

The comparative data lead us to the inescapable conclusion that on June 20 – 21, 2002, during the day and night preceding the loss of television reception, MORE PEOPLE AND OTHER FORMS OF LIFE, ANIMAL AND VEGETABLE, DIED AS A RESULT OF HUMAN ACTION OR INDIFFERENCE THAN IN ANY OTHER TWENTY-FOUR-HOUR PERIOD IN RECORDED HISTORY.

FROM THE "REFLECTIONS," BY HSU-LING HU, ET AL.

. . . The coincidence in time between the massive destruction of biological life — i.e., murder — by humans, and the failure of television is too powerful to dismiss. The message from the children in Chad (see page 722) concerning the mysterious tree in the Sahara Desert constitutes additional evidence of the relationship. Dr. Fisher observed with interest that the tree grew in the same location as the one he photographed from space during the *Inquisitive* mission 82-G, in May 2003. He made contact with Mr. Salih Adoum, the science teacher from Largeau, who confirmed the location and supported an interpretation of the tree as the link between the events of June 20–21 and the failure of television; Mr. Adoum, who is a learned man, noted the universal presence of the tree as a symbol of life in myth and religion. We reprint the complete text of his remarks below. . . . *[TPL note: "Tree of Life in garden of Eden; see also Revelation 22:2: 'and the leaves of the tree were for the healing of the nations,' for instance! Buddha associated with a tree, etc."]*

. . . The path between cause and effect is lit by hindsight, a condition we have not yet achieved. Although we have established a verifiable connection, critical readers will no doubt cite our failure to identify the precise mechanism for the malfunction of television. There has been no shortage of speculations about such a cause over the past eighteen months. It would be irresponsible for us to add yet another conjecture to that list.

It is our conviction that the conclusion disclosed by the research, and its relationship to television, constitutes by itself sufficient grounds for action. . . .

. . . It is our view that failure to act swiftly and universally to end manifestations of murder will lead to consequences far graver than the loss of television reception. . . . *[TPL note: "The critics seized the perceived weakness of the cause/effect argument as an excuse to do nothing, which is why Ms. Hu, Fisher, and the others took their show on the road, and why Fisher had to play all his cards and got assassinated. 'Find out the cause of this effect,/Or rather say, the cause of this defect,/For this effect defective comes by cause.' Shakesp. (Spoken by the windbag Polonius, but nevertheless applicable in this instance.)"]*

Hsu-ling's Story

Some people said the woman who lived in the third shelter from the center of the village had planted the acorn that gave rise to the ancient oak tree shading the school yard. She was so old that no one, not even the grandmothers and grandfathers to whom she had taught the art of storytelling many years ago, could remember having seen her stand upon her legs and walk, a condition of immobility that generated a good deal of prurient speculation among the villagers as to how she eliminated the waste products from her body. One small segment of opinion held that the woman possessed the secret of metabolism, that she consumed and expended energy with such perfect economy that nothing remained as waste.

Every day someone from the village carried her the same foods: upon rising, a bowl of plain tea and twenty-six grains of steamed rice; at midday, a boiled quail's egg; one hour after the setting of the sun, a peach, a pear, or two dried figs, depending upon the season. The singular variation in this rigorous diet occurred after she had finished telling a story, when she would signal one of the children to empty powder from a packet into a glass of clear water. The powders dissolved with the colors of jewels — emerald, ruby, topaz, or amethyst — and the woman sipped the brilliant liquid slowly with a smile of reminiscence. Though she insisted the powders were flavored sugar crystals she had learned about many years ago from a friend in the United States, many people believed they contained grains of eternal life.

The woman, whose name was Hsu-ling Hu, lived alone. This had always been the case, even in her youth. She was rumored to have arrived in the village early in the millennium, a beautiful young woman dressed in white, to escape the world and mourn the death of a lover. As the years passed several desirable men had pressed their affections upon her, but she had never accepted another lover. During the daylight hours she had taught in the school and mingled with the villagers and entertained people with stories in the café. In the evenings, however, having eaten her fruit, she had courted solitude: she had fastened the shutters on her window and bolted her door until daybreak. Thus she had remained singular and childless and grown weary of explaining to one generation after another that solitude and loneliness were not necessarily synonymous.

Some villagers had seen, or *claimed* to have seen — as recently as last week — a peculiar radiance escaping her shelter through chinks in the weathered wood of the shutters. The people commented as well that no one brought fuel for her stove, nor did she ask for any, yet her shelter was warm even on the coldest, darkest days of winter when the solar system was drained of energy. The rationalists who adhered to the theory of perfect metabolism explained both the strange light and the heat as byproducts of the efficient burning of calories. Few people bought into this tidy argument, however, for Hsu-ling Hu had been implicated in any number of queer phenomena. Back around 2032, for example, she had been seen by two young lovers late one Saturday afternoon in a remote meadow, on the arm of a tall man in blue jeans, the two of them strolling casually a foot or so above the nodding scarlet poppies. And not so long ago, on a tender moonless night when the stars shone with exceptional brightness, the baker and his niece spied her sitting on the crest of a hill. Which was impossible, they told one another, because Hsu-ling Hu hasn't been able to walk for years . . . as far as we know. Still, there she was.

Such anomalies aside — and who, after all, could confirm them except the woman herself who never volunteered intimacies? — the people of the village knew Hsu-ling Hu to be regular of habit. When the infirmities of age forced her to abandon her custom of telling stories in the café, she established a storytelling hour at her home, at half past three every day except Monday. Tuesdays through Sundays, at the appointed hour, anywhere from five to fifty villagers of several ages gathered around her chair to listen to whatever story she might choose to tell: an old favorite, perhaps, or something spun straight from her imagination in response to a request from the audience.

On Mondays Hsu-ling Hu rested her vocal cords so that they might retain their suppleness to simulate the voices of the rain, of the red fox, of Xochiquetzal the Aztec goddess of flowers and love, of the Brazilian laborer named Rodrigo, of the thousand sounds that enriched her stories. The years had locked her joints and turned her skin to parchment, but they had spared her astonishing larynx. She could still reproduce a cheerleader's giggle.

Of late, however, certain people had remarked with sadness that time seemed at last to be encroaching on Hsu-ling Hu's brain. Her stories were not as fine and tightly woven as they used to be, the certain people said; there were holes in the plot, and the endings were frayed.

"The old girl's losing it. She misplaces characters or forgets where she was and where she wants to go," a certain person sighed. "Ah well, it had to happen eventually, I suppose. No one's immune to age, not even Hsu-ling Hu."

"Baloney," countered her daughter-in-law. "She's just adopting a new mode. She's probably bored with the old one after — well, who knows how old she is, anyway? She was already an antique when I was born."

"Listen more carefully, child," said the certain person gently. "Didn't you notice that the goat Belita appeared in yesterday's chapter of the Television Tales? Belita isn't supposed to be in Poughkeepsie. I've heard those stories fifty times, and no matter how she told them Belita was never in Poughkeepsie before. Hsu-ling got mixed up."

"The woman's bored," the daughter-in-law repeated. "She's amusing herself. They're her stories. Belita can be anywhere Hsu-ling wants! To tell the truth, I liked her in Poughkeepsie flirting with Zeke. It's an improvement on the tale. Ordinarily Zeke just sits around like a lox taking notes."

The Television Tales over which the two women disagreed anchored Hsu-ling Hu's storytelling ritual. Most of the year the villagers could not predict what story they might hear. But every June 21, on the anniversary of the worldwide failure of television, she started her ten-day cycle of Television Tales — unless, of course, June 21 fell on a Monday in which case she told the first tale on the twenty-second. The Television Tales were the villagers' most beloved, the stories they believed showed off Hsu-ling Hu's mastery of the art to greatest advantage. Whereas five to fifty people came to hear stories the rest of the year, two or three hundred gathered for the telling of the Television Tales. For ten days, punctuated by empty Mondays, they crowded her cabin and spilled into the garden where her vibrant voice reached out and drew them into the center of her fables. They came for the sake of familiarity, and to wonder at how the familiar had transformed itself over the past year.

On the ninth day of the cycle, *this is the tale Hsu-ling told.*

Many years ago a woman came to me with her dream. I repeat it to you as she told it, in the present tense, for in dreams there is neither past nor future, only the immediate.

The woman is stretched out comfortably on her living-room sofa watching a documentary film about African elephants on her television set. Great gray wrinkled pachyderms traverse the screen with their noble grace; a watchful elephant cow retrieves her offspring which has strayed from the herd. The camera zooms in on the massive carcass of a bull, slain to satisfy a poacher's greed. Then the reporter interviews a game warden, a handsome young Kenyan, dressed in military fatigues and armed with an automatic rifle, who answers his questions patiently.

"Have you killed any poachers?" the reporter asks.

"Yes," replies the man.

"How many?"

"Four or five. I think five."

"And does that bother you?" inquires the reporter.

"Not at all," says the game warden. "I have no qualms at all about killing a man to spare the life of an elephant."

The woman watching the program sits up sharply, awaiting the reporter's comment.

• • •

The villagers stirred uneasily.

"Who is the game warden?" someone whispered, "and where did these elephants come from?"

"I told you her mind is failing," whispered a certain person. "She's getting her stories mixed up."

"Shhh," hissed a voice behind them.

• • •

At that moment the image and sound vanish from the television. The woman pushes buttons on her remote-control device and finds all the channels empty. Considering the possibility that the air-conditioning has overloaded the electrical system on this sweltering summer afternoon, she checks the circuit breaker but discovers nothing amiss. She rummages in the kitchen drawer where she stashes the owner's manuals for her appliances, but no description in the instructions that came with her television set matches the condition that afflicts it. She telephones the cable company and is informed by a recorded voice that all lines are temporarily occupied; while the telephone pours generic music into her ear, she remembers what the handsome game warden said about the life of an elephant. She replaces the receiver in its cradle.

The woman finds herself on a city sidewalk, among swarms of people discussing the failure of the televisions. A person approaches, and she recognizes him as a man who was once her lover though he has the face of a stranger, yet in this dream where the strange and familiar exchange places his alien appearance does not alarm her. The lover-stranger reports that all the televisions in the world have stopped, and the woman nods and says, "Yes, I supposed so. Do you think it is a sign?"

"Don't be a jerk," says the lover-stranger. "They'll fix it."

"Who are they?" the woman asks, "and what is it that must be fixed?"

The woman and the lover-stranger are joined by the woman's dead mother. All three enter the football stadium, or possibly it is the abandoned opera house — she can't be sure — which is filling up with people. An usher wearing a crimson-and-gold uniform helps them find three empty places, and they sit down. The woman wishes to thank the usher, but when she looks up she sees his face twisted in a cruel expression, and a powerful weapon slung over his shoulder. She notices now usher-soldiers guarding all the exits which have been locked. She hears sirens, and the president appears in an open car flanked by motorcycles.

The president gets out of his limousine and strides toward the stage, but an usher-soldier approaches him, lays a hand on his arm, and escorts him to a seat in the audience.

The game warden from Kenya stands up and says, "You must help me. You must no longer ask me to choose between the life of an elephant and that of a man. Either decision forces me to kill. My children must not grow up to be the sons and daughters of a murderer."

One at a time people address the audience. The woman is surprised because she has met some of the speakers — one of them is the fellow who cuts her hair — and never imagined the seriousness of their thoughts; they speak about elevated concepts like integrity and natural law and civilization; they make easy references to balance and harmonics and the power of imagination. Their speeches pass through her dream, leaving shallow footprints on her recollection.

Then the president stands up. "Yes, yes, yes," he says, glancing impatiently at his wristwatch, "I know what you mean, but take it from me, the problems of the world are complex. You attack one, and three others pop up in its place. Nevertheless I sympathize with your concern. As a character in a famous play once said, 'One day we are born, one day we die,' uh, 'that's' uh . . ." He snaps his fingers at an aide who hurriedly shuffles through papers and whispers into his ear. "Um, right, 'That's how it is on this bitch of an earth.' Anyway, television relieves the misery in between, and therefore it is the right of every American citizen. Accordingly, I am here today to announce that I have convened a panel of experts who, as we speak, are investigating the failure of television. They are very close to finding what's broken and how to fix it. The chairman reassures me that transmission will resume imminently."

The checkout clerk from the supermarket, wearing green shoes and a pink miniskirt topped by her A & P smock, steps onto the stage. "Mr. President, sir," she says, "forget about the televisions. That's not what we're worried about. The Egyptians built pyramids, the Incas and Aztecs moved emeralds and gold the entire length of Central and South America along the tops of mountains, the Chinese constructed the Great Wall, and the Romans transported water all over the place and soaked themselves in hot baths, so don't tell me we can't manage our garbage or prevent people from starving to death. We have the technology to do practically anything we set our minds to. It's politics that get in the way. For a while there we lost the will and imagination to cut our way through the politics, but I think we've just found them again."

The supermarket clerk starts to walk off the stage. The woman hears the click-click of her kelly green high-heeled pumps. She stumbles at the stairs, tripped up by an afterthought.

"One more thing, Mr. President," she says, "and please don't take it personally. You're a bum, like most of the politicians on earth. That's our fault, because you were what we thought we wanted. But now that it's occurred to us there's meant to be more between birth and death than television, we'd like you to resign. Don't worry. We'll arrange it so you're eligible for unemployment."

The crowd stands and applauds. The checkout girl acknowledges their ovation with a cheerful smile, as though she's just rung up a huge order of groceries without making a mistake.

The president stands center stage, his arms spread wide above his head. "Yes, yes, yes." He grins. "The little missy has made a fine speech. You can count on me. Television will be restored. Thank you, ladies and gentlemen. Have a nice day."

The audience titters nervously. The lover-stranger reaches for the woman's hand. His own is damp and eager. She drops it on the floor.

A child — the woman knows him: he is the bashful boy who lives in the apartment next door, the one she has privately nicknamed "Fat Ozzie" — stands up in the balcony and asks if the time hasn't come to accept that "social commitments and constraints should be viewed as enlargements of the person and are, indeed, essential to the growth of personality."

The child's question lifts the woman close to the surface of sleep. My God, she thinks, the kid is only ten years old. I must be dreaming. But instead of waking she drops back to a lower level where the dream doesn't question its own reality.

The woman's mother is the next to speak. "The elders must become the world's storytellers," she says. "We will relearn the cast-off legends and invent new ones. We will tell the children what the elephant said to the man."

The woman looks to where the president was sitting, but the game warden is there instead. Her mother has flown to the ceiling where she perches on a steel beam, and the lover-stranger is crawling around under the seats in search of his hand, muttering, "What a load of bullshit." The usher returns with a friendly smile on his face and without his weapon. He takes the woman's arm and guides her to the exit.

The woman is tired. She lies down on the ground in the shade of a gigantic tree. An elephant herd grazes in the distance. The game warden stands against the sky. She sees him catch her in the sight of his rifle. She is not afraid. She watches him. He aims the barrel at her, then at an elephant, then again at her. He shrugs. He empties the bullets from the clip and props the gun against the trunk of the tree. He lies down on the sand beside her. She extends her hand to touch him. Her fingers strike something soft and wet —

She wakes: a tuna fish sandwich.

· · ·

Hsu-ling Hu's voices fell silent. Her storytelling hands fluttered to rest in her lap. She closed her eyes and bent her head, as though its weight had grown too great for her neck, on her breast bone.

The villagers coughed nervously and scratched at phantom itches.

"Do you think that's the end of the story?" someone murmured.

"Surely not!"

"Is she okay? Is she breathing?"

"I think she's resting."

"Maybe someone ought to have a look at —"

. . .

— The woman who told me this dream, Hsu-ling resumed, wondered why she had felt so sad upon awakening from it. I explained that there are few things more disappointing than waking up from a dream in which a wish has been fulfilled, that she was sorry to have left the sane world of her sleep, a world in which people immediately grasped the meaning of the television failure. However, as you know, outside our dreams human conduct is all that stuff of which stories are made: imperfections, tragedies, absurdities, comedies . . . which brings me back to where we left off yesterday.

The fifth-graders' research project, which was published under the title *The Book of Follies,* and publicized by Zeke Kramer in a long article for the Sunday magazine supplement to the *Herald,* made no more impression on the world than a flea bite on the back of a rhinoceros. Judy Wackenhut's father more or less summed up popular reaction when he said, according to Judy, "Big deal! There's nothing in here that tells how to fix television. It's irrelevant. The teacher had no right to let you kids waste weeks on such nonsense. Giant trees in the desert, my ass!"

Mr. Wackenhut and other parents complained to the school board which voted unanimously to relieve the teacher of her duties after the Christmas holidays. The *Herald*'s managing editor decided the Fisher story had gotten staler than old Limburger cheese and instructed Zeke to drop it. Susan's scientific colleagues at Yale, who had heard about her signature on the report, snickered when they passed her in the library stacks. The space agency quietly reassigned Jesse Randolph to a dull desk job. The patrons of Moose's Place pointed at Fisher and whispered to one another discreetly behind cupped hands.

"Well, I guess it's all over," sighed Zeke, stroking Belita's silken neck. She pressed against his thigh and looked adoringly at his face.

"No!" objected Bertie. "Not when you've come so close. The trouble is that people simply can't get a grip on the cause-effect relationship. Mind you, it's not a straight line. The tree gets in the way. I had a similar problem last year when so many people came down sick. It took me months to recognize these illnesses are being caused by the television failure rather than by new breeds of viruses. Even now, though I'm absolutely convinced absence of television is precipitating malfunctions in the immune systems of susceptible individuals, I can't cite a shred of laboratory evidence. People in medicine discuss the situation all the time: we know it's correct, but there hasn't been a single scientific paper devoted to the subject. I guess what I'm trying to say is that you just have to keep at it until people come round to seeing the truth."

I forgot to tell you that Fisher's companions in the television venture had collected at his side. Paco arrived from New York minus the enchanting Maria. (Maria's career was taking off like a rocket. She had a three-week engagement at the Café Carlyle, and she had been signed by a recording company.) Bertie, the Florida doctor who had saved Paco from lockjaw and delivered him to Fisher, read about *The Book of Follies* in his morning newspaper, drove straight to the airport, and boarded the first northbound flight. Susan the Kool-Aid lady and Jesse Randolph, who had broken into the photo archives at the Space Center to steal the infamous photograph of the tree and who believed in its authenticity, had helped with the research project and signed their names on the report. Bernice and Nicky, who had saved the Coehlo family from the immigration police, arrived with Paco. And there was Ozzie Elmwood, the child who had the gift of questions.

These oddly matched people sat around the schoolteacher's dining-room table halfheartedly eating a take-out meal of honest food from Moose's, which was featuring curries this month.

"Like it or not, Bertie," Susan observed grimly, "thick-skulled Wackenhuts prevail in this world. By the time they come around to acknowledging the truth, it's too late. We've done everything we can. I don't see that there's anything left."

"Yes there is," announced Paco. "Gregorio must fly!"

"Fly?" gasped Bertie and Jesse, who knew nothing of Fisher's unique gravitational skills.

"He started off by walking on air," Susan explained, "but lately he's been practicing laying himself out flat and using his arms to steer. He's not as fast as Superman, but on the other hand he doesn't have to waste any time in phone booths."

"Is the lady putting us on, man?" Jesse demanded of Fisher.

"I'm afraid not," replied the astronaut. "But like I told Zeke a dozen times, I won't do it in public. I refuse to be a circus attraction."

"Gregorio," Paco continued, "why do you suppose you have suddenly acquired the ability of flight? There must be a purpose, no?"

"Flying's how Mr. Fisher saved me from getting squished in the school parking lot," Ozzie volunteered.

"True enough," said Fisher, "and since Ozzie here's the man who came up with the key questions, I reckon that settles the purpose issue."

"I mean no offense, Ozzie," argued Paco, "but that is not sufficient."

"Well," Zeke admitted reluctantly, "if he hadn't done that walking-on-air stunt, I'd never have believed the photograph."

"That is still too small a purpose for such a great gift," Paco proclaimed.

"How can you be so sure?" asked Bernice.

"I feel I am correct," said Paco.

Fisher sighed.

"Okay, Paco, for the sake of argument let's say you're right," said Bertie, "and Mr. Fisher is supposed to make a spectacle of himself. What next?"

"I only know what I know," Paco said mysteriously. "No more."

"How about it, Greg?" said Zeke. "I can call my editor — "

"Holy cow! I've got it!" cried Nicky, who had been picking at his curried free-range chicken. "What you folks have here is what we call in our racket a promotional problem. You want people to take this report thing of yours seriously, right? So you've got to get their attention. That's where the flying bit comes in, see? I can see the headlines now: FISHER FLIES! You'll have their attention, all right."

"I can have my editor and a photographer up here first thing tomorrow morning," said Zeke. "Just say the word."

"Nah, nah, nah. Forget about it," objected Nicky. "You run a picture of him flying in the newspaper, and you'll screw it up. Everybody will think it's a phony, like the monster tree. Likewise the movies are out and obviously the radio. No, what you need here is a real live performance, an audience, publicity, the whole schmear. But you don't wanna announce ahead that Fisher is going to fly because, sorry about that, Fisher, but you got a credibility rating of minus ten. So what we do is, we use Maria as the hook — "

"No!" Paco interjected vehemently. "My Maria is no hooker."

"A *hook*, not a hooker," Bernice chuckled. "Relax, Paco. It's not the same thing. Nicky means people will come to hear Maria sing; she'll be the hook that pulls them into the show."

"Right," Nicky continued, "and then when she's got the audience all warmed up, Fisher comes out and does his number. And the best thing is, we can get Maria's record company to sponsor the whole shebang, because the free publicity they'll get out of this for Maria's first record will be sensational. They'll make a bundle on the deal."

"You too, I daresay," commented Susan.

"Well, yeah, I guess so. Bernice and I will get our cut of the cake. So will Maria, also Paco because he wrote some of the songs plus which I want him to play for her," Nicky explained, annoyed. "You got a problem with that, babe?"

"No, buster, I haven't," retorted Susan. "I was just wondering how things worked."

"You say the word, I'll get cracking on the deal," said Nicky. "Say, Fisher, how good do you fly?"

Fisher shrugged spiritlessly.

"Good enough to give a few ladies an attack of the vapors," said Zeke.

"Great," said Nicky. He cast a speculative eye at Belita. "What about the goat? She got an act?"

If Gregory Fisher had been able to conceive of any other means of impressing the significance of the fifth-grade report upon the public, he would never have agreed to Nicky's scheme. Recalling his tenure as a media darling back in the days when he'd been an astronaut-playboy with a big mouth, he felt Moose's curry congealing in the pit of his stomach and he knew with certainty that the moment his feet left the platform he could kiss his life good-bye. Flying was not at all the same as declaring one had seen an improbable tree and setting oneself up for insults; other people professed daily to see much funnier things than giant trees. But other people didn't fly.

Not that Fisher didn't enjoy flying. Far from it. He loved flying almost as much as he had loved tumbling around in outer space among his beloved stars, especially lately since he'd established control over gravity to the point where he could float two or three hundred feet above the treetops. He had planned to keep flying a secret vice, like smoking cigarettes, but Paco had strange sources of knowledge, and then it had leaked out to Susan, to Zeke, and on to Ozzie and the others. Odd, Fisher mused, how once they passed through the initial surprise of it, his friends accepted his flying with no more alarm than they would have shown toward a man who could hit a perfect turn-around jump shot every time down the basketball court.

But these weren't ordinary friends, and Fisher understood how other people were likely to react when he soared off the floor and publicly announced himself separate from the human race.

"Why couldn't I just take off my clothes and glow in the dark?" he asked the schoolteacher at night while they lay in bed. He'd grown so accustomed to the radiance he'd acquired after his first space walk that he consigned it to a category above left-handedness but below flight: radiance made him special but not obscene.

"Anybody dipped in Day-Glo paint can glow in the dark," she answered practically. "Before the experts could prove it wasn't a trick, they'd have stripped your skin from your flesh with chemicals. No, my darling, I'm afraid Paco and Nicky are right. You have to fly."

"I'll never get my life back. I'll never be able to grow roses again. I'll never be able to continue my studies of atmospheric chemistry. And what will become of us?" Fisher asked with feeling, for he had at last found a woman he wanted forever and none other. "I can't invite you into my impossible life. Think of what happened to poor Lindbergh, and he had an aircraft."

"Nothing has been predictable since the televisions quit," the schoolteacher remarked optimistically. "I can't promise about the roses, but I'm in your life already. You and I will find a way, I know it."

"It's very disconcerting. *You* know this, *Nicky* knows that, *Paco* has knowledge beyond us all — who knows where it comes from? The only person who doesn't know a damn thing is me, and I'm the freak who has to fly!"

The schoolteacher touched Fisher's glowing shoulder with awed and tender fingers. "You mustn't think of yourself as a freak," she said. "You're like an angel."

"Same difference if you yearn to be a man," he remarked. "What happens if I can't fly when the time comes?"

"You'll fly. I know it."

"Ah, you know it," he echoed wryly. "And do you know if the televisions will start working again?"

"Sleep, my love," said the schoolteacher.

• • •

An old woman in the second row wiped a tear from her cheek. "Did you see the expression in Hsu-ling's eyes when she said 'Sleep, my love'?" the woman whispered to her neighbor. "So beautiful, so sad. It happens every year. Sometimes I wonder if she isn't talking about herself."

"Oh, I shouldn't think so," replied the neighbor.

"Well, suppose Hsu-ling were the schoolteacher, and Fisher her lover. That would go a long way to explaining some of the, er, you know, irregularities about her."

"My dear, it's only a story. It's fiction!"

"And what of it?" sniffed the old woman. "Does that place it farther from truth than the newspapers?"

• • •

In an excess of promotional zeal Nicky talked Maria's record company into booking Madison Square Garden for six nights; "conned" is perhaps a more precise description of his persuasive effort which consisted of talking fast and long, making unspecified promises (and all the while breathing not a word about a man who could fly) until the record company's publicity director gave in just to get him out of her office. Besides, she reasoned, the Garden came cheap what with the Knicks, the Rangers, and the fights all canceled because of the television catastrophe. Nevertheless, the sight of eleven thousand some odd empty seats on opening night, a Monday, did not thrill her.

"You said a full house, Nicky," she hissed, "minimum fifteen thousand."

"So we got nine. Not bad for a little broad with no name recognition." It wouldn't do, thought Nicky, to let Doreen know he was worried, too.

"Don't tell me how to count a house, Nicky. We got seven five, at most eight, definitely not nine. We plastered the city with ads. Do you have any idea what the publicity cost? We'll be lucky to break even."

"Hey," said Nicky, "loosen up, Doreen. Tomorrow night they'll be backed up to Fifty-seventh Street. Once they've seen the reviews you can double the ticket prices."

"I wish I knew where you're getting your confidence," said Doreen, chewing on a hangnail. "Maria's terrific in a nightclub and she sounds great in the studio, but what if she can't carry such a big place? Too bad I let you talk me out of my plan to ease her along, to let her work her way up to the big audiences."

"I have my reasons. I told you I'd throw in something to sweeten the pot, and I will. Trust me."

"Like what?" Doreen demanded cynically. "Is Maria going to sing in the nude? Don't pull anything funny, Nicky. I don't want the cops raiding us."

"I told you. Trust me."

"I don't. Where's your partner?"

"Bernice? Holding Maria's hand last time I looked."

"Has Maria come down with stage fright?" asked Doreen in a panic.

"Maria? She never heard of it." Nicky grinned.

The house lights went down. Three spotlights sliced through the darkness from different directions and joined one another on stage in the center of the arena. "Hey. There she is now. Does that look like stage fright to you?"

Maria stepped into the light. She stood erect and gazed severely around the arena, quieting the audience. The circle of light widened to reveal Paco seated on its perimeter, embracing a guitar. Maria reached for the microphone.

"I sing you a song my husband wrote. It is called 'A Arvore.' Now I sing in Portuguese, but if you like later maybe I sing in English."

Incredible! Bernice reflected as she watched Maria's performance from a mezzanine seat. Maria commanded the Garden with the same authority she ruled the Café Carlyle or Moose's Place. One little woman with an electric green gaze and a voice — my God, such a voice! What phrasing! Talk about poise: nothing fazed her. Not the eight thousand people. Not the eleven thousand empty seats. (Too bad about that. Nicky was stewing.) Her voice reeled you in with a pure gold line until you felt like you were in her living room even when she had her back to you half a football field away.

Too bad though about Fisher's flying stunt. He would upstage Maria. The reviewers might forget about her in the pandemonium that was bound to follow. Maybe Nicky's idea wasn't so hot after all. There was still time to cancel Fisher: he wasn't scheduled until after intermission. But no — there was that report business and the televisions. They were too important. Incredible as she was, Maria couldn't sing the televisions back to life.

Intermission: Nicky and Doreen work the corridors, chatting up the journalists plus a couple of celebrities who have turned out to see if Maria lives up to the gossip of the Café Carlyle crowd. Bernice scoots to the dressing room. Paco, in a sweat, is changing into a fresh shirt. The doctor and the dame with the purple drink are camped out on the floor. Zeke speaks furiously into his tape recorder. Jesse Randolph has his arm thrown around a pale Gregory Fisher who clutches the schoolteacher's hand. Maria sits in front of her mirror repairing her makeup, calm as the doldrums.

The audience regained their seats. Good, thought Bernice. Nobody went home: they're still with her. The house lights dimmed, the spots came up, and the audience cheered as Maria stepped again onto the stage. She sang one song, a brilliant fast-tempo number that had the crowd clapping to the refrain. The song ended. Raising her arms, Maria defeated the applause.

"And now," she said, smiling her soon-to-be-famous smile, "Mr. Gregory Fisher, the astronaut, will fly."

The remarkable thing, Bernice reflected afterward, was that no one in the Garden acted as though Maria's announcement was in the slightest bit peculiar. Possibly they thought she had given them the title of her next song. By contrast, Fisher's materialization in the spotlight set off wavelets of mutterings.

"Isn't he the nut who thinks he sees trees?" Bernice heard a woman ask her companion.

"What's he up to now?"

Fisher, who was dressed in jeans, a navy sweatshirt, and sneakers, stood shielding his eyes against the glare. When the house lights came on, he took a few self-conscious steps around the platform and looked up to the ceiling to measure its height. Then with a little hop off his right foot, he lifted himself off terra firma and soared into the air, arms in the outspread attitude of a swan dive.

Some people in the audience applauded. The rest tried to figure out what they were seeing.

"Must be one of those portable jet things," somebody suggested.

"It's a hologram. You ever been to Disneyland?"

Fisher looked just as you'd imagine a man would look if he

really took flight, Bernice figured: not like a bird or a plane or special effects from Hollywood, more like a creature out of its element — tentative, awkward, with none of the grace of a trapeze artist. Fisher executed a couple of clumsy circles around the arena and came to a halt fifty feet above the floor.

"What do I do now?" he shouted from a standing position.

"Get down into the audience," replied Nicky who was now standing on stage with a microphone. "Show 'em there are no gimmicks."

Fisher made a soft two-footed landing in one of the aisles. Hands reached out to confirm that he was made of matter, that he was neither strung with invisible wires nor propelled by invisible engines.

"Pick up a passenger," Nicky called out.

Fisher took off from the aisle and flew to the other side of the Garden where Ozzie was sitting with the schoolteacher. Fisher caught him by the hand, placed one arm across his shoulders, and carried him aloft. People stood up in their seats, craning their necks to follow the course of flight. The policemen who had been guarding the exits moved up their respective aisles and gazed upward, mouths agape. A woman screamed, then another and another.

"There's nothing to be afraid of," Nicky hollered into the microphone. "The kid's having the time of his life."

"I'm okay, I'm okay," Ozzie shouted reassuringly from on high. "It's great!"

"Any wise-guy journalist out there care to take a ride with Mr. Fisher to check out if he's for real?" offered Nicky. "All front and center, on the double!"

Six or seven people, Zeke Kramer among them, rushed for the stage. Fisher and Ozzie landed gently in their midst. Fisher went over to Zeke.

"Sorry, I know you deserve your scoop," he apologized, "but

you're too closely identified with me. I have to take someone else so it doesn't look like a fix. You choose."

"In that case you might as well take him." Zeke jerked his thumb at a rumpled middle-aged man. "He's so cynical he wouldn't believe an egg came from the butt end of a chicken unless he had a worm's eye view of the action."

Fisher tapped the rumpled man on the shoulder. "I hope you don't mind heights, sir," he commented. "All you have to do is relax, okay? Let me do the rest."

They took off, crisscrossing the arena, flying high among the lights. When they came back down, the rumpled man seized the microphone from Nicky.

"Ladies and gentlemen," he announced in a trembling voice, "Mr. Fisher flies. This is no humbug!"

Eight thousand people went into psychic shock. Then a woman sitting near the stage stumbled into the aisle and fell on her knees. Others imitated her, and within minutes worshipers jammed the aisles.

"What am I supposed to do now?" the bewildered Fisher whispered to Paco.

"I do not know," said Paco. "Perhaps wait."

"Who are you?" a man called out from the crowd. "What do you want from us?"

"The tree I saw in the desert was real," Fisher replied, "and what is written in *The Book of Follies* is true."

"Will you fix the televisions?" another voice asked.

"No, I don't think so. I don't have the power."

"Then how will we get the televisions back?"

Fisher looked frantically at Paco. "What do I tell them?" He leaned down, and Paco spoke into his ear. Fisher addressed the audience.

"Read *The Book of Follies,*" he commanded. "You will find the answer. And please, take your seats. Maria will sing."

He replaced the microphone in its stand and turned to Nicky. "Now get me the hell out of here," he hissed.

"Cut the house lights!" Nicky shouted. He guided Fisher to the edge of the stage. Maria resumed her place in the spotlight.

"Now I sing for you again 'A Arvore.' In English it means 'The Tree.'"

Paco played the opening notes of the enchanting melody which Maria engaged with renewed conviction; when she reached the refrain, eight thousand voices joined hers.

Nicky tugged at Fisher's sweatshirt. They slipped off the stage through the arena into the dressing rooms.

"Hey! Did you see that?" squealed a girl who was sitting on the aisle.

"See what?" asked her boyfriend.

"That *thing* that just ran by. Something glowing, it looked like a man."

"Must've been your imagination."

Gregory Fisher's exploits made the late night radio broadcasts and dominated the early edition newspapers; by midafternoon the news had circulated around the globe. People started lining up at Madison Square Garden five hours before the box office opened. Disk jockeys besieged Doreen, the record company publicist, with requests for Maria's song; luckily, the studio had a prerelease tape from which several copies were hastily produced. The immediate popularity of "A Arvore" gave new meaning to the expression *overnight sensation*.

Meanwhile Bernice and Nicky fended off journalists, rival agents, promoters, and other miscellaneous predators. "Mr. Fisher will not grant any interviews," Bernice announced at a midday press conference. "He has asked us to say on his behalf that his only public message is what he said last night, quote: 'The tree I saw in the desert was real, and what is written in *The Book of Follies* is true.' Unquote. He expects to take part in future performances at Madison Square Garden. I am not at liberty to reveal his whereabouts to you. As for Maria, we've put together a press kit to give you background information and so forth. We'll let you know as soon as possible when she'll be available to answer your questions. In the meantime she joins Mr. Fisher's request that you attend to his message as well as to the lyrics of the song 'A Arvore.' "

"So what you're telling us is," said a journalist, "that Fisher's gone into hiding, right?"

"Mr. Fisher, as you can imagine, goes wherever he pleases," replied Bernice with a sly smile.

In truth, Fisher and the schoolteacher were freely exploring New York City streets where the astronaut passed unrecognized in an old New York Mets baseball hat and a pair of horn-rimmed glasses, wondering if anonymity might not be possible after all.

The Garden sold out before noon. The evening's performance proceeded approximately as it had before, except that people, owing to both greater numbers and amplified expectations, pressed themselves urgently on Fisher as if he might touch them with immortality, so he resolved to stay in the air or on stage — but out of the aisles. As flying companions that night he transported a woman who taught metaphysics at Yeshiva University and the Tanzanian ambassador to the United Nations. Everybody stayed to the end to sing "A Arvore" with Maria.

"Two down," Fisher sighed after the show, "four to go."

"What do you mean?" snapped Doreen. "You're not coming on the tour?"

"If they haven't gotten the message in a week, they'll never get it! Right, Paco?"

"That is correct, Gregorio."

"What would you say to three million cash — "

"No."

" — *plus* five percent of the gate?" pressed Doreen.

"I'd say you hadn't been paying attention."

Two men from the Pentagon, a Russian Nobel physicist, and a representative of the Vatican were in the audience for Wednesday's performance. Thursday's attracted still other officials and skeptics who, like their predecessors, quit the auditorium in puzzlement.

By Friday Fisher had almost gotten into the groove of a routine. He and the schoolteacher slept late in the morning. After breakfast he slipped into his thin disguise, out of the apartment Nicky had borrowed for them in Queens, and into the stinking subway station. That day, Friday March 12, in the year 2004, Fisher and the schoolteacher spent part of the afternoon in a secondhand bookstore near the corner of Broadway and Eighty-eighth Street. When they tired of browsing they stopped at a delicatessen. The schoolteacher ordered a grilled Reuben sandwich and a lime Kool-Aid, for which she had recently developed a taste; the waiter scowled and said they did not serve Kool-Aid so she settled for seltzer. Fisher asked for a hot pastrami and a beer which, he claimed, enhanced the amplitude of his flights.

Around four o'clock the lovers walked to the Museum of Natural History where they watched the last projection of stars onto the domed ceiling of the Hayden Planetarium. Afterward, the weather being mild, they meandered south along Central Park West, their footsteps skirting that patch of sidewalk in front of the Dakota where John Lennon had spilled his life's blood, past Columbus Circle, and down a few blocks on Seventh Avenue. Here they stopped again, this time in a nondescript bar between Fifty-sixth and Fifty-seventh streets. They occupied a back booth and split a chicken sandwich; the schoolteacher drank two cups of coffee, Fisher one draft beer. Holding hands across the table, they lingered a long time and pretended not to listen to the conversation at the bar where people talked only about the man who could fly and argued over definitions of divinity.

Fisher and the schoolteacher left the bar around ten to eight.

Five minutes later they boarded a bus which dropped them at
Madison Square Garden at 8:20, late enough to avoid the worst
of the crowd yet in ample time for Fisher's scheduled appearance
at 9:15. They exchanged a kiss on the sidewalk. The schoolteacher, who wanted to watch Maria, walked right toward a public entrance through which she was admitted upon presentation
of her pass. Fisher turned left, flashed his credentials at a policeman, and entered the dressing area. He stretched out on a sofa
and listened to Maria over the loudspeakers.

Maria came back during intermission and greeted him with a
kiss before sitting down to touch up her lipstick. Paco, who looked
tired, complained of influenza symptoms. Bertie felt his forehead
for fever. Bernice fished through her purse and produced a pair
of aspirins. Susan furnished orange Kool-Aid to wash them down.
Jesse Randolph's mouth tightened as he observed Fisher.

"What's up, Jesse?" inquired Fisher, catching the look.

"Maybe nothing," said Jesse. "I'll be glad when this is over,
though."

Maria opened the second half of the program with a new
song, a sexy samba number, after which she made her artless
introduction of Fisher. The crowd cheered his name, but when
he appeared in the spotlight it held its breath. The house lights
came on. Fisher hopped off his right foot into the air and made
one and a half circles of the arena as usual. Then, perhaps feeling
playful, he uprighted himself and went into his Fred Astaire imi-
tation, the same funny routine he had once performed for Zeke
in a meadow in Strangeways, New York, except now he was fifty
feet above ground, not three. He danced his way down two flights
of imaginary stairs and alighted on the stage with a deep bow
from the waist. The crowd rose to its feet with a din.

A small man seated near the stage stepped into an aisle, took
aim with his pistol, and fired a single expert shot. The bullet
struck Fisher as he was coming up from his bow. He crumpled.

Paco dropped his guitar. The schoolteacher, Zeke, Nicky, Bernice, Susan, Bertie, and Jesse Randolph dashed for the stage. Maria screamed into the microphone.

A young man in the audience spotted the little man with the gun racing toward the exit.

"Assassin!" he sobbed, hurling himself into the little man's path. The gunman stumbled and fell and was in turn fallen upon by a mob with murder on its mind. People stood up on their seats and howled for blood. Twenty jittery policemen converged on the writhing heap with drawn weapons.

Jesse seized the microphone.

"DON'T KILL!" he commanded. His voice rose from his belly out through the sound system, resonating in the arena with an unearthly echo. "Have you not yet understood Gregory Fisher's message? He flew to tell you the murder must end. AND IT MUST END NOW!"

The crowd froze.

Jesse handed the microphone back to Maria. He looked down at Fisher's fallen form.

"Come on, Nicky," he said. "Let's get him out of here. I'll take his shoulders."

Jesse leaned over, grasped Fisher's upper arms, and lifted. His muscles, which had tensed themselves for the dead weight of his friend, went slack with surprise.

"My God!" Jesse whispered to Nicky, "no wonder the man could fly. He's lighter than air."

Even so the two men, accompanied by their friends, carried Fisher off the stage and through the stilled crowd. They were halfway up the aisle when Paco plucked the soulful theme from "A Arvore." As Maria sang the first verse, the audience stood solemnly. One by one they joined their voices to the refrain, an anthem to Gregory Fisher.

• • •

Hsu-ling leaned back against her cushions and signaled one

of the children to prepare her a potion of yellow powder and water.

A woman blew her nose. "It's a shame Gregory Fisher had to die," she commented aloud.

Hsu-ling looked uncharacteristically flustered. "Die? Did I say Fisher died?" she inquired. "I can't recall having used that word."

"What happened to the televisions? Did they ever come back on?" called a small boy from the garden.

"Dear child," replied Hsu-ling, "surely you already know the answer to that question. Just ask yourself: Do we or do we not have television?"

O z z i e ' s   S t o r y

Osgood Elmwood extracted the precisely folded handkerchief from his jacket breast pocket, shook it out, passed it twice across his perspiring forehead, wiped his clammy hands, and jammed it back into the pocket in a lump. He knew he shouldn't have let his wife talk him into wearing his dark blue suit, but she'd insisted. She claimed it made him look thinner.

"This meeting isn't about thin, it's about storytelling," he argued. "Besides, I've been fat for eighty-three years. It's an accident of nature that can't be rectified by a blue suit."

"But dear, you look so *dignified* in that suit. And they've given you such a big honor that the least you can do is show your appreciation by putting on your best suit."

"It's too heavy. I'll sweat."

"Then ask them to turn down the heat. Surely as the main speaker you have that right."

"It has nothing to do with heat. I'll be nervous, and when I'm nervous I sweat. I can't control it."

"Nervous? Why should you be nervous? All you have to do is tell a story. Don't be silly, Ozzie. I'm packing your blue suit, and that's that!" She took an immaculate white handkerchief from the dresser drawer, deftly turned over its edges, and tucked it into the breast pocket of the jacket so that one corner showed as an equilateral triangle. "There," she said, patting the pocket fondly, "that way I won't forget it at the hotel. Very elegant."

Which was why Ozzie was sitting in the auditorium now, on the edge of a too-small seat, sweating like a hog and destroying his wife's linen geometry. He hadn't been able to make her understand that being voted Storyteller of the Year was a pain in the ass. Sure, he was glad he won, would be proud to have the certificate framed and hanging on the living-room wall next to the old autographed photograph of Gregory Fisher, but the award ceremony was torture, like play period in the fifth grade before Fisher and Ms. Hu rescued him.

"All you have to do is tell a story," his wife had said. She couldn't see the difference between telling stories to children or to the old people he taught in his Master classes and getting up in front of three hundred and fifty Grand Master storytellers.

Ozzie, who had been to these events twice before, knew that many of the Grand Masters never attended to the story; they listened only for the *flaws*. Later you'd hear them in the bar gloating over how the Storyteller of the Year had started with a blond heroine who had turned up midway through the tale with raven tresses. Tresses indeed! someone would snort; does anyone still use that word? Or how the storyteller's voice had gone dry, and she'd had to interrupt herself in midsentence for several sips of water. Really, you'd think with her experience . . .

"Pssst, Ozzie," his wife hissed, "pay attention. He's saying such lovely things about you."

Ozzie heard the master of ceremonies droning on, piling up

clichés—founding member this, incomparable artist that, yak, yak, yak—and pulled out the handkerchief again. He closed his eyes and inhaled deep breaths of stale air.

The audience broke into applause. Ozzie's wife elbowed the ample upholstery of his rib cage.

"Go on, it's your turn." She smiled, kissing him on the cheek. "And don't worry: you'll be great."

The applause grew louder as Ozzie hauled himself out of the seat and lumbered down the aisle. He took the steps slowly and made his way to the center of the stage. He put on his reading glasses, pulled out a piece of paper, and cleared his throat.

"I am deeply honored to be the recipient of this year's award," he read in a flat voice, "and I dedicate my story to Hsu-ling Hu from whom I first heard stories as a fifth-grader. As you know, Ms. Hu originated the Television Tales, the beloved cycle of ten stories about the television failure. It is her custom to retell the stories every year to the people of her village and to visitors so fortunate as to be passing through during the third week of June. I myself have heard the complete cycle twice, the tellings several years apart.

"Like all great storytellers Ms. Hu improves, embellishes, or otherwise alters her stories from one telling to another and therefore never repeats the exact same story. She particularly delights in surprising her listeners with different versions of the tenth and final Television Tale. Therefore tonight it gives me great pleasure to honor the special place Hsu-ling Hu occupies in my memory with my own variation on the last Television Tale."

As the audience clapped politely and shifted in their seats, Ozzie put the paper from which he had been reading into his pocket, removed his glasses, and stood stiffly behind the lectern. He took a swig from the water tumbler.

This is the tale Ozzie told.

———

In the high valley of the Ecuadorean Andes that lay some-where between the mountains of Chimborazo and Cotopaxi, there lived the only people on earth who had not heard about the television failure and who, if they had heard of it, would not have cared, for they possessed no knowledge of the device called tele-vision.

· · ·

Ozzie coughed a couple of dry coughs and took another sip of water. He looked down at his shiny black shoes, then up at the ceiling.

"Get on with it, Elmwood," shouted a voice from the audi-ence, "the bar closes down at eleven-thirty."

Ozzie grinned. "The truth is," he announced, "I came down with a case of the stage frights and forgot where I meant to start this story. You know how it is, you've got a choice: either you can barge ahead and fiddle with it as you go along to try to make everything come out right in the end, or you can admit you flubbed up and start over. Since I haven't gotten very far, I'd like to start over."

The Grand Masters gave Ozzie a warm round of applause because never before had one of their own stood in front of them and admitted to a mistake. They knew then that they had chosen wisely, that he was indeed a great storyteller, a man who would not sacrifice a well-formed story at the altar of his vanity.

"And if you don't mind," Ozzie continued, "since I'm a little overheated, I'll take off my jacket and loosen up my necktie. Okay? Here goes:"

· · ·

In the latter half of the twentieth century, in a city on the great North American plains, there lived an ugly male child. Even as a newborn his deformed features were cause for the unspoken shame of his parents, both of whom were exceedingly handsome. Yet, though they loved him little, they named him Archibald and raised him dutifully, keeping him hidden from company lest his disfigurement distract them from more symmetrical thoughts. When Archibald was two and a half his mother gave birth to a second child, also a boy, who arrived in the world as fair of form as his older brother was imperfect, and who gave great joy to his parents and commanded their attentions. They named the second child Daniel.

From the day he arrived home from the hospital, Daniel occupied the center of the family universe, with mother and father revolving close around him and consigning little Archibald to a distant orbit, a situation the older sibling accepted with equanimity, for he could hardly be displaced from a position in his parents' affections that he had never held. Sensing himself superfluous, he withdrew into fantasies fed by television—to which he had unrestricted access because when he sat in front of the screen quietly, he was almost out of his parents' sight and mind.

In the absence of parental oversight, television served as Archibald's first teacher, and in some respects it served well. By the age of three and a half he had mastered his ABCs and his numbers from his favorite program which was called "Sesame Street." Otherwise his tastes gravitated to fictions about wholesome families unlike his own; but hundreds of hours of viewing did not reveal to him the secret of unlocking the cuddles and praises of parents.

Apart from television, Archibald enjoyed listening to music of which his family had a large collection. One day in the middle of his fourth year, when none of the fifty-three TV channels had captured his interest and when his mother had left him with Hattie the housekeeper to take Daniel to the playground, Archibald climbed up on the piano bench, lifted the lid to the keys, and started to play *The Goldberg Variations.* The housekeeper, who had been on her feet all morning, plopped herself into an overstuffed chair and let the healing fingers of the notes massage the aches and pains of her soul.

"What's that tune you're playin' there?" she interrupted.

"Music," replied Archibald who did not know it had a name.

"It sure is pretty," she said. "Did your momma or poppa teach you?"

"No," said Archibald. "I never tried the piano before."

Hattie, aware of Archibald's peripheral position in the household, scrunched her brows in thought.

"If I was you," she advised, "I'd keep this a secret between you and me and the piano. I got a funny feeling your folks would be spooked."

This was most likely bad advice since evidence of a prodigious talent might have compensated for the child's ugliness in his parents' eyes, but Archibald took it anyway since Hattie was the only adult who hugged him. From that day on, whenever his mother and father went out, and provided "Sesame Street" wasn't on television, Archibald spent hours at the piano playing by ear pieces he had heard on the stereo system or—and this came somewhat later—making up his own melodies. One day Hattie gave him a present.

"I was down at the video store," she explained, "and they were running this movie about that Goldberg tune I once heard you play, so I thought maybe you'd like it. Here. You just pop it into that VCR like I showed you." She smothered him in a sweaty hug and dispatched him to the television with a pat on the rear.

That videotape, of Glenn Gould playing Bach's *Goldberg Variations,* was Archibald's prized possession during the year before he entered kindergarten. Over and over and over he studied the eccentric Canadian pianist coaxing transcendental sounds from the piano, sounds that he himself could not reproduce if for no other reason than that his feet did not yet reach the pedals.

School, which Archibald had been looking forward to, turned out to be an ordeal, for it was there that he was made to understand that he had committed the sin of ugliness. Whereas his parents had done him the kindness of ignoring him, Archibald's classmates assaulted him with insults, taunts, and teases against which his enclosed nature left him defenseless. Lacking any instinct either to clown around or fight back, he retreated deeper into fantasy. The only people who treated him with unforced affection were Hattie and Daniel, whose innately generous disposition miraculously survived his parents' overindulgence, but those two could not protect Archibald against his tormentors.

The older Archibald grew, the uglier he got, and the more cruelly his peers persecuted him. Though he continued to find solace in music, the images of cute children and beautiful adults that dominated the television screen reminded him painfully of his own flaws; he further observed that except on "Sesame Street," which he had outgrown, characters with irregular features were usually villainous. He gave up watching television because it depressed him.

Luckily, however, Archibald's defection from the tube coincided with his discovery, during a third-grade class excursion, of the public library. His earliest literary experiences were of fairy tales, particularly those stories in which frogs turn into princes and ugly ducklings into swans. Well advanced in his reading skills, he rapidly moved on to more adult literature and by the age of twelve had read deeply into Dickens, Mark Twain, James Fenimore Cooper, and Edgar Allan Poe, whose invented worlds became for him more vivid than his own unhappy existence.

It must have been around this time, or perhaps a little later, that Archibald discovered the writings of H. G. Wells, specifically a story called "The Country of the Blind," which he checked out of the library and never returned, preferring to pay the penalty for the "lost" anthology from his allowance. He hid the volume under his pillow and reread the story often; at night before falling asleep he imagined himself among the blind, beloved by people innocent of his ugliness. He learned from the story that he must not commit the same error as the mountaineer Nunez who, having fallen (literally!) into the Country of the Blind, had endeavored to become its king and whose ability to see had gotten him into trouble. No, Archibald wished only to exist unseen and unscorned among gentle people, and to achieve that he decided he must acquire their skills and live by their rules. Therefore, after Daniel and his parents had gone to bed, Archibald tied a bandanna tight around his eyes and explored the house and yard with his hands in order to sharpen his senses of touch, hearing, and smell; though his hands and ears became quite skillful, he didn't make any noticeable progress with his nose. He also resolved to purge his vocabulary of sight-related words—or, rather, not to acquire them in the Spanish course which he was taking so as to be able to converse with the people when he arrived in their land.

"Don't tell anybody, but as soon as I'm finished with school I'm going to go live in the Country of the Blind," he confided in Daniel one day.

"I won't tell," promised Daniel. "But I never heard of the Country of the Blind. Where is it?"

"It's in Ecuador," said Archibald. "Here. You see?" He handed his brother a much worn three-year-overdue library book.

Daniel, who was a bright boy, scanned the first few pages and leafed through the remainder.

"But, Arch,"—he frowned—"this is a story. It isn't a real place."

"No, it's real all right. It's just that you don't hear about it because nobody goes in or out. I'm pretty sure I've figured out where it is on the map."

"If you say so," said Daniel doubtfully, "but it's a big risk. What if it turns out not to be there? Then what? But I do see your point, I mean about blind people. Maybe you could do something like be a teacher in one of those special schools."

"I want to live where nobody ever sees me and where they don't have mirrors!"

"But what about me?" asked Daniel. "I'd miss you, Arch."

"I'll miss you too, Danny. You and Hattie."

Archibald did not after all complete his high-school education. In April of his junior year, about ten days before the Junior
Prom, a boy classmate informed him that the girls had organized
a lottery, the loser of which was condemned to invite Archibald
to the dance. Arriving as it did at a time of life when Archibald
was taking a keen but distant interest in girls, this item of malice
made the sum total of his humiliation almost unbearable: one
more insult would flatten his will forever.

So that night while his family slept, Archibald stuffed a few
belongings into his knapsack and tiptoed down the hall. Just before he reached the back door, he had an afterthought. He returned to his room and wrote a note to Daniel. "Dear Danny,"
it read, "I've gone where I always said I would. I don't suppose
Mom and Pop will worry, but just in case tell them not to. That
goes for you, too. Take care. Love, your brother, Arch." On his
way out the second time, and for no particular reason, he picked
up the old Glenn Gould tape Hattie had given him.

"What's that supposed to mean—'where I always said I
would'?" demanded Pop of Daniel at breakfast.

"A place he read about in a story," gulped Daniel, "called
the Country of the Blind. It's somewhere in Ecuador, I think."

"That's insane! There's no such place. It's fictitious."

"I guess we'd better call the police," sighed Mom. "Archibald
shouldn't be hard to spot."

"Let him be," counseled Daniel. "He doesn't want to be
found. Or if he does, he'll come home by himself."

"I sure am gonna miss that boy and them songs he used to
play on the piano," snuffled Hattie as she poured another round
of coffee.

"What songs?" inquired Mom and Pop in a single voice.

"You know, that Goldberg song, and those other piano tunes.
Sure was pretty."

"Daniel, do you know what Hattie's talking about?" asked
Pop suspiciously.

"Well," Daniel began . . .

Archibald traveled five and a half months in search of the
Country of the Blind. Like many desperate adventurers, he had
no sound plan and hardly any money. He spent his savings to
purchase a bus ticket from his home on the North American
plains to New Orleans where he hoped to find a ship that would
carry him to Guayaquil. However, no such vessel anchored in
port for several weeks, forcing Archibald to look for work to pay
for food. He applied for several jobs as a waiter, but no one would
hire him on the grounds that his appearance would spoil the
customers' appetites. Then his luck turned and he was employed
to play the piano in a whorehouse where the madam considered
his ugliness an asset: the girls would not be distracted, and all the
clients would feel handsome.

Though Archibald rather enjoyed the dim lights of the
whorehouse as well as the whores, who liked his music and who,
being well-trained professionals, did not subject him to personal
offenses, he left after two months when he discovered a rusty
Panamanian freighter en route to Ecuador via Veracruz, Belize,
Bluefields, through the Panama Canal, on down to Buenaventura,
and finally, Guayaquil. He signed on as second cook. The voyage
was miserable. Archibald, who had never been at sea, got sick
three hours out of port and, except for shore leaves, stayed sick
for the duration. The crew was brutish. The cook, with whom
he was cooped up in the reeking galley for hours on end, was a
mean drunk. Though Archibald's high school Spanish lessons had
skirted the grosser obscenities, he understood the word *feo* and
suffered it a hundred times a day for seven weeks.

Archibald jumped ship in Guayaquil, a rathole of a port populated by mosquitoes and misery, and proceeded by bus to the

more salubrious altitudes of Quito. He lived for a while among the homeless Indians who had quit their villages in pursuit of the twentieth century, practicing his Spanish and advancing tentative inquiries concerning the Country of the Blind. The Indians had never heard of it and called him a crazy gringo. However, one sympathetic fellow advised him that if he really meant to look for it he had best start soon, during the drier months of summer when the mountain passes were easier to negotiate. So Archibald took a bus south to Mulalo, near Mount Cotopaxi, and then headed on foot southeast in the general direction of Mount Chimborazo.

Archibald wasted several weeks in the mountains owing to H. G. Wells's inaccuracies; in fact, the Country of the Blind lies *north* of Mount Cotopaxi, not south as Wells stated, and Archibald might never have found it at all had he not misread his compass and gotten lost. Also the valley was no longer quite as inaccessible as it had been at the time of Nunez's visit; some time since then a geological event had created in one of the surrounding cliffs a crevasse through which a man might squeeze himself in dry weather. Neither the blind people who made their home in the valley nor the llamas who grazed in the pastures had discovered this passage. But Archibald did.

The moment he saw the valley spread out before him, Archibald knew he had reached his destination for, except for the annoying matter of sloppy geography, the Country of the Blind looked exactly as Wells had described it — the orderly paved paths lined by queerly patched and plastered windowless houses, the remarkable irrigation system, the boundary wall. He was further reassured by the absence of people at midday, for he had read that the inhabitants slept during the day and rose to work in the cool of the night. Knowing their hearing to be extremely acute, and wishing to respect their ways, Archibald crept with caution to the edge of the village, where he lay down in the shade of a tree and fell asleep.

As you must imagine, Archibald's presence startled the local population who had never encountered an outsider apart from the legend of Nunez whom they called "Bogota." Archibald awakened in late evening to the touch of many fingers whispering across his person and the murmuring of voices.

"Where am I?" he inquired in Spanish, as though he were lost.

There followed an avalanche of questions of the kind he had expected: Who are you? Where did you come from? Why are you wearing such funny fabrics? Why do you speak with an accent? Are you related to "Bogota"? and so on—to which he had prepared a single answer.

"I don't know," he said.

"How can a man not know his name and where he has been?" demanded a cranky village elder after a while.

"I don't know," replied Archibald for the eleventh time, with a small sob now, for he was hungry and scared.

"He's only a boy," scolded a woman reaching out for his smooth cheek, "and a fine-feeling one at that. But the poor child weeps."

The Country of the Blind admitted the foreigner as an immigrant of unknown origin and faulty memory. Within a few days he acquired a name of his own choice: Archibald, which the natives struggled to pronounce but which was a piece of continuity Archibald kept because he was accustomed to it. He was, of course, clumsy and poorly educated—he couldn't smell one llama from another, for instance, and his fingers hadn't been taught to read books—but he learned quickly, worked hard, and shed the strangeness of his ways. He was also much admired for his tallness and the irregularity of his features, which were exotic to the touch. He guarded the secret of his sight, using such advantages as it conferred upon him with the utmost care.

Archibald adjusted easily to the absence of conveniences he had taken for granted—electricity, cars, radios, telephones, for example, as well as television. The only invocation of his post-industrial past was the random jet flying overhead, which the blind people heard as a sign of godly displeasure. True, he sometimes craved a slice of Hattie's banana cream pie, but the distractions of his new life left little room for remorse.

Transformed by the magic of invisibility from a frog into a prince, Archibald became the most desired bachelor in the valley. He played the field for a while, then fell in love and settled down in wedlock with a sweet girl named Yna who eventually gave birth to a baby boy. Recalling his biology classes, Archibald worried lest his own genes prevail and his child be cursed with sight, but Yna evidently carried a mightier chromosome for blindness. His child preoccupied him as he lavished upon the infant the attention he had never received from his own parents. When his son was three Archibald, wishing to share one of the few pleasures of his youth, determined to present the boy with a piano for his fifth birthday. To that end he asked permission from the village elders to cut two of the trees from the east cliff—trees that secured the slope against avalanches.

"Describe to us again what you want to do with the wood," said the elders.

"I wish to construct a piano," said Archibald.

"And what, pray tell, is a piano?"

"An instrument of music," explained Archibald. "It makes noises that bounce off the smooth shell of heaven and return with the sounds of angels."

The elders, who knew only the music of a crude wooden flute, were seduced by a promise of sound and approved Archibald's petition.

Archibald spent two years building his son a piano from memory. Owing to the cramped quarters of his workshop, he constructed a modest upright rather than a grand piano, but even so it was a tremendous, often maddening task, from the felling of the tree to the carving of the intricate pieces that controlled the piano's action. Lacking standard materials, Archibald had to improvise. He stretched and treated llama guts for the strings, wove llama hairs into a fabric approximating felt, and substituted finely cut and polished llama bones for ivory keys. On the day—or rather the night—before his son's birthday Archibald played the umpteenth scale on the instrument and detected flaws in its tune, his ear after years in the Country of the Blind having grown fussy and so keen that it registered every wavelet of sound. He labored throughout the night—or rather the day—and at three o'clock prepared to test the piano before the public.

Archibald's birthday child was long in bed but his curious neighbors clustered in his parlor cocking their heads as he pressed the keys that made llama felt hammer upon llama strings.

"Ahh . . .," they exclaimed in admiration even of the false notes.

"That's nothing," Archibald declared. "Wait till I've got the damn thing in tune."

Two and a half hours later, after more tightening and loosening and fiddling with a homemade tuning wrench, he pronounced his product finished. He sat down on a bench and began to play the first thing that popped into his head, Schumann's *Fantasy in C Major*.

The blind eyes of the people of his adopted country wept tears unseen by all but Archibald.

"Surely," the chief elder said, "that is the sound of heaven."

"No," countered Archibald, "anybody can learn to do it. It's easy. I can teach you."

"And where does this music come from?"

"I don't know," replied Archibald, falling back on his standard answer. No point trying to explain Schumann to these folks; he'd only get himself into a pickle. "Maybe I dreamed it." He ripped off a Scott Joplin rag, and his listeners started clapping in rhythm.

Archibald's piano was the biggest thing to hit the Country of the Blind since Archibald himself. Because everyone wanted to learn how to play it, Archibald was relieved of his agricultural assignments and pressed into service as a piano master. Unfortunately, ownership of a great talent does not guarantee the ability to communicate it (or even the mechanics of it) to others, and Archibald, who had never suffered lessons himself, turned out to be a rotten teacher. Therefore only two children who possessed innate gifts akin to his own learned to play the instrument; one of them, to Archibald's delight, was his own son who demonstrated a particular aptitude for jazz improvisation. Feeling sheepish that he had failed to produce more players, Archibald apologized to the community and said he would return to the fields.

"Never mind," said the elders. "It's enough for us if you play concerts and take care of the instrument."

Archibald passed more than a decade in perfect contentment, beloved by family and friends, giving concerts every week and happily tinkering with the piano which, owing to the materials of construction and the climate, required constant mechanical maintenance. He observed the musical maturation of his son and the second child with pride. He also polished his own performance skills and started to compose new music.

And he might have lived out his life in this blessed condition had he not returned to the first music he had ever played, Bach's *Goldberg Variations,* with the notion of performing them privately for Yna as an anniversary present. Though he had worked on the *French Suites,* the *Well-Tempered Clavier,* and other Bach compositions, Archibald had not attempted the *Goldberg Variations* since leaving North America, and on his initial run-through he realized he had misplaced several measures of the epic twenty-fifth, the slow variation in G minor, in his prodigious musical memory. With a frown he started the twenty-fifth again, hoping to retrieve the missing notes by an act of repetition, but they were lost, lost, and nothing in his bag of mnemonic tricks worked to find them.

Surely Yna would not have remarked on one variation more

or less; or surely she would have been thrilled with Chopin or Liszt or Scarlatti. Not Archibald, however, who was dead set on the *Goldberg Variations, all* the *Goldberg Variations.* Though he tried to tell himself that a few unremembered notes were no big deal, he couldn't get what wasn't there out of his mind. He began picking at his food and tossing in his sleep. He played a weekly concert so lacking in luster that some villagers who had developed sophisticated listening habits actually booed his performance. One day he was so restless in bed as to arouse Yna and cause her ordinarily sweet temper to sour.

"For God's sake, Archibald," she moaned, punching her pillow, "give me a break. If you insist on making such a ruckus, go do it on the living-room couch! What's your problem anyway?"

"Nothing to worry yourself about," said Archibald. "Go back to sleep. I think I'll go for a walk."

He threw on his clothes, plunged out into the blaze of daylight, and strode through the sleeping street in the direction of the southwest pasture, all the while trying to empty his head of the twenty-fifth variation on the theory that if he didn't deliberately seek the missing measures they would pop back into place of their own accord. Certain memories didn't take kindly to force.

As he crossed the open field the midday light made him squint, so he cast his eyes down to the ground; the sun broiled the back of his pale neck. He passed close by a llama who spit at him.

"If I concentrate too hard on the twenty-fifth," he fretted, "I may soon forget the twenty-fourth or the ninth."

Archibald had sunk so deep into his worries that he failed to notice the man wearing blue jeans, a sweatshirt with a hole in the front, and a faded New York Mets cap until he nearly ran smack into him.

"I don't suppose you speak English," muttered the man.

"As a matter of fact, I do," snapped Archibald irritably, realizing in the next microsecond what a blunder he'd committed.

As any fool could see, the man was a stranger in the Country of the Blind: he was wearing horn-rimmed eyeglasses. Oh my God, thought Archibald.

"Where am I?" asked the stranger.

"Who are you?" replied Archibald.

"It doesn't matter who I am," said the stranger. "The point is, I'm lost."

"How did you get here?"

"How I got here isn't the question. The question is, *where* is here. Don't make it so complicated."

"Where are you trying to get?"

"That's not important either. If I know where I am, I can get to where I want to go."

"How can you be sure you're lost?"

"If I tell you how I got lost, will you please tell me where I am?" asked the stranger impatiently.

"Maybe," said Archibald, "but you also have to tell me where you want to go."

"I got lost somewhere in the Amazon basin because of the cloud cover. I couldn't see the stars, which is how I usually keep track of my bearings. By the time the sky cleared, I was in the Andes—I don't know exactly where, somewhere in the eastern foothills. These mountains and villages all look alike to me. When I don't have my stars I sometimes screw up." The stranger rubbed his temples. "It's hot as hell in the sun. Couldn't we mosey over under those trees?"

"Okay."

The two men walked silently side by side to the edge of the pasture and settled in the shade of a great tree.

"Well?" said the stranger. "I lived up to my end of the bargain. It's your turn."

"You didn't say where you wanted to go," Archibald observed.

"I guess I didn't, did I?" acknowledged the stranger. "Right now I want to go to either Buenaventura or Guayaquil, whichever is closer, so I can pick up a ship to the Far East. It's too far for me to, uh—I'm following a woman whose name sounds like wind chimes."

"Ahh," sighed Archibald in relief: the man wasn't interested in the Country of the Blind, probably hadn't even heard of it. Nevertheless, it would be best to hustle him out of the valley pronto, before the villagers woke up and discovered him and started asking unanswerable questions.

"No problem," Archibald continued, recollecting the maps he'd studied as a teenager. "Guayaquil's nearer, a little less than two hundred miles southeast as the crow flies. And the easiest way to get there is to take the bus from Quito which is about sixty miles almost due north, or better yet catch a bus for Quito in Mulalo which is even closer. So first you have to go back to the place where you entered this valley, and then—"

"How do you know where I entered? Did you see me?"

"No. But I know for certainty there's only one way in or out of this valley unless you fly. You didn't come by plane, did you?"

"No," said the stranger.

"I didn't think so. Somebody would have heard the noise. And since I don't see any strange vehicles, I assume you're traveling on foot."

"Perhaps," said the stranger. "But I don't have any money for bus fare to Guayaquil, so tell me more about how the crow flies."

"That way." Archibald pointed in the general direction of Guayaquil. "And if I were you, I'd be on my way long before the stars came out. Ordinarily I don't like to speak ill of my neighbors, but the folks in this valley aren't exactly hospitable when it comes to outsiders. If they find out you're here, things could get ugly."

"I appreciate the advice, although that doesn't explain how you happen to be here. You're an outsider, aren't you?"

"Let's just say I'm a special case," said Archibald.

"A special case," echoed the stranger wryly. "Yeah, I know all about special cases." He hoisted himself off the ground and stretched his long limbs. "Well then, I'd better get moving. Can I ask you one last favor?"

"Maybe. Make it snappy!"

"Please don't tell anyone you saw me. It will just confuse the issue, which is already confused enough."

"Buddy," Archibald laughed, "whatever your secret is, it's safer with me than in the Bank of England. As far as I'm concerned, you're a dream who dissolved when I woke up."

"Thanks," said the stranger. "By the way, you haven't heard anything about the televisions, have you?"

"Huh? Televisions? What do you mean? Should I?"

"I guess not. Never mind."

What a funny question, Archibald reflected. Why should he want to know about television?

As the word *television* was crossing Archibald's brain for the third time, it tripped a languishing memory: the old Glenn Gould videotape, Hattie's present. He still had it. If only he could watch it he would remember the forgotten sections of the twenty-fifth Goldberg Variation and, who knows?, maybe pick up some subtleties of tone and phrasing from the incomparable Gould. He'd have to leave the valley for a few days, of course, but the crevasse would be passable at this season and it might be interesting to see what had become of the world.

The notion so excited him that he didn't remark on the stranger's departure, let alone his unique means of locomotion. And when at last he turned around to look for him and found him gone—definitely vanished—Archibald shrugged. The stranger would never come back, he was sure of it. Good riddance. The important thing was to play that tape! He headed back home, spinning stories to tell his wife.

"The piano has developed some problems," he remarked with
artificial casualness to Yna when she woke up, "which I think I
can solve by replacing some of the balancers and hammershanks.
They take special wood though, so I'll go to the forest for branches.
Don't worry if I'm gone for a few days. You know how long it
takes to feel for the proper pieces."

"I'll pack some food for you, then," said Yna cooperatively.

"Thank you, my love," said Archibald, at once ashamed of
his lie and proud of its success.

Archibald left home on June 24, 2004, carrying the fruit and
cold llama-loaf Yna had packed for him, along with Hattie's videotape and a compass for guidance. When he reached the crevasse shortly after nightfall, he remarked that the dense growth
of vines that choked the entrance to the passage appeared undis-
turbed, and offered silent thanks to the stranger for having covered his traces so thoroughly. Very carefully, Archibald cut himself
an entrance in the vegetation and squeezed through the cliff, out
of the Country of the Blind. During the night he passed two
mountains and traversed a barren valley; he stopped to rest in
the late morning and started through a mountain pass the next
evening. Emerging from the western side of the pass he saw the
unmistakable glow of the electric lights of a town. He ducked
behind a bush as the headlights of a car swept around the bend
of a road.

Though panicked at the prospect of meeting sighted people
and being seen by them, Archibald remembered his sweet wife
Yna and proceeded warily toward the town. After all, he was
asking for such a small favor, smaller than a piece of bread, merely
an hour or so with a VCR. Perhaps he could slip into a bar and
use the equipment after closing hours. Or maybe he'd find a
house temporarily emptied of its occupants . . . Archibald was
nearing the edge of the town and examining his options when
he noticed, off to his right, two or three hundred yards in the

distance, the curve of a television dish antenna outlined against the sky. As he drew closer he caught sight of a low-slung building which even in the dark had a forsaken look about it.

Curious, Archibald circled the building cautiously. He located an entrance and tried the knob. When it yielded, he gave the door a push, and it swung open creakily. He stepped inside. A furry creature scooted ratlike past his ankles into the night. He took a few steps forward until his foot landed on a dead snake— no, it wasn't a snake after all, more like a fat cable. His eyes really couldn't make out anything at all in the darkness, but he felt his way with practiced hands: cool metal, hard plastics, rubbery syn- thetics, materials he hadn't touched in years molded into almost forgotten forms. One by one they added themselves up in his mind, and Archibald realized with a chuckle where he was.

A television studio. An *abandoned* television studio—aban- doned for quite a while, judging by the accumulation of dust and cobwebs. He supposed the station, if that's what it was, had gone out of business, but that didn't explain the equipment sitting here unsold. He retraced his steps back to the entrance and ran his fingers along the wall next to the door, feeling for the lights, on the odd chance the electricity was still connected. He found a set of switches and flipped them all. The lights came on with a blaze that caused him to cover his eyes.

Archibald lowered his elbow from his face and surveyed the scene. A television studio indeed: big cameras on dollies, small cameras strewn about the floor, lighting equipment, banks of television monitors, video recorders, an electronic control panel— dusty and with traces of animal feces here and there, but never- theless first-rate equipment by the standards he remembered: Sony, Panasonic, and so on. He toyed with levers and switches on the control board which lit up like a video arcade, flashing signals he couldn't decipher. He hit the ON button of one of the televisions, and the set came on though it didn't seem to be receiving any broadcasts. Weird! In the old days thieves would have picked this place bare as a baby's bottom in a few hours.

Something must have happened in the world, Archibald reflected: something big. A nuclear war. Maybe this stuff was radioactive—but then what about the town? And the car? Or maybe—yeah, that was more like it: the equipment had been contaminated by some horrible disease, a weapon of biological warfare, and people were afraid to touch it. He inspected his hands anxiously for rashes or peeling skin, then remembered the furry animal that had brushed by his feet, alive and scampering. Still, there must have been something. The stranger in the pasture had inquired about television, remember?

The hell with it, Archibald instructed himself; whatever happened means nothing to me: I don't belong to this world anymore, I'm only a tourist. He pulled Hattie's tape out of his knapsack, inserted it into a VCR, pressed the PLAY button, and fast-forwarded the tape past the credits to the beginning of Gould's performance.

No one knows precisely when the televisions started to work again, although I am of the personal opinion that it must have been at that moment when the angry mob surrendered its desire to kill the man who shot at Gregory Fisher. But it might have been later. Or earlier. The fact is that the experts had long given up testing television, and no programs had been broadcast for more than a year.

You remember, however, that some people who were as accustomed to the glow of television as a green plant is to sunlight had left their sets running long after the picture and sound had disappeared. Others arrived home tired and turned on their televisions out of habit, a Pavlovian response to another working day survived. And still others eagerly scanned their empty screens for messages from extraterrestrials. Altogether then, perhaps a million of the half billion TVs on earth were ready to receive on

June 25, 2004, when the visitor from the Country of the Blind inserted his tape into a VCR in an abandoned studio in the mountains of Ecuador.

Those people who happened to be in the proximity of a working television told about hearing a funny click, followed by the whir of rushing videotape. Next there is video static, then credits racing by too fast to read. Another click: the tape slows to normal speed. An unfamiliar image inhabits the screen, an untidy, bespectacled man wearing a dark blue shirt with unbuttoned cuffs. He is balding, badly shaven, sickly. He looks as though he might have eaten his last meal standing next to a dumpster at the back door of a Chinese restaurant. Now, however, he hunches over a piano keyboard, his mouth slack, his nose inches from his hands.

The man makes a spectacle of himself. He groans and sings and waves his arms around.

He plays like God.

Archibald viewed the entire tape, replaying the twenty-fifth Goldberg Variation three times to fix the notes in his memory. When the concert ended, he turned off both the television and the VCR, leaving the tape in the machine, for he had no further use for it. He turned off all the switches and lights in the studio, closed the door, and walked back to the Country of the Blind.